*For Mia, Replied.*
—S.I

Printed in USA
First edition 2023.

Our books may be purchased in bulk at a discount for promotional, educational, and business use.
Please contact The Little Press sales department by email at
info@littlepresspublishing.com
Library of Congress Control Number: 2023937380
ISBN 978-1-956378-14-6 (paperback)

Book design by Harini Rajagopalan
Text by Sierra Isley
Cover Art by David Habben
Edited by Michele McAvoy and Monique Jones Brown
Copyedited by Crystal Branson

The Little Press
P.O. Box 35 Wood-Ridge, N.J. 07075
www.littlepresspublishing.com

# IN THE RING

## SIERRA ISLEY

THE LITTLE PRESS • NEW JERSEY

"I saw the best minds of my generation destroyed by madness."
—Allen Ginsberg, *Howl*

# CHAPTER ONE

**THIS PARTY FEELS LIKE A PANIC ATTACK.**

I can't breathe through the clouds of cigarette smoke. Vibrations from the stereo shake the ground beneath my boots. The green and blue strobe lights are disorienting.

"Rose!"

Gemma's voice cuts like a dagger through the music. She flashes a smile that lights up the dark chamber of drunk high school students. They clear a path for her. A pink striped jumpsuit hugs her body tightly. She looks superhuman in comparison to the other girls. Judging by the glares, they know it as well as I do.

"Drink," she says, shoving a cup into my hand.

Clear liquid spills out of the lid and drips onto the carpet. Months have passed since I've had alcohol, but I don't hesitate. It burns, sharp as fire, as it drips down my throat.

"Want to dance?" Gemma asks.

"No," I say, even though there's no point in arguing with her.

She pulls me into the middle of the cramped living room. A boy to her right shoots me a dirty look. Gemma scowls at him, her thin nose and sharp jawline further defined in the purple light.

"Ignore him," she whispers. She lifts my hand into the air and twirls me like she did the first night we met. When I saw Gemma Shao at our homecoming dance freshman year, I was speechless. It took me hours to work up the courage to ask her to dance. Our horrible attempt at a line dance sparked a friendship that's lasted us through to today: the third week of our senior year of high school.

"Is there any more to drink?" I ask.

Gemma snatches two more cups. This time, the alcohol goes down easily. I hold the empty cup into the air like a trophy and Gemma laughs.

Suddenly, the music stops. The room is silent except for one, booming voice.

"Whichever idiot parked in my driveway; you have forty-five seconds to move it before I sit my drunk ass in your driver's seat and do it myself!"

Elliott King, the host of the party, towers over the stereo system. His black tank top shows off several tattoos scattered across his arms and shoulders. I remember entertaining the idea that he might be illiterate after peer-reviewing his essay on *Pride and Prejudice*.

"Now!" he demands.

A short haired girl jolts to the door. Elliott grabs the solo cup out of her hands as she leaves, downs the beer in one gulp, then screams, "Let's fucking go!"

The music starts up louder than before. Elliott reaches for the closest girl he can find, pulling her in for a public make-out session that threatens to resurface my drink. Gemma and I take shots of what I think is vodka, then dance and sing until my throat is sandpaper.

"Water," I mutter, forgetting the other parts of the sentence.

Cups litter the carpet around us. I stopped counting after four. Gemma, noticing my lack of coordination, smiles. This isn't something she sees often.

"I'm on it. Stay here."

As soon as her hands leave my shoulders, I lose my balance. I grip the granite countertop of the large kitchen island to keep myself upright. Gemma makes her way toward the fridge but doesn't get more than a few feet before a group of guys stop her to chat.

My spit barely makes it down. I'll get it myself.

When I let go of the counter, the room spins. Red, blue, and green lights mix into a messy rainbow so bright it burns. I manage to make it to the corner of the living room before the nausea hits. My hand slaps over my mouth.

I tap on the shoulder of the first person that walks by: a tall, muscular boy in a football jersey. His shaggy brown hair barely reaches past his shoulders. Only one word escapes my lips.

"Bathroom?"

To my relief, he smiles warmly.

"Sure. Follow me."

He snakes through the crowd. There's a number printed on the back of his jersey: eighteen. My lucky number. He guides me out of the living room, across the foyer, then toward the main staircase. I take a deep breath of air less tainted by smoke.

"You're Rose Berman, right? We had Math together last year."

My stomach sinks to the floor.

Of course. Harris Price. Star quarterback of the football team. The only varsity athlete in advanced calculus. I swallow down the sick taste that accompanies the memory of what happened in that classroom.

"Yes," I whisper.

If Harris notices my discomfort, he doesn't react. He grins as he leads me upstairs. One of my hands grips the railing, the other instinctively falls onto his back to steady myself. His shoulders tense, but he doesn't stop moving.

"This way."

We creep down the long, towering hallway of Elliott King's mansion of a house. He hosts parties here almost every weekend. The walls are bare of any family pictures, and most of the expensive furniture is destroyed. I wonder where his dad is tonight.

To the left, an open door reveals a group of freshmen passing around a joint. One of them waves. Harris, uninterested, continues down the hallway. He stops at the last door on the right and ushers me in with his hand.

"Thank you," I utter, relieved.

A queen-sized bed and a night table face me.

It's a bedroom, not a bathroom.

I turn around. "I really need—"

Harris shoves me forward. I stumble into the side of the bed, piercing pain shooting through my knees. Amused laughter erupts from the corner. I look up to find a huddle of seniors watching us. A blonde girl giggles at the shock on my face as she leans her head onto Elliott King's shoulder. He's eyeing a thin line of white powder on the table in front of them.

"You brought Berman?" barks the blonde.

She takes a hit off a joint, then passes it to Elliott. He winks at her before pulling in a cloud of smoke. The fog fills up the small space and I cough.

"I thought she might be fun," Harris replies. He takes a step toward me. I take a step away from him. My ankles hit the bed frame and I fall backwards onto the mattress; the sudden movement makes the liquid in my stomach rise to my throat.

"I need to go," I moan, sitting up.

Harris acts like he doesn't hear me. Or maybe I'm not speaking loud enough. I say it again, with conviction this time. He rubs his rough hands over his brown hair and flashes a sly smile. From my position on the bed, his height is amplified.

"You haven't been at school in a while," he says.

I wince. I thought that after two months of summer break, gossip about what had happened in calculus would have finally died down.

"Well," I say, "I'm back."

A flash of heat raises my body temperature, and the blonde girl notices. She twists her face as she stares at the sweat pooling around my bangs.

"Do you think she's possessed?" she jokes.

"Maybe she needs some pot?" Elliott suggests innocently.

Much to the girl's annoyance, he offers up the joint to me. Instead of taking it, I bend over and puke onto the checkered brown and white rug. Which probably costs more than anything in my house.

*Shit.*

I freeze. The smell of what I've done wafts upwards, threatening to make me puke again.

"Well, fuck," says Elliott "You couldn't have aimed for the trash?"

Harris chuckles. The rest of the group joins in, creating a chorus of laughter at my expense. The quarterback, unde-terred by my sickness, creeps closer. He takes a seat on the bed beside me and places his hand on my shoulder. His skin is ice cold. I lift my eyes to meet his. Nothing. They're clear as glass, void of any emotion.

"You know, I think the psycho thing is kind of hot," Harris comments as if noticing me for the first time.

The corners of his lips curl like a butcher ogling a slab of meat.

"Isn't that what everyone calls you? Psycho?"

"Don't bother. She's a prude," the blonde girl retorts.

Maddy Davis. She moved here only a few months ago from Virginia. Elliott whispers something in her ear that makes her giggle.

Harris's hand moves from my shoulder down my left arm like he's marking my skin. I open my mouth to defend myself, but my words disappear when his fingertips touch my neck. He gently grabs a piece of my dark brown hair and twists it.

I stop breathing.

"You're not a prude," says Harris, unashamedly exploring my curves.

I feel naked in this tight black dress. I shouldn't have listened when Gemma suggested I wear it. Gemma. She's one floor beneath me. I will her to save me from this humiliation, begging her to somehow hear my thoughts . . .

She doesn't.

I want to scream. I *should* scream. But my throat is raw, incapable of making any sound except for a whimper.

"Are you?" Harris asks.

The walls of Elliott's bedroom are covered in posters, and I focus on one hanging to the left of the bed—a jazz musician playing a guitar. I count the strings on it.

*One.*

Harris places his hand softly around my neck.

"Stop," I finally manage, my voice uncooperating.

*Two.*

Harris's hand travels down to the top of my chest where he traces my collarbone with his index finger. His hands are calloused and prickly.

"Stop," I say louder.

Harris shakes his head. Instinctively, I try pushing him away, but as my palms meet his shoulders, he knocks me flat on my back.

This time I know I'm shouting.

"Stop!"

*Three.*

It all happens so quickly. A pair of inked hands grabs the back of Harris's jersey and pulls him off of me. I sit up when Elliott slams him into the table, shattering the glass.

Maddy dives away from the commotion. "What the hell, Elliott?" she exclaims.

Tiny pieces of glass litter the floor around the two boys. Blood pools from a fresh cut in Harris's arm and drips onto the puke-stained rug. He pulls himself back onto his feet, his anger rising.

"Never thought you'd play the hero, King," he spits.

A hint of amusement flashes across Elliott's face. He doesn't seem afraid. In fact, he relaxes. Like this is his usual Saturday night. He crosses his arms and lets out an annoyed groan.

"Get out," he commands.

It's a stark contrast to the comical tone I'm used to when he cracks a dirty joke in class. Harris kicks over a piece of the broken table, spilling more glass shards onto the rug. White powder sticks to the saturated fabric.

Elliott takes another step toward Harris. Elliott might be an inch shorter, but his arms are twice the size, and so is his presence. He lifts his chin, daring the quarterback to make a move, but to my surprise, Harris doesn't.

"Fine," Harris concedes, "but don't expect any more favors from me."

He turns to me, and I scoot backward on the bed.

"Tell anyone about this and you're dead. Got it, Psycho?"

I nod once, then Harris storms out of the room. Maddy rises from her spot on the ground. She hops over the mess on the floor like she's puddle jumping, then pauses in the doorway.

"Come on, Elliott."

His feet stay planted. "I'll meet you downstairs."

Maddy huffs before disappearing into the hall. Only after she leaves do I notice my hands are shaking. Elliott comes to the side of the bed and crouches down to my level. The power that radiated from him only moments ago is gone. He's calm, his blue irises dripping with concern.

"Do you want me to take you home?"

I can't tell if he's being sincere. His pupils are dilated, the whites around them bloodshot. I glance between him and the white powder stuck to the rug. I've heard rumors about Elliott's drug use but seeing it close up is more disturbing than entertaining.

"Rose?"

He sounds like he's talking to a child. I lift my chin, desperate to prove I'm not a kicked puppy.

"No, I'm fine."

I stand up from the bed, ready to get the hell out of here, but my body moves in slow motion. I should thank him for helping me, but my brain is screaming, and my throat hasn't recovered.

I hold on to the walls as I creep out of the disaster of a bedroom without another word from either of us.

Somewhere in the crowd is Harris, chatting girls up like he does at pep rallies. I don't look up from the floor of Elliott's house until I'm safely outside.

The wind blows my thin dress. Atlanta usually isn't this cold in September. I rub my hands against my arms to keep the goosebumps away. A few classmates from the party follow behind me, engaged in their own loud conversation. Is the story already making rounds? I stop to listen.

"You guys want to go back to my place?"

"Totally."

For the first time since entering Elliott's bedroom, I exhale. His house is only steps away from my own. We've been next door neighbors ever since the third grade when his family refurbished the abandoned mansion.

Climbing the stairs to my front door, someone grabs my shoulder.

Cold hands. Sharp nails.

Harris followed me!

He squeezes, and my blood stops flowing. I gasp from the pain, throwing my palm over my mouth to silence my scream. My heart pounds against my rib cage. When I work up the courage to face him, my hand curls into a fist in the same way Elliott's did.

Nobody is behind me.

The street is empty. I shove my key into the door. Quickly step into the foyer and turn the bolt. The sound of my father snoring from the recliner settles my nerves. I take a deep breath, tiptoe around him, careful not to make any noise. The clock on the coffee table reads a quarter to midnight.

I was only gone for an hour. It felt like an eternity.

The stairs creak, but my father's snoring doesn't falter when I reach my bedroom. Next to the stack of unfinished homework on my desk, my phone vibrates. I should have brought the damn thing with me.

**Gemma: I got your water. Where r u?**
**Gemma: Helloo?**
**Gemma: Did you leave?**

*Crap.*

**Rose: Hey, sorry. Got sick and went home.**

Three dots appear on the screen as she types. Everyone must know what happened by now. Gemma won't even get to hear it from me.

**Gemma: Feel better. Nishi kissed me!**

The adrenaline cascading throughout my body finally slows its course.

News hasn't spread. Not yet, at least.

A sour smell wafts from the bottom of my dress to my nose. I saunter into the bathroom, pausing when I reach the mirror.

I look like absolute shit.

My curls are bunched together in dark, matted knots. The choppy bangs across my forehead are soaked with sweat. Red blotches clot the pale skin on my neck. I trace the outline of one with my pointer finger.

I put the shower on the hottest temperature. The water is probably burning my skin, but I can't feel it. I can't feel anything except Harris's fingers tracing my arm. I scrub every spot he touched until it's raw. Even then, no matter how hard I scrub, the outline of his dirty fingers won't fade.

*Behind me, Maddy laughs. Harris smirks viciously. Elliott lunges. The violent symphony of the glass shattering replays again and again and again.* How did I not notice that Harris's eyes had no color in them when I spotted him? Why did I assume he was safe to follow?

Salty tears drip onto my lips. I sink down to the floor of the tub, tucking my head between my knees. I've been warned a thousand times by my friends, my father, even my mother before her death, that something like this could happen. It could happen to anyone.

*Anyone,* I thought, *except for me.*

I stay seated on the shower floor until the water runs cold.

# CHAPTER TWO

**SUNLIGHT STREAMS THROUGH MY WINDOWS, WAKING ME UP EARLY.** Too early. I groan, throwing a pillow over my face to block the golden light. The innermost part of my skull pulses as if it has a heartbeat, and my stomach rumbles from the alcohol lingering in my system. I slept for no more than an hour or two.

My phone vibrates from my nightstand. If news about what happened in Elliott's bedroom was going to make rounds at the party, it would have by now. I whisper a silent prayer in Hebrew before opening the text.

**Gemma: Got home safe.**

The stiffness in my shoulders ease. If nobody else finds out about last night, I might be able to forget it ever happened. I can lock up the memory and bury it.

Tossing my phone back onto the nightstand, I drag myself out of bed. Last night's black dress taunts me from the floor. Scowling, I kick it beneath my desk, out of my line of sight. Maybe Gemma will help me burn it later.

My reflection in the mirror is slightly less monstrous, but my eyes are still hooded with tiredness. I rub a layer of concealer across my skin to cover up the red spots. Even after brushing my teeth for five whole minutes, I still taste vodka on my tongue.

I'm *never* drinking again.

The smell of bacon grease wafts from downstairs and my stomach growls. I can't remember the last time I had anything to eat. After one last peek at the mirror, I follow the smell to the kitchen.

My father's disheveled dark hair is sticking out in multiple directions. I hold back a giggle as he tries and fails to flip a pancake. He's been cooking breakfast every Sunday morning since my mom died. It's one of our few remaining traditions.

"How was the movie?" he asks.

*Right. I lied about my plans.* He wouldn't have cared much if I went to a party; in fact, he probably would have been excited about me hanging out with other people again, but the movie excuse seemed better than suffering through his "don't drink or you'll die" speech for the tenth time.

"Pretty good."

He passes me a plate stacked with pancakes and pork bacon. Before my mother died, we used to keep kosher. Now we don't even go to synagogue.

"Sleep okay?"

I lift my chin and smile with as much energy as I can muster. "Yeah. I had weird dreams."

I've been using "weird" instead of "bad" recently.

"Do you want a ride to your appointment?"

I've told him a thousand times I'm getting better, but he insists I keep seeing Dr. Taylor, my therapist, an aging man with too much patience for his own good. Although, after last night, complaining to somebody doesn't sound like as much of the usual inconvenience. I shove a forkful of food into my mouth.

"Sure, thanks."

We slip into small talk about our plans for the upcoming week. I toss my cleared plate into the sink, then head upstairs to change. My room is a disaster. I throw the purple comforter over my sheets and straighten up the rest of the bed. One of the posters on the wall, the album cover of Nirvana's *In Utero*, threatens to fall onto my head. I grab an extra tack from my desk and pin up the bottom.

"Ready?" calls my dad from downstairs.

I glare at the black dress on the floor once more before leaving.

My dad hums along to the radio as he drives. Apart from a few solo cups peeking out of the bushes, there is no sign at all there was ever a party at Elliott's.

Grady Hospital is less than a ten-minute drive from our house. A security guard waves the car into the covered parking lot. Dad picks the closest spot to the entrance.

"Do you want me to come in with you?"

I shake my head. He always asks even though I never let him. I attempt a reassuring smile, but the concern on his face doesn't fade. These appointments end differently each time. Sometimes I leave feeling better; other times not so much.

Rain sprinkles onto my hoodie. I take my time walking to the front entrance, sucking in a lungful of cool autumn air.

Inside, the smell of sterilization is overwhelming. The walls are coated in a thick layer of white paint. I asked Dr. Taylor once about the choice of color. He told me that white raises the moods of patients, but I disagree. Too bright.

"How have you been?" Dr. Taylor asks.

A pair of thick-rimmed glasses sit dangerously close to the edge of his nose. One tiny movement and they'll fall right off.

"Good," I reply half-heartedly.

He motions for me to take a seat, which I do. Compared to the white of the hallways, the brown hardwoods in his office are comforting. I run my hands over the three marks dug into the hand rest of the chair. Months ago, during a boring session, I determined someone must have forced their nails into it.

"Is the Prozac still working?"

I respond truthfully, "I haven't had a panic attack since I started it."

I never thought something as small as a pill could help so much. I take one every morning like clockwork, never missing a dosage. Dr. Taylor scribbles in the notebook in his lap. His gray, speckled hair bounces around as he writes.

"You mentioned last week that Gemma invited you to a party? How did that go?"

Some of his features are similar to Harris's. Their lips are identical in size and shape, and they prefer the same musty cologne.

"It was alright."

I try not to react to the weight of his question but hiding even the slightest negative reaction from him is an Olympic feat. I swear he was born for this gig—body language is his natural dialect.

"You seem on edge. What happened?"

I speak through gritted teeth. "Some people made fun of me while I was there."

"What did they say?"

"A lot of stuff. One of them was in class with me. When *it* happened."

I remember Harris's reaction, now. He was sitting in the front row of the classroom when the EMTs guided me out of calculus. That day disrupted the rest of my junior year; Dr.

Taylor and I have spent the last few months working toward some form of normality again.

"Did this person say something about the incident?"

"No. But he called me *Psycho*."

Dr. Taylor groans. He's become as annoyed with the nickname as I am. He really does care, which makes admitting the bad stuff even worse. I sink into the chair.

"High schoolers are incredibly immature. We both know that."

"I know," I mumble.

Dr. Taylor's guided me through a thousand different exercises where I learn to ignore the *Psycho* thing, but I haven't found the courage to tell him it's an impossible task. High school is literally all about being defined by the nicknames given to you by people like Harris Price.

Suddenly, Dr. Taylor's green eyes light up. He pushes his glasses farther up on his nose and flashes a smile that makes me nervous.

"I have an idea, but I don't think you're going to like it."

Not the most intriguing start.

"What if you tried out a sport?"

I can't stop myself from laughing. Loudly.

Dr. Taylor rushes his words. "I think the physicality of it might help you forget about all the stuff going on mentally. It would give you something consistent to look forward to."

Just entertaining the idea of myself playing a sport is nightmarish. I'm uncoordinated and the opposite of a team player. I've been picked last for kickball every year since sixth grade when I accidentally hit Angela Thomas in the face.

"I'm not joining a sports team," I proclaim. To my surprise, Dr. Taylor doesn't back down.

"How about something more individualized? Yoga?"

"Too slow."

"Track?"

"I hate running."

"What about boxing?"

I pause.

Elliott wrangled Harris off of me without effort. He could have easily beat the school's quarterback to a pulp if he wanted to. Elliott exuded the power I've been trying to get back ever since that day in calculus.

"Maybe," I say.

Dr. Taylor beams. "There's a place close by that my friend goes to, Midtown Ring. First lesson is free."

He rips off a piece of paper, scribbles down the name of the gym, then passes it to me. I slip it into the pocket of my blue jeans. We spend the rest of the meeting discussing my plan for graduating on time.

"Same time next week?"

I nod, and he narrows his gaze on my pocket. "I truly hope you give it a go."

"I'll think about it."

Exiting the hospital, I take out my phone and type Midtown Ring into Google. The gym's website hasn't been updated since 2005. Apart from a calendar with an address and a time for a class tomorrow, there's no other information.

"Lovely," I whisper.

The sprinkle of rain earlier has turned into a thunderstorm. I sprint to the car.

"How was it?" Dad asks.

"Dr. Taylor suggested I try boxing."

He stares at me like I've grown an extra head. "But . . . you hate sports?"

"I know," I sigh.

Dad seems to go through the same thought process I did—minus the visual of Elliott King throwing Harris Price into a glass table.

"Well," he finally says, "I guess there's no harm in trying." He sounds hopeful. He's been desperately searching for something—anything—that might help me. A few boxing lessons aren't going to magically get rid of my anxiety, but I keep my mouth shut.

I spend the rest of the day catching up on my reading for class, the piece of paper heavy in my pocket.

*

Gemma wraps me in a hug when I step out the front door. Her hair, naturally black but dyed red, is pinned up into two Princess Leia buns.

"I have so much to tell you!" she exclaims.

"Why do you have this energy at eight in the morning?"

"Coffee, obviously."

I turn my nose. Caffeine makes my anxiety act up, so I've been staying away from our local Starbucks as much as a seventeen-year-old girl can. We start toward our school, Dekalb High. Other seniors pass us by on the other side of the street.

I need to tell her about Harris, but the words are glued to my throat. If Gemma finds out, she'll freak. She'll want to talk to Harris, and if the whole school is around to hear her, I may as well be dead.

*Later. I'll tell her later.*

"We played spin the bottle after you left the party. Nishi spun and it landed on me. She wouldn't kiss me though, which was super embarrassing."

Gemma talks so quickly; I have to slow down my walk to understand her.

"Then she took me to this quiet corner in the back of the house and was like, 'I didn't want our first kiss to be in front of everyone else.' And then she kissed me!"

I grin. For months, Gemma's been pining after Nishi Kapoor, lacrosse player and president of the Gay-Straight Alliance club. For someone so outspoken, Nishi can't form a coherent sentence in front of Gemma. I don't blame her. Gemma's intimidating. She's never found it difficult to turn a crush into something more. The only time it didn't work out for her was when I was her conquest.

"Was it good?"

"More than good." Gemma drools. "I think I'm in love."

My eyes roll to the back of my head, but I'm thrilled for her. "You say that at least once a month."

"It's true this time!"

As we approach the school gates, I practice Dr. Taylor's exercise: Breathe in. Hold your breath. Count for three seconds. Release. Repeat. As always, it doesn't help my anxiety. The only thing that does is the Prozac, which I forgot to take this morning.

*Shit.*

"Rose?" Gemma questions, "You good?"

"Sorry, yeah."

The brick building is buzzing with students. Sophomores chat with each other, embracing their last moments of freedom before the first bell rings. I scan the crowd for Harris, but he's nowhere to be found.

Hopefully, he caught the flu. Or something worse.

Gemma waves goodbye as we head to our respective classrooms. Math is emptier than usual. I have class in the same room that I took calculus in last year. Harris used to sit two rows in front of me. I spent hours staring at the words printed on the back of his jersey: H. *Price, Eighteen.*

"Rose?"

Mrs. Smith. She's waiting on an answer.

"What?"

Two girls in the back chuckle. I crane my neck and glare. It shuts them up.

"Can you solve the equation for us?"

"No. Sorry."

She lets me off easy. They usually do. I try to pay attention throughout the rest of the class, but I can't stop thinking about Harris. If he's not at school today, he'll certainly be back tomorrow. It's impossible to hide from him.

When the bell rings, I shiver.

I've been dreading this.

English class with Elliott King.

His back is facing me when I take my first step into the classroom. Girls crowd around his desk like moths to a flame. They laugh in perfect unison over the sight of him attempting to balance a pencil on the bridge of his nose.

He doesn't notice when I enter the room. No one ever does. I doubt he even knows      we're in the same class. The desks to the left and right of me are empty, so I utilize the extra space for my notebooks. A girl to Elliott's right runs her hands across the collar of his green polo.

"Cute shirt," she purrs.

Maddy Davis. The girl from Elliott's bedroom. She moves her hand down the side of Elliott's chest and intertwines their fingers. His eyes wander absently toward a different girl across the room, narrowing on the shape of her butt.

*Classy.*

Mr. Ruse stands up right as the clock hits eleven. He's the oldest, quirkiest teacher I have and his taste in fashion shows it. Today, he's dressed in a bright purple suit with a polka-dotted tie. He scribbles the first few lines of *Annabel Lee* onto the white board.

"The last complete poem written by Edgar Allan Poe," Ruse says, tapping a marker against the words. "One of my absolute favorites. Has anybody read it before?"

A few hands shoot up, including my own.

"Well, you all will be happy to know that we're beginning our poetry unit today. I want each of you to choose a poem that you admire and discuss it in a paragraph or two. Write about what you think it means or how it makes you feel. Turn it in before Friday."

I scribble down the assignment. Ruse dives into a lesson on Edgar Allan Poe, but my attention drifts to the bruise on the back of Elliott's neck.

Did Harris get a hit in?

I swallow the bitter taste of guilt on my tongue. If only I had stayed in the kitchen and waited for Gemma to come back. Elliott's room wouldn't be destroyed. His skin wouldn't be turning purple. And I wouldn't want to die when he glances in my direction.

As class comes to an end, I can't stop thinking about why I couldn't sleep last night. I was too busy debating if I should

25

take up Dr. Taylor's suggestion, and I still haven't come up with an answer.

I wait for Elliott and Maddy to clear the classroom before leaving my desk. Elliott wraps his arm around her shoulders and pulls her close, laughing obnoxiously about someone who fainted at his party. A freshman half Elliott's size crosses his path.

"Move," Elliott commands.

The kid jumps like a scared cat, earning an amused chuckle from Elliott. He's the king of the school when Harris isn't around.

Harris. His hungry expression as he stared down at me won't escape my mind. The rough touch of his fingers on my skin hasn't faded, and I'm not sure if it ever will. If I knew how to defend myself, things might have gone differently.

I know what I need to do.

# CHAPTER THREE

**FROM THE OUTSIDE, MIDTOWN RING IS A TOTAL SHITHOLE.** Some of the letters on the sign have fallen off, so it reads "MIDTN RNG." The only real sign of civilization comes from the chattering of people at the coffee shop next door.

After two minutes of awkwardly standing in the empty parking lot, a red car pulls into a spot near the gym's entrance. A twenty something man with brown skin and teased, bushy coils steps out from the driver's seat. He's dressed in athletic shorts and a tank top that shows off his toned arms. A pair of light green gloves peek out of his backpack. He definitely belongs in a boxing gym. I glance at my own outfit. My converse, jeans, and an oversized hoodie don't exactly scream pro-athlete. I don't even have gloves.

I wait until after the man enters the building before making my way toward it. There are no windows, nothing at all to hint at what might be going on inside. I pause in front of the entrance. Take a deep breath. Shake out my hands. Every rational part of me screams, "*turn around and leave!*"

But then I think of my father. The hopeful smile on his face when I brought up Dr. Taylor's idea was exactly what he's been waiting for. He would want me to do this.

I want to do this.

I open the door.

The inside of the gym is nicer than the outside. A graffiti mural of two purple boxing gloves covers the exposed brick wall in the back. Weight training equipment is scattered around the perimeter of a boxing ring. The ring itself is massive; the building reeks of sweat and people stronger than me. Punching bags hang from three of Midtown's walls. An enormous weight set takes up the fourth wall. To my left, the man from the parking lot waves.

"Are you here for the class tonight?" he asks.

I survey the rest of the room. A few other lurkers with muscles protruding from their tight clothing watch us. The only other woman here is at least three times my size.

Maybe this was a bad idea.

"Uh, this is the beginner's class, right?"

He chuckles. "Our adult classes are a mix of all skill levels. What's your name?"

"Rose."

He holds out his hand to shake. I do. His grip leaves a mark.

"I'm Andre." He peeks behind my shoulder at my backpack. "Do you go to school nearby?"

"Yeah, I'm a senior at Dekalb."

"Oh! We have a kid in our group from that school. Maybe you know him. He's—"

We both turn around at the sound of the gym door opening. Elliott King, holding a pair of black boxing gloves in his tattooed right hand, strolls inside.

"Right there," Andre finishes.

*Kill me.*

Andre waves over the one person I've been trying to avoid all day. He has changed out of his school clothes and into gray sweats and a black tank, but it's without a doubt Elliot King. He approaches the two of us with a surprised expression. I calculate the best way to make a quick escape. *There's a back door in the corner behind the mural . . .*

"Have you two met?" asks Andre.

"Yep," Elliott answers casually.

"Cool. Show her how to wrap?"

He gives Elliott no time to respond before leaving the two of us alone. I open my mouth to try and offer up an explanation as to why I'm here, but Elliott turns and walks off before I'm able to get a word out.

"Come on," he says, motioning toward one of the benches.

He takes a seat beside me, and as he does, I get a whiff of his tank top. Cigarettes. The cheap ones my father used to smoke. Elliott opens his backpack and passes me two long, red strips of cloth.

"I used to do this wrong all the time. Fucked up my knuckles. So, pay attention."

He opens his right hand, exposing a tattoo on his middle finger of the King of Hearts playing card. He slides his thumb through the small loop on the piece of cloth. I do the same. Then, he twists the cloth around his palms.

"Shit," I grumble as my wrap comes undone.

He grabs the cloth and pulls my hand toward him as he ties it around my wrist. His skin is rough and battered, but his touch is gentle.

"You'll get better," he reassures me. Nicotine lingers on his breath.

"Thanks."

Elliott shoves his backpack into one of the lockers that line the area around the gym. I throw my own bag onto the floor, then grab a pair of brown communal boxing gloves from

29

the crate by the locker room. They reek of death. I strap them on tight, but they're still too big.

The group of boxers gather in a semicircle in front of the ring. I stand on the right side of Elliott. *Do you remember what happened? Are you pissed I'm here?* I force myself to turn my attention to other members of the pack. There are six of us in total: Andre, two men—one of which has a stiff, long mustache and shoulder-length locs—a muscular tan-skinned woman, and of course, me and Elliott. We're certainly an eclectic group, but I didn't expect much else from the gym recommended to me by my therapist.

"Everyone, meet Rose," Andre announces.

My cheeks flush as the remainder of the group notices me. The strong woman scans my body and shakes her head.

"Oh, geniál. Una niña débil."

She calls me a weakling. She's right. But I don't let on that I understand her. After four years of Spanish class, something was bound to stick.

"Calláte, Sofía!" Andre shouts, nudging her. He faces me. "Sorry. She's not the biggest fan of newcomers."

"I can speak for myself," Sofia interrupts. She looks me up and down again, pursing her lips. "You know, you need muscle for this sport."

My mouth turns dry. Andre talks over her, "You'll get stronger."

Sofía raises her hands in a mock surrender. Mustache guy, noticing my discomfort, flashes a friendly smile. His dark brown skin contrasts with the white of his tank top, making his muscles appear even more defined. He's tall. Stubble lines his cheeks and there are subtle scars across his body. He's definitely been doing this for a long time.

I really don't belong here.

"Rose, why did you decide to try out boxing?" asks Andre.

*Well, I was assaulted by my classmate at a party, so I want to learn how to punch someone in the face in case it happens again. Also, my therapist, who I see because I'm probably losing my mind, suggested I come here.*

"I need more exercise," I grumble.

"Fair enough."

Andre leads the group in a few stretches. My calves burn from even the slightest movement, but I follow along with the rest of the boxers, not wanting to paint myself as an outcast more than I have. Elliott stands to my right. Our shoulders are only inches away from touching, and I silently hope that my deodorant holds up until the end of practice.

"Line up!" Andre exclaims, herding us toward a heavy bag. I go to the back of the line.

"Give me eight jabs. Rose, just watch for now."

I step aside. Mustache guy goes first. He places his left foot steadily in front of him, bends his elbows and points his chin down. He punches with his left hand, glove bouncing off the bag with a loud snap. It shakes from the force of each hit.

"That's Riley," Andre whispers to me. "He's a doctor at Emory. He's been coming here for years."

A boy closer to my age takes his turn.

"Max is also new."

Max punches with less power than Riley, but his hits are impressive. Next up is Sofía. She uses the perfect combination of strength and precision in her punches. The sharp noise from the impact echoes throughout the gym.

Andre, noticing the shock on my face, muffles a laugh. "Sofía's practically a professional. Don't be intimidated."

*Easier said than done.*

As Sofía steps away from the bag, she finally smiles at me. It's not comforting.

"And of course, you know Elliott."

He positions himself the same way as the rest of the boxers, but the punches he throws are quieter. They don't shake the room in the same way as Sofia's, but they're thrown with so much power that the whole gym submits into perfect silence.

Elliott is usually obnoxious and noisy to a fault. His punches should be the loudest ones here. I don't have a second to ponder the weirdness of it all before Andre declares that it's my turn to try. I open my mouth to object, but Sofía nudges me forward with her shoulder.

"You got this," Andre says.

I do my best to copy the same stance as Riley: left leg in front, fists curled. Andre touches the bottom of my elbows and moves them upwards toward my chin.

"You want to protect your face," he instructs. "Keep your elbows tight. Aim like you're going for the nose."

What's the point in tightening muscles that barely exist? Just as I'm about to make a beeline for the exit, I think of my father. He would want me to try, even if I might fail. Otherwise, I came here for nothing.

I throw my first jab.

Strength travels from the tips of my toes to my clenched fists. The weighted bag swings slightly when my skin comes into contact with the thick material.

It *moved.*

It *did what I wanted.*

The rush of adrenaline and power is sudden and overwhelming, and I find myself relaxing, *really* relaxing, for the first time in months. Andre breaks into a slow round of applause, followed by the rest of the group.

"I knew you could do it," he says. "You'll only get better from here."

His prideful smile inspires me to keep going. I hit the bag a couple more times to complete the warm-up. Each time, my confidence improves. I feel strong, which is a word I've never used to describe my frail arms.

When I turn back toward the group, Elliott winks.

"You could cause some real damage with a punch like that."

I bow, quietly laughing as I do. Maybe this doesn't have to be weird.

The rest of the lesson passes by in a blur. I watch as the rest of the group does more challenging routines. Andre makes me try out a right hook and an uppercut. I stumble, but Andre brushes it off, claiming again I'll improve with practice.

We end the lesson by watching Sofía and Riley spar. They each have their own strategy that balances the other out. Riley surrenders when Sofia knocks him to the floor, and they both collapse.

"Wow," I whisper.

Elliott takes the place at my side. I pass him the hand wraps.

"Thanks for letting me borrow those."

A bead of sweat drips from his buzzed blonde hair onto his forehead as he tosses the wraps into his bag.

"No problem."

From behind, Andre grabs my right shoulder. The sudden, familiar pressure of the touch makes me shudder. The panic passes in an instant, but not before Elliott notices. He frowns.

*So, he does remember.*

"Will you be back Wednesday?" Andre asks.

"I think so."

He grins. "Sweet. Rest your muscles!"

He doesn't have to tell me twice. I feel like a worn-out rag doll.

Outside, the wind cools the layer of heat across my body. I make my way through the parking lot, glancing behind me as Elliott climbs into his black convertible. He holds a cigarette in his left hand and uses his right to turn the key in the ignition. I could pick out the sound of his car in a concert of engines. That damn convertible speeds past my bedroom window every morning, music blasting so loud it serves as my alarm.

When I get home, Dad's recliner is empty. He's been taking on extra shifts at work ever since Mom died. I've asked a hundred times to let me help with the bills, but he refuses, insisting school should be my only concern. An untouched box of pizza is waiting on the counter. I shove two pieces of pepperoni into my mouth before heading upstairs to shower.

The hot water soothes my aching muscles. I coat my body in a thick layer of lavender soap to wash away the grime and sweat. Harris's fingerprints across my body fade with the waves of rushing water.

For the first time since Elliott's party, I'm clean.

\*

"How was it?"

My father perks up when I walk into the kitchen. He takes a sip of morning coffee from a "World's Best Dad" mug I bought when I was ten. I grab a bottle of Advil from the cabinet and down two. The muscles in my arms haven't stopped hurting since I left the gym yesterday. Collapsing into the chair next to his, I notice the dark circles around his eyes.

"Didn't you work last night? You should sleep—"

"I want to hear about boxing."

I'm glad to relay some good news to him.

"It was great! I tried some punches, and my teacher is cool. The class meets twice a week, so I'll go again on Wednesday."

He pauses mid-sip. "Sorry, did I hear that correctly? My daughter is going to exercise twice in one week?"

I stick out my tongue right as the doorbell rings. "I'll tell you more after school. Get some sleep!"

He nods. I snatch my backpack from the floor of the kitchen and make my way out the front door. Gemma smiles. She's wearing a blue dress with strawberries and blackberries embroidered into the neckline.

"I ran into Nishi after school," she declares.

"Good morning to you too."

She trips down the stairs, cursing in Mandarin under her breath. I grab a hold of her arm to steady her.

"Heels," she spits. The extra inch of height from the shoes makes her tower above me. "We talked for like three hours," she continues, not missing a beat, "I think it became a date, but I didn't ask."

She stops walking, opens her mouth, and frowns in horror. "Should I have asked?"

"You're asking *me* for relationship advice?"

The two of us are polar opposites when it comes to relationships. Gemma dates around, while I've only ever dated her. When we met at homecoming, only weeks before my mother's death, I thought she was the most beautiful person I'd ever seen. There was an undeniable attraction between us, but I was terrified of my own feelings. Gemma talked to me about her experiences with girls from her hometown like it was the most casual thing in the world.

"I'm so scared!" I admitted.

She giggled. "Rose, it's just a kiss. You don't have to be scared."

"But what if I mess up? What if it's weird?"

"Do you want me to kiss you?"

"What?" I asked, eyes widening.

"You know. To get it over with."

I froze, contemplating the idea of Gemma kissing me. She was gorgeous, and I thought she might like me, and I didn't want to screw it up. My heart was racing so fast I thought it might explode. All I could do was nod. Gemma grinned, then leaned in and pressed her lips to mine. It was the opposite of terrifying. It was wonderful.

Weeks later, we both got drunk at a friend's birthday party. I kissed her, and her lips tasted like honey and strawberry lip gloss.

"We should try this," Gemma said. "Being together. Right?"

Right? Didn't we owe it to ourselves after months of friendship? I agreed, but it went downhill quickly. Our conversations were suddenly awkward, like we needed to start our friendship over but on completely different terms. We decided after only five days of "dating" that we made better friends. Both of us were so relieved that the other felt the same that we agreed to never try anything like it again.

"Hello? Earth to Rose?"

Gemma's voice snaps me out of the memory.

"Sorry."

"What did you do after school?"

I tell her the truth, as crazy as it sounds. "I took a boxing class at the place downtown. Elliott King was there."

Gemma gasps. "Boxing? Since when are you into that?"

"Since yesterday, I guess."

The sharp sound of an engine revving stops me in my tracks. I recognize it immediately.

"Speak of the devil," Gemma murmurs.

We watch as Elliott's black BMW approaches the stop sign, rap music blasting through the open windows. He takes a drag of a cigarette. In the passenger seat, holding his free hand with hers, is Maddy Davis. Her blonde hair, curled to perfection, floats wildly in the wind. Elliott doesn't check for pedestrians before speeding through the stop sign.

"Believe it or not, he was actually pretty nice."

Gemma sneers. "I don't believe it."

We make plans to hang out later in the week before splitting up for class. I spend the morning doodling over my notes, rendering them useless. In English class, Mr. Ruse looks suspiciously like he's dead. I'm relieved when he blinks. He breaks into an enthusiastic smile once the bell rings.

I'm the only one to smile back.

"I hope you all are working on your poetry assignment."

Maddy leans over and whis pers in Elliott's ear. He smirks, muttering something back to her, but not quietly enough to get away with it. Mr. Ruse locks in on them.

"Did you pick a poem, Luke?" he asks.

I vaguely remember seeing Elliott's older brother, Luke, at school last year before he graduated. They could have been mistaken for twins if not for Elliott's array of tattoos. Luke was even more of a ladies' man than his brother.

"Sorry, wrong King," Mr. Ruse grumbles. "Elliott?"

"Yeah," he barks, "I read 'Fire and Ice' by Jack Frost."

"Robert Frost."

"Whatever."

Elliott sinks farther into his chair. He taps his foot against the floor.

"Did you like it?"

"Sure," he says, monotone. "If you like watching paint dry."

Ruse's eyebrows furrow. My gaze drifts to the bottom of Elliott's desk. His hands, littered with healing scabs, grip the bottom of the wood.

Ruse presses on. "Well, which do you think it will be?"

Elliott plays off his agitation, but I can tell he's uncomfortable. He must have the lowest GPA of the entire school. "What?"

"The end of the world. What will destroy it?"

"Fire," Elliott replies, unflinching. "I think everything will burn."

Ruse doesn't ask him any more questions. Elliott's grip on the desk loosens. He stays quiet for the rest of our class discussion, only occasionally making comments at inappropriate times. I do my best to concentrate on Ruse, but as always recently, my attention drifts to my phone.

**GEMMA: Coffee after school?**

I'm so distracted by answering Gemma's text that I crash into someone on my way out of the classroom door. The impact of our bodies knocks the wind from my chest. I turn to apologize, but the words disappear when I realize who it is.

Colorless eyes stare into mine. I could never forget that cold stare.

"Careful," he hisses.

Harris Price, dressed in the same football jersey he was wearing at Elliott's party, examines me. I stand frozen in place for at least a full minute before I disintegrate.

I need to leave, but my feet won't budge.

Harris observes me with the utmost curiosity, like I'm a specimen to be studied. I can only put together one coherent thought: *I can't do this again. Not in front of the entire school.*

I scream at my body to listen to my brain, commanding my legs to work. The women's bathroom is around the corner. If I can make it there, Harris can't touch me.

Laughter erupts from the doorway to Ruse's classroom. Elliott walks out with a different girl than Maddy at his side. His laughter fades when he notices Harris.

*Please,* I beg my feet. *Please move.*

I've never been able to describe my anxiety to my dad. Every time I try, he doesn't understand the panic isn't entirely in my head. I wish he could see me now, with my hands shaking and my face ghostly white, so he might finally understand how physical this truly is.

An eternity later, my feet finally move again. I sprint away from Harris, Elliott, and the other students into the bathroom.

I count. It helped last time. Didn't it?

*One.*

My own words play back to me, "I haven't had a panic attack since I started it."

*Two.*

How stupid was I to think that boxing might somehow fix this?

*Three.*

A few girls watch as I push my way into an empty stall. I heave into the toilet. There's nothing in my stomach, but I still try to rid myself of the weight in my body. Tears drip down my cheeks, and my vision goes white. I crash onto the floor and throw my head between my knees, trying once again to practice Dr. Taylor's damn breathing exercise that never works.

"Rose?"

The dizziness fades when I finally let go. My movements still as the world around me fades into darkness.

# CHAPTER FOUR

**A SMELL AS SOUR AS ROTTING FRUIT WAKES ME UP IN A PANIC.** The school nurse is staring down at me. "How are you doing honey?" Nurse Callie asks.

We've become familiar with each other since my incident last year. Her nose, coated in freckles, scrunches up with concern. In her hands is a jar of something pungent. She tucks the nasty gel into a drawer.

"I'm okay," I sigh. "I'm so sorry."

"Don't apologize! We're glad that you're okay."

*We?* That's when I spot Elliott beside her. Embarrassment flushes my face. He must have called the nurse when I ran into the bathroom.

Once again, I owe him for helping me.

"Your father didn't answer when I called. Is there someone else you want me to contact to come get you?" asks Nurse Callie.

"No. I can walk home."

I press my fingers against my throbbing forehead. At first, the pressure worsens the pain, but then the aching stops. A migraine, not a concussion.

To my surprise, Elliott says, "I'll drive her."

Nurse Callie, confused, considers his suggestion. She turns to me.

"Is that okay with you?" She draws out her words as if to say, *blink twice if you need help.*

"Sure," I respond with a shrug. I don't want to be alone with him, but it might be my only opportunity to talk about Midtown Ring.

As I place my feet on the floor, Elliott rests his hand on the back of my shoulder to keep me balanced. My muscles tense as he does. Harris made the same move. Fortunately, Elliott notices my discomfort and pulls his hand away before the feeling of his skin against mine fully registers. I exhale my nerves away and regain my composure.

The parking lot is empty. School must have already ended. *How long was I out for?*

Sunlight illuminates Elliott's face, exposing the shadow of a bruise around his eye. He walks me to the black convertible that I've been seeing way too much of lately. As I open the passenger door the scent of air freshener mixed with tobacco worsens my headache.

"I'm sorry about all of this," I say, slipping into the passenger's seat.

"It's cool. Not like you live far away."

Placing my bag beneath my feet, something catches on my shoe—a lime green thong. I hold it up to Elliott.

"Shit," he grumbles, grabbing the thin piece of cloth from my hand. He chucks it into the back seat. A moment of awkward silence falls between us. Then, I burst out laughing.

"You should really clean your car."

Elliott smirks mischievously. He turns the keys into the ignition. Music blasts through the speakers, vibrating the seats and the dashboard. Elliott quickly turns the volume down, chuckling at the startled look on my face.

He passes me a half empty bottle of water from the cupholder. "Drink."

I untwist the lid. Suddenly, Elliott grabs the bottle back, holds it up to his nose and sniffs. He nods approvingly.

"Not vodka?"

"Nope," he confirms.

The water is warm and stale, but I ignore the bad taste and chug most of it down. Elliott pulls out a pack of cigarettes from the glove box and lights one. Smoke travels from his lips to my lungs. Much to his amusement, I roll down the window and cough.

"Sorry," he says, but I know he doesn't mean it.

I narrow my gaze on the destroyed skin beneath his eye. "What happened?"

"Sparring after practice yesterday. Andre got me."

I'm almost positive Elliott and I left Midtown at the same time, but I let it go. Ever since that day in calculus, my memory has been nothing short of useless. He turns out of the parking lot and onto the main road. As he does, I ask the question that I've been avoiding.

"Are you okay with me taking classes at Midtown?"

Yesterday was the best I've felt in a while, but if Elliott doesn't approve, I can't keep going. He was there first, and I already owe him enough favors.

He shrugs. "I don't own the place."

It's not exactly the enthusiastic *yes* I was hoping for, but it's good enough. Elliott parks his convertible in my driveway. My father's car isn't there. *Good.* He doesn't need to know that our friendly neighborhood alcoholic gave me a ride home.

"Thanks for driving me," I say, reaching for the door handle.

"Sure. See you."

I'm desperate to ask if he's heard anything about Harris's plan to blab about what happened at his party, but the question sits like a rock in my throat. Saying Harris's name out loud will open up a can of worms I'm not ready to face. Without another word, I climb out of the car and shut the door behind me.

Elliott parks in his driveway. Despite us being neighbors, we've spoken more in the last few days than throughout our entire lives. His family never once showed up to any of the neighborhood block parties.

Inside, my house is eerily quiet. It always is these days. I go straight upstairs to lie down, letting the darkness of my bedroom ease my migraine.

"Hey."

My father's voice wakes me. I glance at the clock: 9:00 p.m. My nap may as well have been a full night's sleep.

"I got a voicemail from the nurse," he continues. "What happened?"

*Crap.* I should have known that she would get a hold of him eventually. He'll freak out if I tell him the truth, but I'm too exhausted to come up with a convincing lie.

"Panic attack," I admit. "I'm okay now."

His eyebrows crease with concern. He brushes his hand over mine and squeezes.

"Do you want me to call Dr. Taylor?"

"No! I'm okay. I promise. I just got overwhelmed with school stuff," I say. "Like any *other* teenager would."

I emphasize the last bit, but my dad still doesn't appear convinced. I keep talking.

"I never got to tell you the rest of the story about boxing. Two people from my class tried sparring, and we all got to watch. I think I want to get good enough to try that."

"You do?"

"Boxing is a test of physical and mental control. If I can do that, I can do anything. Right?"

"Alright," my dad replies, sounding both confused and relieved. "Why don't you stay home from school tomorrow? You can catch up on your work."

"Sounds good."

My father refills my glass of water and tells me to go back to sleep. When he leaves, I take out my phone and scroll through Instagram.

The first picture on my feed is a group of sophomore girls posing together in front of a restaurant. In the middle, dressed in his football jersey, is Harris Price. Morbid curiosity gets the best of me. I click on his profile. He has hundreds of pictures; most of them feature him posing shirtless in a mirror. One in particular stands out from the rest. Harris is holding a solo cup in one hand and snapping the photo with the other. Behind him, Elliott King lights a cigarette. His profile is tagged, and I click before I can stop myself.

Elliott's only posted three pictures: one showing off a lion tattoo on his ribs, one of him standing in a crowded room at a party, and one from when he first got his car. Nothing worth commenting on, but there are compliments from random girls on each one. Gemma will flip when she learns he drove me home.

Gemma. I never responded about meeting her for coffee. I text her an apology.

**GEMMA: WTF happened?**
**ROSE: Long story. Please don't be mad.**
**GEMMA: I'll forgive you if you go shopping with me.**
**ROSE: Fine.**

We chat about our plans for the rest of the week until I can't stay awake any longer.

\*

My dad wakes me up before my alarm with a plate full of breakfast. I shove a spoonful of scrambled eggs into my mouth, taming some of the hunger pains in my stomach.

"How are you feeling?" he asks.

"Much better." I'm grateful he's letting me stay home today.

"Do you have work?"

"Tonight."

He works at a call center downtown. He makes nothing compared to what he used to as an accountant, before he quit to take care of my mother. He tells me he likes his colleagues at the call center more than anyone he met in finance, so I've never commented on the pay.

"I have boxing later. Could you give me a ride?"

He nods. Although the thought of seeing Elliott makes me want to run away screaming, I need to go to practice. I have to give Dr. Taylor's suggestion a fair chance; otherwise, my dad putting half of his savings into therapy appointments was for nothing.

Mr. Ruse's poetry assignment takes up most of my afternoon. Inspired by our class discussion of *Annabel Lee*, I select another Poe poem, *Alone*. My essay is half-assed, but it's enough to get by with a passing grade.

Before that day of junior year in calculus—one of the worst days of my life, second only to my mother's funeral—a project like this would've excited me. But I'm tired and eager to be done with an essay that I'm not at all proud of.

Around three, my dad knocks on my bedroom door.

"Work wants me early. Do you want me to take you to the gym now?"

Boxing isn't until five, but I agree. Throwing my hair into a high ponytail, I slip on my pair of black and white Converse, which press uncomfortably against my toes. I need to get some real sneakers if I'm going to keep this up.

Skyscrapers on both sides of the road pass us by in a blur. On the rooftop of one is a billboard featuring a familiar face: Damon King, Elliott's father. He's posed with his hands on his sides on a black velvet couch. The words "King Law Firm" are printed underneath the photograph. I snicker. Ever since the billboard went up, the creepy expression on Elliott's dad's face has been a running joke at school.

A train briefly exits the underground before dipping back below the street. Atlanta's public transportation, MARTA, runs on an unpredictable schedule and only reaches a few destinations (Gemma and I call it the Metropolitan Atlanta Rapid Transit Asshole), but I can't complain. The subway is the reason why I've been able to survive life without a driver's license. I've been meaning to get it for a year now, but every time my dad tries to teach me, I end up having a panic attack at the wheel.

My father pulls up in front of the coffee shop next to Midtown Ring. A few adults are seated at the outdoor tables, busy with work and their own private conversations. I order a peach tea and sit in the corner, then pull out my notebook and finish Ruse's poetry assignment.

When I go over to the gym, I see Elliott first. He's dressed in a black T-shirt and dark blue athletic shorts. His hands are already wrapped and ready to hit. The skin around his eye has darkened into a plum color.

"You're back."

The voice comes from Riley, whose mustache is somehow creepier today. "My body feels like it went through a paper shredder," I reply.

"That's a good sign. Means you're getting stronger."

He's one to talk. His arms are three times bigger than mine. Despite his size, he doesn't make me feel small. Compassion radiates from him.

*Can't judge a book by its cover.*

"How long have you been boxing for?" I ask.

"Here at Midtown, only five months or so. But I went to a gym in Boston for two years."

He tells me that he studied at Boston University and left with a degree in neuroscience before taking a job at Emory, a hospital on the other side of town.

"Alright, everyone, let's get started!" Andre announces.

I jog over to Elliott. "Can I borrow your wraps again?"

"Sure," he replies.

He points to one of the lockers. I manage to wrap my hands without his help, though it's not as neat of a job. The communal gloves are loose around my hands. Turning my nose at the smell of rotting eggs wafting from them, I join the rest of the group in a stretch exercise. A few quiet conversations break out between them. Everyone is so comfortable with each other that it's hard not to feel like an outcast.

An outcast within a group of outcasts. *Oh, the irony.*

"We're going to begin with a partner activity," says Andre. "Elliott, you'll be with Rose. Max, you're with Sofía. I'll be with Riley."

I exhale a nervous breath as Elliott approaches me. He doesn't seem as bothered as I am by the pairing.

"You weren't at school today," he states.

I didn't think he would notice. "I wasn't feeling well."

"But you're boxing?"

"Yep," I reply.

He doesn't pry any further. Andre goes over the instructions for the exercise: each partner will hit the bag ten times while the other watches their form. I turn to Elliott, hoping he'll lead    as an example, but he doesn't make a move. My confidence lacks when I throw my first jab knowing Elliott's watching. I instantly forget everything Andre taught me on Monday.

"Keep your weight on your right foot," Elliott instructs.

Again, I try to punch the bag and lose my balance—one mistake away from falling face-first onto the ground. The image of Harris smirking at me in the hallway burns into my brain every time I make a move.

*Focus on the physical. Focus on something you can feel.*

Shaking out my hands at my side, I inhale a breath of salty air before trying again. The force of my punch is much stronger this time. By the fifth attempt, I manage to hit the bag without making any major errors.

Elliott applauds. I silently accept the victory before stepping out of the way for him to take my spot. The tattoo on his left arm of a bouquet of flowers bends and curves with each hit, yet the image of the rose in the center remains intact. His knuckles clash against the bag, and the sound is like an earthquake. Anyone watching would know that he was born to do this.

"Any notes?" Elliott asks.

He was flawless, and we both know it. "Your posture needs serious work."

"I'll keep that in mind."

I'm not sure if I'd call him my friend yet, but I'm much more comfortable around Elliott than ever before. He's a lot less intimidating outside of school grounds.

"I saw your dad on my way here," I say.

Elliott pauses. He drops his hands to his side, chest heaving as he catches his breath.

"He was here?"

"On the billboard. He's kind of terrifying with his face scaled so big."

He nods, saying nothing, so I drop the subject. We alternate a few more times before Andre calls the group back to the center of the room. Elliott takes the spot next to me. I still need to thank him for what he did at the party, but talking to him about Harris is ten times scarier than telling Gemma, and I haven't even found the courage to do that yet.

"We're going to do some interval conditioning next. Alternate between hits for two minutes, jump rope, and push-ups," explains Andre.

I groan. I'd rather eat glass than do cardio.

"Rose, I'm going to work with you while they're doing that. I want everyone caught up so we can work on sparring next week."

Score.

I follow him to one of the empty bags. He shows me an example of what he calls the "orthodox stance," with his left foot leading in front of his right. I try to copy him, but my balance is off. He gives the same speech as Elliott about not putting all my weight on my toes.

By the time practice ends, I'm drenched in sweat. Hot blood pumps throughout my body. I'm exhausted, but I'm alive.

Crashing onto the wooden bench, I peel off the smelly gloves and toss them on the ground. Elliott sits beside me. He's as sweaty as I am, but he belongs in a sporting goods ad while I feel like a wet dog.

"You're better already," he says with a flicker of pride in his crooked smile. "How does it feel?"

"Good, not counting the cramps in my foot."

He chuckles, then tosses his own pair of gloves into his bag. "You going to the party this weekend?"

The question catches me off guard. The only reason I was invited to Elliott's party was because Gemma pulled some strings. Usually, I don't make the guest list. I push a piece of hair out of my face and try not to show how surprised I am by the invitation.

"I didn't know there was a party," I reply, proudly handing him my pile of damp hand wraps. He snickers.

"Alex is hosting."

Alex is another member of the Dekalb football cult. He's less intimidating than Harris Price, but definitely not a friend of mine. I have zero interest in spending any more time with their group.

"Probably not then," I murmur.

He shrugs. "Suit yourself."

He throws his backpack across his shoulder, black boxing gloves peeking out from the open zipper.

"I'll get some of my own gear for next week. I promise."

"Don't worry about it."

Elliott leaves the gym, the light from the doorway illuminating a few scattered bruises across his body. I wait until his car clears the parking lot before leaving myself.

*

I recognize her from behind.

Her dark mess of hair matches mine. A few freckles line the tops of her shoulders. People said we could've been twins. Doris Berman faces me, alive and smiling. She's holding a book with a cover I recognize from my childhood. I used to draw in the margins of the beaten-up pages.

My mother tells me about a princess who doesn't need a knight. When she reads, her voice is soothing, each word flowing from her lips like a music note. I try to memorize the unique way that she pronounces the letters, as if she's speaking in cursive.

But her tone becomes less musical with every sentence. Her pupils expand until her eyes are an all-consuming black. She opens her mouth to scream, but no sound comes out.

I beg her to hear me, but she can't.

I'm too late.

Again.

"Rose!"

My father is shaking my shoulders. I shoot up from my bed and gasp for air. Moonlight trickles through my bedroom window. *When did I fall asleep? I can't even remember getting home from practice.*

"You were screaming," my dad whispers.

He passes me the cup of water from my nightstand. I drink it all in one gulp. My pulse slows to a normal pace.

"I'm sorry I woke you up."

All the color in his face has vanished, and I know exactly why. My mother used to wake up the house when she had nightmares. Dr. Taylor told us that her bad dreams were a symptom of her anxiety disorder, a way for her fears to materialize. She tried sleeping pills, exercise, even sound machines, but none of them could rid her of the bad dreams.

"I'm okay," I insist. "I promise."

He glances down at the time on my phone. It's midnight, on the dot. I left Midtown Ring around seven.

*Five hours. I can't remember five whole hours.*

"What were you dreaming about?" my father asks.

"Ghosts," I lie.

I can tell he wants to believe me, but there's doubt in his eyes as I explain the details. He's been watching me like a hawk ever since my panic attack in calculus, and I hate it. I don't want him to worry; he has enough on his plate as is. When I've convinced him that the nightmare is all my fault for watching *The Conjuring* again, we go back and forth discussing mind-numbing topics like the weather tomorrow.

"How was boxing?"

I perk up. "Fun. We did partner exercises. Elliott King was mine."

At the sound of Elliott's name, he pauses. My father might be the only person to know any details about Elliott's family having lived right next door for the last nine years.

"Damon King's son?"

I nod. My father tilts his chin, pondering the memories he must have of Elliott.

"Your mom wanted the two of you to get to know each other. Damon was a jerk about it."

"You met him?"

I can't recall ever talking to Elliott's father, though I'm familiar enough with his face from the images plastered all over the city.

"We talked occasionally. He didn't spend much time at the neighborhood barbecues."

"Does he have a wife?"

"Not that I ever met."

My dad stays by my side for a while before heading back to sleep. As he slips out of my bedroom door, I pick up my phone and type Damon King's name into Google. Two hundred results pop up. Most articles are about his successful law practice. A few highlights him giving back to the community, donating part of his vast salary to local charity organizations. Elliott's older brother, Luke, shows up in a couple articles, but Elliott's name is never mentioned.

I finally accept that I'm being a total stalker and put down my phone.

# CHAPTER FIVE

**ON FRIDAY, EXCITEMENT SEEPS THROUGH THE HALLWAYS OF DEKALB HIGH.** The school has a different energy with the weekend approaching, especially one with a big party planned. I waste away the minutes of English class counting the bruises on Elliott's neck. Today there are four. Two more than yesterday.

"You're hanging out with Elliott, King of STDs?" Gemma exclaims during lunch, shoving a bite of turkey sandwich into her mouth.

I made the mistake of telling her about Elliott inviting me to Alex's party, and she hasn't stopped talking about it since. I shush her. Elliott's only a few tables away from us, surrounded by a group of football players even though he doesn't play. To my relief, Harris isn't one of them. I haven't seen him since our run in on Tuesday.

"Hanging out is an overstatement," I reply. "We're in the same boxing class."

She grins. "You're sweaty and fighting each other? That's hot."

I grimace. I'd have to be blind to not find Elliott attractive, but there's no way in hell that anything would ever happen between us. He has every girl in our school hanging on his arm. Literally, there's one grabbing his bicep as Gemma speaks. I have zero interest in becoming a tribute in their boyfriend *Hunger Games*.

"You should go to Alex's," Gemma pleads. "Elliott told you he would be there, right?"

"Yes, and I told him I wouldn't be. Do you really think I want to get with someone who can barely spell his own name?"

"Touché."

Last year, I would have jumped at the opportunity to go. But after what happened at Elliott's house, the thought of walking into a crowded room of drunk football players makes my stomach turn. Harris will be there. He never misses a party.

If I could find the right words to tell Gemma about what happened with Harris, she would understand my hesitation. I peer over my shoulder. Students crowd my left and right. Anyone could hear us. I swallow down the truth for another time.

On our way out of the cafeteria, Gemma stops walking. "Just consider it, Rose."

I sigh. I can't fight with her all day about this.

"I'm not going."

She pouts theatrically. Gemma never hesitates to do anything at all, even with the threat of her conservative parents constantly breathing down her neck. How they haven't figured out about the parties she's been attending, I'll never understand.

"I really won't have a wingman tonight?"

*So Gemma was already invited.* The realization hits me harder than I expect it to, and I suddenly feel stupid for thinking I was special. Half the cafeteria was probably invited before me.

"I'm sorry, Gem."

She leaves the cafeteria without another word. I spend the rest of the day listening in on conversations about beer pong tournaments and hookups. Gemma meets me outside in our usual spot in the courtyard.

"What should I wear tonight?" she questions.

I glance at her high waisted blue jeans, pink tank top, and hoop earrings. "Why not that?"

She stares at me like I have three heads. "Hell no. Not enough cleavage. I gotta show off these killer curves." She twirls, moving her hips in a circle. I burst out laughing.

"Your mom is going to kill you."

"Actually, I told her I'm going on a date with Jeremy Toh. She'll let me wear whatever I want."

I stop walking. "Jeremy Toh? I thought he was in rehab?"

"I told her he's studying at a super prestigious boarding school. She loves it."

Elliott's convertible shoots down the empty street beside us. Gemma nudges her elbow into my side at the sound of the growling engine. I huff, crushing a patch of wildflowers with my boot.

"Nishi and I are going to grab food from Simone's. You want to come?"

Gemma's been trying to get Nishi alone for weeks now. Crashing her first unofficial date would be a betrayal. I shake my head *no*.

She walks me all the way to my front door, then hugs me.

"Love you," I whisper.

"Love you, too. See you later!"

She skips down the driveway. I force myself to turn away from her and drag my feet through my front door. The possibility of something bad happening to Gemma tonight makes me want to lock her inside and throw away the key.

I expect to find my father on the couch, but the living room is empty.

**DAD: At work. Call me if you need anything.**

I hate when the timing works out like this. Our house is creepy at night. I try to distract myself from the weird sounds in the attic by cooking dinner. My attempt at alfredo pasta tastes like cardboard. I spit out the bite in my mouth and warm up a frozen pizza instead. The microwave clock reads 7:00 p.m. The party starts in an hour.

*Please, Gemma. Stay away from Harris Price.*

I turn on the Leonardo DiCaprio version of *Romeo and Juliet*. My eyes shut against my will right before Romeo dies, but I don't get the chance to fall asleep before the piercing sound of my phone ringing sends me into cardiac arrest. I fall off the couch trying to grab it from the coffee table. Gemma's contact picture lights up the screen.

"Hello?" I pant, throat parched. I gulp down the rest of my water.

"Rose? It's Nishi."

"Hey, Nishi," I respond. "What's up?"

"Gemma is sick. It's bad."

Her words are rushed and panicked. I instantly straighten up, propping myself up against the table. My nails dig into my palm, the pain waking me up fully.

"Where are you?"

"About half a mile east of the school. You know where Crystal Springs is?"

I know the neighborhood. My mom used to attend a book club there when I was young.

"Yes," I say. "I can come over but I'm—"

"It's the third house on the right," she interrupts. "Call me when you're here."

Through the phone speaker, I can vaguely make out the sound of Gemma moaning. Rising from the floor, I snatch my father's windbreaker from the coat hanger and race through the front door. The sight of my bike in the garage porch, wheels coated in rust, stops me in my tracks. *Faster than walking.*

The bike makes it down my driveway without falling apart, so I decide to ride it all the way to Crystal Springs. Streetlamps guide my path down the sidewalk. I recognize a few familiar landmarks: Dekalb High School, Simone's Chinese Food, and finally a large, gated neighborhood. The security gate is propped open by a brick.

"Idiots," I say, biking through the entrance.

Music blasts from the first house. I drop my bike in the middle of the lawn, then dial Nishi back.

"I'm here," I huff. Sweat trickles from my forehead onto my neck. If not for the cardio Andre forced me to do this week, I doubt I could've made this trip without fainting.

"We're upstairs. Hurry!"

Two drunk girls stumble out of the door. I catch it before it closes, slipping inside of the smoke-filled living room. Freshmen pressed up against each other spill drinks and cigarettes across the hardwood floors. My gaze travels to the group of football players gathered around a beer pong table. Harris lurks between two of them, his long, shaggy hair pinned up in a bun. I turn around before he notices me.

*Focus. You're here for Gemma.*

"Excuse me," says a girl who doesn't give me a chance to move before plowing into me. I glare and push past her.

Something cold and wet brushes against the back of my arm. My heart hammers. I prepare to come face to face with

Harris Price, begging my body to listen to my brain and not throw up this time, but it isn't him who greets me.

"Sorry," says a sophomore boy, as he moves the wet solo cup in his hand away from my skin.

I dash up the spiral staircase. The hallway that it leads to is coated in darkness, but I don't need my vision to hear Gemma's moans echoing from the shadows.

*Bingo.*

Four doors line the walls. Marijuana smoke floats out from one on the left; Gemma's groaning comes from the right. To my relief, Nishi opens the door when I knock. Her thick eyebrows are furrowed with fear. Behind her, Gemma is slumped over on the toilet. Something green and sticky peeks out from her red ponytail. She's awake, yet she barely responds to the sight of me.

Nishi locks the door after I step inside the bathroom.

I glare at her. "You let her drink this much?"

My tone is aggressive, but I don't apologize. Gemma's my best friend. My *only* friend.

And I wasn't there for her.

"I didn't know she took so many shots. I freaked out—"

"It's fine," I hiss. "Move."

Nishi steps out of my way, and I crash onto the cold bathroom tile next to Gemma. Her lips twist into a small, helpless smile as I place my palm on her forehead. Not feverish.

"How are you feeling?"

Gemma crinkles her nose. "Gross."

Her green dress reeks of cheap cinnamon whiskey. I rub my hand across her back.

"How many shots do you think she had?" I ask Nishi.

"I don't know. Maybe five? Seven?" Nishi's shoulders sink as she realizes the weight of her words. "I should've stopped her."

I try to remain calm. Panicking won't get us out of here. "Let's get her up."

We wrap our arms around her and pull. She makes herself a dead weight against us.

"No," Gemma moans.

Nishi frowns hopelessly, but I just roll my eyes. There's a simple way to get Gemma to do anything I want.

"If you cooperate, I'll buy you coffee for a week."

She perks up. A piece of reddish black hair falls into her face. Even in her worst moment, she's still beautiful. Nishi seems to come to the same conclusion. Her mouth waters. But Unlike Harris, her hunger is innocent, fueled by adoration rather than mindless desire.

"Two weeks," I plead with Gemma. "Pumpkin spice lattes. Anything you want."

She nods. She straightens her back so we can get a better grip on her. Nishi and I manage to keep her on her feet as we guide her up from the floor.

"I'm dizzy," Gemma whispers.

Nishi nudges the bathroom door open with her elbow. Step by step, we lead Gemma from the bathroom into the smoky hallway. A sophomore girl passes us by, shooting Gemma a sympathetic frown before making her way down the stairs.

*The stairs.*

There's no way in hell Gemma will make it down without falling on her face. Even if we can manage it, our only form of transportation is my bike—if someone hasn't stolen it.

"Shit," Nishi whispers, apparently coming to the same conclusion as me.

With the rush of adrenaline coursing through my veins, an idea I hadn't considered before comes to mind.

"I think I can get us a ride. Stay with her."

Carefully, we lean Gemma against one of the walls to keep her from falling over. Nishi's arm remains locked across her shoulders. I start my search upstairs, peeking into the room with the smoke, but Elliott is nowhere to be found.

He'll be downstairs, where the real party is.

I muster up every ounce of courage I have, but my anxious trembling doesn't stop as I descend toward the living room. I follow the sound of shouting. In the middle of the room, a football player guzzles beer from a metal bucket. Beer drips out of his mouth and stains the Persian rug. One of the girls admiring him spots me. Maddy.

"Hey," I stammer.

She scowls, pursing her red lips. "What do you want?"

"Is Elliott here?"

She hesitates for a moment, as if deciding if she should tell me the truth. Then, she says, "Upstairs."

Elliott wasn't in the bathroom or the smokers' room, which means he must be in the room with the closed door. A thousand different nightmarish scenarios flash in my mind of what could happen if I open it—Harris waiting for me with nobody around to stop him, Elliott passed out in the corner . . .

"Thanks," I say, turning away from the crowd.

Nishi shoots me a nervous look when I return without any help. Gemma's skin is translucent, her knees twisted, but she's standing. I jog to the door at the end of the hallway and knock three times.

No answer. I knock again.

Still nothing. Behind me, Gemma whines, a pained sound that implies she's going to throw up again if we don't get her out of here quickly.

*Fuck it.* I open the door.

It's a closet. In the darkness, I'm able to make out the shapes of two people: Elliott and a red-haired girl. Her lips are pressed against his. She wraps one of her hands around his head, pulling him closer. They don't notice the sound of the door opening.

I cough. Elliott pulls away, jerking his head when he notices me.

"Rose?" he gawks.

The girl flashes a murderous glare in my direction. That's when I notice her lack of clothes. She crosses her arms against her bare chest, and I turn away, embarrassment heating my cheeks. I keep my gaze trained on Elliott, who, fortunately, is fully dressed.

I rush my words. "I need your help. My friend is sick. I need to get her home."

For a moment, Elliott hesitates, hands still lingering on the girl's waist as he glances between the two of us. Then, he breaks away from her. Elliott picks up the girl's shirt from the closet floor and tosses it into her hands. Her mouth drops into a surprised O.

"Don't worry, babe. We'll reschedule."

The girl shoots me a death stare. I'm being an asshole, but I really don't have another option. Silently, I mouth to her, "Sorry."

"Let's go," Elliott commands.

I don't have a second to react before he brushes past me into the hallway. The door to the closet closes behind him, leaving the shirtless girl inside it alone.

Elliott pulls out a pair of car keys from his pocket and tosses them to Nishi. She glances reluctantly between the two of us, probably trying to piece together how the hell we know each other. I wish I had a different answer than the truth.

"My car is the black BMW. Can you drive it up front?" asks Elliott.

Nishi nods, pocketing the keys before rushing down the stairs. I move to get a better grip on Gemma's waist, but Elliott stops me.

"I got her," he says. He wraps his arm around my best friend's lifeless body. "Grab her stuff."

I do. Elliott scoops Gemma up as if she weighs nothing. She lets out a small whimper at the sudden movement but doesn't struggle. I squeeze her hand as the four of us make our way down the stairs. Partygoers stare and whisper. Someone pulls out a cell phone camera, to which I stick up my middle finger.

Elliott's car is waiting in the driveway when we slip through the front door. Nishi jumps out of the driver's seat, throwing open the back door so Elliott can lay Gemma there. My bike has vanished from its spot on the lawn.

"Assholes," I grumble under my breath.

"Can you drive?" Elliott asks Nishi. His slurred words imply that he's had more than enough to drink tonight. She nods and grabs the keys.

Elliott climbs into the passenger seat and blasts the heat onto Gemma's trembling body. She must be freezing in her thin green dress. I take off my jacket and lay it across her.

I wonder out loud, "Should we go to the hospital?"

Through the rearview mirror, Elliott observes Gemma. "We can go to my house," he decides, after a few seconds of deliberation. "If she gets any worse, we'll take her." Considering he has more experience drinking than all of us combined, I trust his judgment. The ride back to his house is quiet; the only noise comes from Nishi occasionally asking Gemma if she's okay. Elliott rolls down his window and takes a puff of a cigarette. I consider asking him to put it out, for Gemma's sake, but this is his car, and he's the one letting us use it. I shut my mouth and peek out the window.

And then I see her.

She's gone in a moment, just the outline of a person. Her shoulders are hunched and motionless. But it's my mom's smile lit up by headlights that I recognize. My vision blurs, stomach plummeting to my feet. I pull a muscle in my neck trying to get a better look.

Nothing but darkness.

I shiver. It wasn't really her—I know it wasn't—yet she looked so real. Suddenly, this tiny car is suffocating. As soon as Nishi parks, I fling open the door. Gemma leans over me and throws up onto the driveway. Something wet hits the bottom of my shirt, but I ignore it. Her sickness is the least of my problems right now.

"Come on," Elliott whispers, guiding Gemma out of the seat.

Standing at the front door, Elliott's house makes the hair on my arms stand up. I've passed it every day since the night of the party, but the nighttime amplifies its eeriness. The upstairs windows and the front door form a taunting smile.

Elliott holds Gemma with one hand and puts out his cigarette on a brick with the other. The spot is covered in ash stains.

"Welcome home," Elliott mutters.

He twists the key into the lock and flips on the lights inside. The interior of the King mansion is as unsettling as I remember. The living room is spotless, floor clear of any solo cups or empty shot glasses. In the light, I can make out the Victorian furniture in its entirety. A grandfather clock looms over the wood fireplace. Two dark leather couches reside behind a wooden coffee table. The room is exactly what I would imagine you might find inside of a rich lawyer's home.

Elliott guides Gemma to one of the couches. She lies down. Nishi grabs a garbage can from the nearby bathroom and places it at Gemma's side. I end up in the kitchen searching for a glass for water. The kitchen cabinets are white, a stark contrast to the rest of the design of the house. The counters lack a single crumb. I grab the only plastic cup and fill it from the sink. To my annoyance, Gemma refuses to drink when I offer it to her. It takes several attempts of coaxing from both Nishi and I until she takes a sip.

"I'll walk her home once she can stand," I tell Elliott.

He blinks, confused. "She can sleep here."

"Are you sure? What about your dad?"

"He won't be home until Sunday. It's cool."

He glances between Nishi and me. "You both can crash here, too."

"Thank you," Nishi exhales, voice rich with gratitude. She ties Gemma's hair out of her face, so it won't keep falling into her mouth. "I'll stay awake with her."

Her brown eyes never leave Gemma. I shouldn't have been so harsh with her earlier.

"You okay?" I ask Gemma.

She grips the side of the metal trash can and exhales. Some of the color has returned to her cheeks. "I'm never drinking again." We both know she'll drink again next weekend. I just hope that it's half of tonight's endeavor. Gemma rests her head against the pillow, left hand reaching out to clutch Nishi's. They're cute together. I have to tell Gemma when she's functioning again.

Surveying my T-shirt, I scowl—it's stained brown and smells like the dirty gloves at Midtown Ring.

"You want a shower?" Elliott asks.

"That would be great."

"Follow me."

I stand. He guides me away from the living room. My phone dings with a text from my dad asking about my plans.

**ROSE: Sleeping at Gemma's. I'll be back tomorrow.**

**DAD: Have fun, love you.**

A wave of guilt rushes over me for lying to him, but I push it down. It's better that he doesn't know. Elliott leads me upstairs, stopping at a door on the left side of the hallway. Every step farther into the house brings back memories of last weekend. I can't stop the nervous sweat dampening my armpits. Inside the door is a bathroom. The bathroom. The one I was searching for during the night of the party. It's only steps away from Elliott's bedroom. The onslaught of frustrated thoughts in my head are so loud that I'm surprised by my lack of words. I bite my lip. A small trickle of blood drips onto my tongue, the iron thick and rich. I swallow it before Elliott sees.

67

He leaves, then returns moments later with a pair of purple sweatpants and a black T-shirt. The tag on the back implies they belong to a girl. I don't want to know which one.

"Thanks," I whisper.

"Towels are under the sink. You need anything else?

"I'm good."

He nods. "Cool."

And with that, Elliott leaves me alone.

The two of us never had any reason to get to know each other before. I never considered him a friend more than a neighbor, but over the last few days, he's done more for me than most people have. I owe him more than a thank you, but I decide to at least start with that tonight.

The piping hot water relaxes my strained muscles. As the bubbles run across my skin, clearing away the dirt and grime from tonight, I recognize the smell of the soap as Elliott's.

The water feels impossibly good, but I don't linger. I hop out of the shower and get dressed. The black shirt is a V-neck that does my flat chest no favors. The sweatpants are one size too big, but I tie them twice to keep the cloth from falling off my waist. My bangs drip water down my face as I leave the bathroom.

Elliott's bedroom door is propped open. The walls, a dull gray color, match the blankets on the bed. And there's that damn poster on his wall, the musician and those guitar strings mocking me. They know all about what happened here.

Elliott sits on the edge of his unmade bed with his cell phone pressed against his ear. His brows are tensed, cheeks heated with aggravation toward whoever is on the other line. He doesn't notice me pass by.

Downstairs, Nishi and Gemma watch an animated television show. Gemma relaxes on an air mattress on the ground that Elliott must have set up while I was showering.

"How are you doing?" I ask Gemma.

"I can't lie down without the room spinning. Good thing *Rick and Morty* is on all night." She pauses, then looks around, as if she's just now noticing we're no longer at Alex's party. "Uh, where are we, exactly?"

I laugh. This place is more like a movie set than a home. I still haven't spotted a family photo.

"Elliott King's house. He drove us here."

"That was really nice of him."

"I know," I mumble.

I still can't figure out why Elliott was so willing to help tonight, but the more I think about it, the more confused I get. Reaching into the pocket of Elliott's sweatpants, I realize my phone isn't there. I must have left it upstairs.

The door to Elliott's bedroom is closed when I walk by again. I snatch my phone from the bathroom counter and head back toward the staircase, but Elliott shouting distracts me.

"Seriously? I said five hundred! You'll get at least a thousand back."

I pause.

"I told you nobody's going to find out."

I inch closer, trying to hear better, but the bedroom door swings open before Elliott says another word. He stares down at me, blue eyes wide with shock. I may as well be holding a sign that says *eavesdropper*.

"Sorry—" I stammer.

He cuts me off. "Can we talk?"

His stance is rigid, his broad shoulders stiff. I talk without answering his question. The words come out in a jumbled mess.

"Thank you. For everything. I should've said that earlier."

Elliott drops his phone into his pocket. "You don't need to thank me. That's why I wanted to talk. I've been trying to apologize."

*Elliott apologizing? For what?*

He takes a step to the side, welcoming me into his bedroom, but I hesitate. I'm safe, yet my subconscious begs me to run far away from this space. Glancing between me and the bed, Elliott's lips part as he recalls what happened here.

"Shit. Sorry."

I can't avoid everywhere that Harris has been—the entire city of Atlanta would be off limits if I did. "It's fine," I state, stepping into the bedroom.

There's nothing in the room that would leave anyone to believe something bad went down here. The checkered rug and glass table have vanished.

Nothing broken remains—except for me.

"Harris didn't used to be this way," Elliott continues, lowering his voice so only I can hear. "I would never be friends with somebody who—"

"I know."

He takes a seat on the bed, kicking away an empty bottle of Grey Goose on the ground. I remain standing.

"Did you start boxing because of what happened with Harris?" he inquires.

There's no reason for me to lie to him. "Yes."

I have other motivations, of course. One of those being that my therapist recommended I try it to cope with my crippling anxiety, but Elliott doesn't need to know about that part.

"You're good at it, you know. Andre wouldn't be so patient with you if he didn't think so."

A major compliment coming from the boxer who commands the gym at Midtown. I know he's just trying to be nice, but I can't keep the proud smile off my face. Maybe Dr. Taylor's suggestion wasn't such a bad one.

"How long have you been boxing?" I question.

Elliott leans farther into the bed, flashing a grin that shows off his crooked white teeth.

"I started classes when I was twelve, but I had plenty of experience fighting with my brother."

Cautiously, I sit down beside Elliott, leaving at least a foot of distance between us. From this angle, I can make out the shapes of three overlapping triangles tattooed behind his ear.

"I like that," I say, pointing to the ink. "How do you have so many? Aren't you seventeen?"

"There's a guy under the bridge with a tattoo gun. He does it cheap."

I wait for Elliott to laugh, but he doesn't.

Not a joke.

"Well," I state, "That sounds like a recipe for hepatitis."

Elliott considers the idea as if he had never thought about it before. Then, he shrugs. "It hasn't happened yet."

He runs his hand through his buzzed hair, further exposing the set of triangles. When I first saw Elliott King after summer break between eighth grade and freshman year of high school, I was stunned. His long, blonde hair was shaved down to practically nothing. Tattoos littered his arms. The sight of a fourteen-year-old with ink on his body wasn't something I was accustomed to.

I wonder what his father must think.

As I'm about to get up from my spot on the bed, Elliott speaks again.

"Are you applying to any colleges?"

"A few, yeah," I say. "You?"

He shakes his head. He's the first senior I've met who isn't making college plans. I've been counting down the days until applications open, crossing my fingers I get into a school with a good creative writing program. But all those plans are on hold until I'm deemed mentally stable enough to move out.

"What do you want to do after graduation, then?" I ask, perplexed.

Elliott blinks. I can tell that he hasn't given the question much thought.

"Maybe join the army. I'm not sure they'll take me."

"I don't think they're very picky."

He leans back, folding his hands under his head, revealing the image of a dagger inked into the skin of his inner bicep. The edge of the blade is pointed in the direction of the rest of his body, as if one wrong movement could cause it to sink into his heart.

"You know, I see the way that you look at me," he says, a smirk dancing on his lips.

I pause. I wasn't trying to stare, but he's a difficult person not to stare at. Blush creeps into my cheeks.

"The way I look at you?"

"Like I'm an idiot."

"What?" I retort. "No, I don't!"

"In class, when I said I chose *Fire and Ice*, you totally thought I was a dumbass."

"Sorry. It wasn't intentional."

He chuckles. "It's cool. I'm not much of a school person."

There have definitely been a few times over the years where I caught Elliott cheating off of my tests, but I never stopped him. I figured if he needed help that badly, I shouldn't be the one to deny him. Elliott relaxes into the queen-sized bed, and I'm surprised by how comfortable I am beside him. Still, I can't shake the feeling that there's something he's keeping from me.

"I should check on Gemma," I mutter.

This time, Elliott doesn't stop me from leaving. His eyes are soft in the dim bedroom light, and a fleeting thought crosses my mind of what it must be like to look further into them. I could drown in the color of the waves.

I brush it off and leave the room, shutting the door behind me.

Downstairs, Gemma and Nishi clear a spot for me on the air mattress. Gemma falls asleep after only a few minutes. Nishi and I carefully move her head from my shoulder to the pillow.

"Nishi," I whisper, "I'm sorry for how I acted earlier. This wasn't your fault."

"You don't need to apologize," she replies. "I don't know what I would've done if you weren't there."

Elliott trudges downstairs. He tiptoes when he notices Gemma sleeping, but even his gentle walk is an earthquake.

"Who's there?" Gemma croaks.

"Nobody," I reply. "Go back to sleep."

She does, grabbing Nishi's hand with hers as her breathing steadies. Elliott slides onto the couch behind us.

"What the hell are you watching?" he asks.

"It was *Rick and Morty*, but now . . ." I pause. "Crap. George Lopez. Why is it always him?"

Elliott chuckles. "What did George Lopez do to you?"

"Plague my childhood nightmares."

I grumble and change the channel to a nature documentary. Nishi is the next one to fall asleep. Her legs stretch across my lap.

"I'm going to need the name of the girl you were . . . *with*," I tell Elliott. "I think I owe her an apology."

"The red head?"

I nod.

"Don't know it."

"But you told her you'd reschedule?"

"Figure of speech," he answers.

The narrator on television drones on about beluga whales. We sink into silence, but my mind won't relax. I finally work up the courage to ask, "I didn't mean to eavesdrop when you were on the phone earlier. But is everything okay?"

Silence.

I turn around, but Elliott is already asleep.

# CHAPTER SIX

**"MORNING."**

Elliott's voice is a hoarse whisper. He wears a curious expression, the corners of his lips curled into a playful half-smile. Sunlight spills through the lofted windows of the living room. Slowly, I sit up from my spot on the couch. There's a crick in my neck from sleeping without a pillow. I must have knocked it off in the middle of the night.

"Hey," I whisper.

Face down on the air mattress, Gemma is snoring. My bangs, which came unpinned as I slept, fall across my forehead. I brush them away. Elliott watches me intently, like every move I make is of the utmost importance, and for a moment, I wonder to myself how many other girls have woken up to the sight of him like this: tired but beautiful, too exhausted to put up a facade. I don't think I want to know the answer.

"What time is it?" Gemma mumbles.

I answer, "Ten."

"What day is it?" adds Nishi.

Nishi rises from her spot on the mattress. She yawns, which makes Gemma yawn, which makes me yawn, which makes Elliott yawn.

"I should probably get home soon," Gemma says. "I didn't even tell my parents that I'd be sleeping out."

Nishi replies, "I texted them for you. Your mom kept calling."

We take turns reminding Gemma of the details of what happened at the party. Nishi explains that Gemma started out the night by playing beer pong but sucked so badly she gave up and took shots.

"Sore loser," Elliott teases.

Gemma snorts. "Like you're any better. I've seen you at parties."

Elliott sticks up his middle finger.

"How's your head?" I ask Gemma.

She presses her hand against her temple and sighs. "It hurts. And I'm starving."

"There's plenty of food. Make whatever you want," suggests Elliott.

Nishi and I wander into the kitchen. The fridge is stocked with unopened containers. We find eggs, milk, and a sealed box of pancake mix. I pour chocolate chips into the batter without asking permission. As Nishi cooks, I tell her about the time my mom and I tried making latkes and almost burnt the house down. It's strange to talk so casually about my dead mom, but Nishi doesn't make it weird, so I don't either.

In quiet moments, I can hear Elliott and Gemma talking from the living room, but I can't make out their words. Something about all of this still feels . . . *wrong*.

"Yum," Elliott exclaims, his mouth watering at the finished stack of chocolate chip pancakes.

The room smells heavenly, and the pancakes taste as good as they smell.

"This is amazing," I affirm in between forkfuls of syrup and chocolate chips.

Elliott eats an entire pancake in one bite. All of us giggle as he attempts to swallow it down. Breakfast with one of the most popular guys in school was not on my list of potential weekend activities, but I'm enjoying it more than I care to admit.

"Thanks again for letting us crash here," Gemma says.

Elliott waves her off. "You guys are good company. And I can't complain about the breakfast."

Gemma burps loudly. I laugh so hard a tear drips down my cheek. We stand up to clean our plates. Then, Gemma, Nishi, and I head toward the back door.

Elliott unlocks it. He turns to me. "I'll wash your clothes."

Gemma and Nishi raise their eyebrows. I blush.

"Thanks," I reply, for what must be the millionth time this weekend.

"See you at school."

The three of us slip out the back door into the morning air. We cut through the patch of woods in Elliott's backyard, so my dad doesn't see us. The leaves are changing color, creating a beautiful array of red and yellow. Gemma basks in the warmth. We step into the street a few houses down from mine—the opposite direction of Elliott's place.

"That was really nice of him," says Gemma. "Who knew Elliott King was a halfway decent person?"

I shuffle to a stop. "You don't think it was weird at all?"

"I mean, I guess it's a little weird he helped us, yeah. But I think he likes you."

"No way." I'm not the type of girl Elliott crushes on. *Anyone* crushes on. Unless they're interested in social suicide. So why risk it?

"Shopping tomorrow?" Gemma asks.

"Sure," I reply. "After therapy."

Nishi and Gemma both hug me when we reach the bottom of my driveway. Reaching for the handle on the front door, my dad answers before I can open it. He waves to Gemma and Nishi.

"Where are they going?"

I lie, "Walking to breakfast."

"Don't you want to go with them?"

"They're on a date. And I have homework."

He watches as they disappear over the hill. I walk through the door, dropping my dirt-covered boots on the mat.

"Clean your room while you're up there," he orders. "I can't see the floor."

He's right. My bedroom looks like a tornado hit it. Clothes, including the thin black dress that I've been too afraid to touch, litter the ground. Half-read books form stepping stones from my bed to the bathroom. As I'm reaching for the vacuum, my phone vibrates with an Instagram notification. I open the app to twenty-seven new comments on my profile from Harris Price. Beneath all of my pictures, he's typed the same thing.

**@hprice13 Psycho Bitch.**

I throw my phone onto the bed.

Pressure builds in my chest.

My grasp on the world around me slips away suddenly. I pause at the sight of myself in my full-length mirror.

My reflection is unrecognizable. She smiles knowingly at me. Then, the scene from Elliott's bedroom fills the mirror. *Harris's calculated movements play in slow motion. I open my mouth to scream at him to stop, stop it now, but all that I can get out is a whimper.*

*Her face returns to my reflection but quickly changes shape; it looks like Harris instead of me. His long brown hair blends with my dark curls. His eyes narrow. His fingers reach out to touch my shoulder. And his taunting smirk transforms into a new one that I can't bear: my mother's.*

*She's beautiful—alive—but impossibly cold.*

*Her skin cracks like ice.*

Reality is slipping from my grasp, shaking my body, destroying my sanity.

I punch her image, my reflection, whatever it is, it has to stop.

She shatters into an array of small pieces that crumble onto the floor. The pain is searing as my torn knuckles scream at the bits of jagged glass sticking out of my skin.

My trembling slows. The dizziness stops. Pain is so much easier to understand when the source is real. Tangible. Not some bizarre hallucination.

*I can breathe.*

*I can breathe.*

*I can breathe.*

"Rose?" My father shouts from down the hallway. "What was that?"

I sprint from my room into the bathroom and grab a roll of bandages from under the sink. Blood oozes through immediately, but I keep layering the cloth around my hand until the roll runs out. Then, I take the closest object to me, an old water bottle I had left on the counter, and chuck it into my bedroom on top of the mess of shattered glass. My dad's lips part with shock as he takes in the scene of the crime.

"I was aiming for the bed," I state, pointing down at the water bottle. The false words come out smoothly, but I'm not sure if he believes my unlikely story.

"Are you hurt?"

My hand is tucked into my jacket pocket. He doesn't notice it.

I shake my head. He inches closer to the mess, brown eyes dripping with worry as he picks up a large piece of glass.

"I'll clean this up," he says. "Why don't you go pick up some food from Simone's?"

He doesn't want me in the vicinity of sharp objects.

I nod. "Okay. Vegetable fried rice?"

"Sure."

He passes over his wallet. I grab it with my left hand before escaping down the stairs. Once I'm out of sight of my house, I take a seat on the curb. The bleeding has stopped, but moving my knuckles sends a wave of pain up my arm.

In the months before her death, my mother became confused. She didn't know what was real and what wasn't. Derealization, Dr. Taylor calls it.

Punching that mirror wasn't an impulse. It was instinct. Survival.

First the nightmare, and now this. I should tell Dr. Taylor, but when I bring up the similarities between myself and my mother, he tells me the same useless spiel about how we aren't the same person. But I see the way he twitches uncomfortably when I talk about my panic attacks. He's afraid I'm getting worse.

*Focus, Rose.*

I think of Midtown Ring and the control I felt when I stood over the bag, and my racing heartbeat slows.

I use my left hand to delete all of Harris's comments. There's no telling how many people saw it, but for now, at least it's gone. Then, I force myself off the curb and shift my focus to the walk ahead. The pain in my hand worsens with every step that I take, but I ignore it. I ignore everything except my own two feet.

Because I'm fine. Totally normal.

Simone's restaurant probably should've been torn down years ago for health code violations, but they survive on the glowing recommendations of locals. My dad and I became frequent customers after my mom died. We spent every night there in the week following her death when neither of us had the willpower to cook. Mr. Lin, the old man who owns the place, has been giving us the family discount ever since.

When I walk through the door, Mr. Lin smiles from behind the wooden counter.

"Rose! What can I get you?"

I order enough food for leftovers. He puts in my order then asks about school. I give him the short and easy reply that everybody wants to hear. "Pretty good. Lots of homework."

"College?"

"I'll be applying soon," I assure him. "Georgia State is at the top of my list."

"Great! You can still come to see us then. What would we do without our number one customer?"

I laugh. We make small talk until the food is ready. I grab the paper bag with both hands, forgetting to hide my wound. Mr. Lin shoots me a concerned stare. I raise my brows, silently challenging him to ask about it. If I can lie to my father, I can lie to anyone.

He turns away without questioning me.

My walk home is uneventful. I try to focus on normal things. Shopping with Gemma tomorrow. Pancakes this morning. Finishing my poetry assignment.

Before calling my dad downstairs to eat, I wipe away a trickle of blood dripping out from beneath the layer of bandages.

\*

"I've been thinking about my mom a lot recently. She was around my age when things started to get bad, right?"

Dr. Taylor studies me. He pushes his glasses farther up his nose. "Late twenties. Much older than you are."

My mom had me at twenty-four and died at thirty-eight, when I was fourteen. For a few months after her death, I felt physically fine; just mentally terrible as I tried to cope with teenage life without a mom. But then the panic attacks began, and the nightmares. The first night that my father woke me up from one, his skin turned as white as a sheet. I thought his expression was one of terror or confusion. Then, I realized it was recognition.

The bad dreams became less frequent after I started seeing Dr. Taylor, but last week was worse than all the previous combined. I saw her for the first time in years.

*Mom* . . .

"I'm afraid," I admit. "What if my anxiety gets as bad as hers did? What if I start feeling like I'm not really here?"

My grip on the chair handles tightens, but my right hand remains hidden inside of my jacket pocket. If he finds out I hurt myself, he won't let me leave this hospital.

"Rose, if your symptoms worsen, we'll learn to manage them."

"Nobody managed my mom's symptoms."

"That's different."

Dr. Taylor speaks slowly, consciously choosing his words so as to not anger me, but that pisses me off even more. Heat rushes through my cheeks.

"She was prescribed medication," he continues. "She stopped taking it."

"So, it's that easy?" I challenge him. "She decided to give up, so everyone else did too?"

"Of course not."

"Then why did nobody stop her from killing herself?"

Dr. Taylor doesn't have the answers I need. If he did, I would've stopped coming to this office a long time ago. He leans back into his chair, resting his mop of gray speckled hair on the wood. His steady gaze doesn't falter.

I hate when he watches me like this—like I'm a specimen rather than a human.

"Anxiety and Derealization are difficult to treat. They manifest in unique ways and require unique treatment. I don't know exactly why the hospital staff didn't watch her more carefully," Dr. Taylor explains.

"Is it really that hard to keep somebody in a locked room?" I growl.

When my mother checked into inpatient, we were promised that she would receive the best of the best care. Yet, she somehow made it out of the facility and walked back home. I found her lifeless on our bathroom floor holding an empty pill bottle. The coroner said the plastic bottle was dented; she had squeezed it so tight.

I've always wondered why she had squeezed that bottle. Maybe she was afraid of what she had done. Did she regret it in her final moments? Did she think of me?

"No, Rose. It isn't hard to keep somebody locked up. But the system failed. It's infuriating and wrong, but there's nothing we can change about that now. All we can do is focus on you and make sure you're healthy. Just being in this room with me, talking about your feelings, shows how strong you are. I will not let what happened to your mom happen to you. You can have my word on that. We won't let the bad stuff win."

*I think it might be winning.* From within the pocket of my sweatshirt, my hand throbs violently.

"Okay?" he asks.

"Alright," I respond. "I'm sorry."

That seems to appease him. Dr. Taylor scoots his chair closer to mine. He takes out his notepad and scribbles something on it.

"Did you go to the gym that I suggested?"

"Yes!" I exclaim. "I went twice last week, and I really liked it. I told my dad I want to take it more seriously."

Dr. Taylor tilts his chin. "Yeah? Why?"

I swallow. I'm still not sure what it is about the gym that I'm so attracted to, so I speak the first thought that comes to my head.

"The bag moves when I want it to."

He nods like he understands. That rush of power that I felt when I punched—something physical to prove to me that I still have control over my own body—is what I've been searching for ever since my mom died.

"Then keep it up. We can discuss your progress during our appointments."

After the session ends, I text my dad to let him know that I'm taking MARTA to the mall. The speeding train passes by patches of trees in a blur of green, yellow, and red. Therapy, boxing, Harris, my mother—all of it feels far away when I'm speeding through the sky.

Gemma's waiting for me when I reach the station near my house. We race to the next train, diving in right as the doors close. I pant against the cold orange seats.

"I really shouldn't be this tired from running up one set of stairs," Gemma heaves. "Maybe I should get into boxing."

"You could, but I'm as exhausted as you are."

"Good point."

Gemma points at a man a few seats down from us. He puts on a pair of bright yellow sunglasses as the train dips underground. When he opens his mouth to yawn, he reveals a startling lack of teeth. He's the perfect subject for a game Gemma and I love to play called *guess their story*.

"He lost his teeth in a carnival accident," Gemma whispers.

"What the hell is a carnival accident?"

"He was running the Ferris wheel and got a little too close. Some kid's foot knocked all of his teeth right out."

"You're right. He despises that kid. He has a vendetta against him."

We giggle, so distracted by our complicated story that we almost miss our stop. The station platform leads directly into the shopping mall. It smells like cinnamon pretzels and expensive perfumes. Gemma goes straight to her favorite store, a boutique with cute blouses.

"What exactly are we searching for?"

"Something that brings out my curves. Nishi likes them," she says with a wink.

We split up to conquer more ground, but I quickly get distracted by the athletic section. I pick up a handful of leggings and tank tops in my size. I have to admit, I'm motivated to look better than I have at the gym. The clothes are on sale, so I feel less guilty about buying something I'm going to sweat through. By the time I find Gemma again, her hands are full of dresses. She chooses a purple satin dress and a silver chain link necklace.

We celebrate our shopping victory with ice cream in the food court.

"We haven't talked in forever," Gemma says as I pile a spoonful of mint chocolate chip into my mouth.

"What do you mean?"

"We haven't *really* talked in a while. What's new? How are you?"

"I'm okay."

Gemma is open minded, but she's never fully understood what goes on in my head. Whenever I try to explain my anxiety to her, she asks more questions than I have the answers to. It's not fair to either of us that I'm keeping secrets, but it's so difficult to tell the truth when I know a panic attack might come on at any moment. I take another bite of ice cream. "Actually, I need to tell you something."

I say it before I can talk myself out of it again. Gemma puts down her spoon. One of my favorite things about her is that she's never pretending to listen. I inhale a deep breath of perfumed air.

"At Elliott's party, I tried to find a bathroom and got lost. Harris took me upstairs into a room with some people. He made comments, like he wanted to . . ."

"What?" Gemma leans in. "He didn't touch you, did he?"

"Well, sort of but not really . . ." I shake my head remembering. "Elliott stopped him. Threw him into a table, actually."

Her mouth falls open. She seems to go through every emotion that I did that night: fear, shock, then anger. "God, I'm so sorry, Rose. He's such an asshole. If you want to tell the principal—"

"No," I say. "No way." They'll never expel the star quarterback based on my word alone. Besides, telling the principal means everyone finds out, including Dr. Taylor and my father, and I'm not ready for that. "Boxing is helpful."

She half smiles. I continue, "There's something else, though. When we were sleeping at Elliott's house, I heard him talking on the phone. He was acting super secretive. And the next day, Harris commented 'Psycho Bitch' on all my Instagram posts. Do you think Elliott is in with Harris?"

"I don't think Elliott's like that," Gemma murmurs. "Why would he kick his ass if he was?" But there's unease in her voice. She adds, "Maybe you should keep your distance."

Elliott has been approachable, even nice to me at Midtown Ring, but he's nothing like that at school. Why would he choose to be kind to me, out of all people? The more I think about it, the more I doubt him. If I let myself trust Elliott only to find out that he's playing me, I might lose whatever fragment of sanity I have left.

I huff. "We go to the same gym. He's in my class. I can't avoid him forever."

"That doesn't mean you need to be his best friend."

"Yeah. I don't want to quit boxing," I confess. "It would be stupid to leave when I just started."

"Then don't. It's your place as well as his. Show him that he should be scared of you, not the other way around." Gemma grabs a hold of my arm. "There's somewhere I want to take you. Come on."

She doesn't let go of me until we're halfway across the mall. Gemma stops in front of a sporting goods store on the second floor. My eyes widen at the racks of leggings, sports bras, and equipment displayed in the window.

"Let's find you some cute gloves!" Gemma squeals.

She must have guessed that I would never go into a store like this alone. I smile as Gemma walks up to an employee, unafraid, and asks about boxing gear. He leads us to a rack of gloves, wraps for hands of all different sizes, punching bags, and more. I pick out a pair of pink gloves. The white stitching is strong, and they don't reek like the communal pair at the gym.

"Try them on," Gemma suggests.

I shake my head. I can't try them on without using both hands, and Gemma's had enough heartache for today. She can't find out about my shattered knuckles.

"I don't need to," I state. "They're perfect."

She beams. I grab a pair of black and white checkered hand wraps, so Elliott won't need to lend me his again. The last item I pick out is a mouthguard. It will be a while until Andre lets me spar, let alone in a way that requires a mouthguard, but I'm too excited not to buy it.

"Trying out a new sport?" the employee asks as he rings up my items.

I nod.

"Great. You look like a fighter."

# CHAPTER SEVEN

**MONDAY MORNING, MR.** Ruse spends the rest of class dissecting a poem I didn't read. Even Elliott makes more comments in our class discussion than I do. I'm dreading practice tonight; I want to perfect my left hook, but I don't want to see him. I haven't stopped thinking about the weird phone call. He helped Gemma, sure, but does that really mean Elliot can't be in with Harris? They've been friends since middle school.

I hide my injured hand throughout the day. Writing with my left is difficult to say the least, but I manage to turn in something legible. Gemma's waiting for me in the courtyard after the final bell rings. Ever since our conversation at the mall, she's been overly clingy. She texted me motivational quotes at least twelve times last night.

"Want to come over?" she asks.

"I have boxing."

"Right." She pouts. "Well, do you want a ride then? I got the car for the day."

I can't say no to that. We blast Marina and the Diamonds from the stereo of Gemma's mother's Jeep, the breeze through the open windows cooling down the skin on my neck. When we arrive at the gym, Elliott's BMW is already parked in the lot. I grind my teeth.

"He's punctual," Gemma says. "Shocking."

"What if he talks to me?"

"Ask him if he's secretly conspiring against you."

I roll my eyes.

"Play it cool," she says, "you'll be fine. If he messes with you, I'll kill him."

Gemma drops me off in front of the entrance to the gym. I grab my backpack, filled to the brim with my new equipment.

Gemma grins from ear to ear like a proud parent. "Have fun!"

I stick up my middle finger. She exits the parking lot, leaving me alone next to Elliott's car. I head inside and go straight for the benches in the back corner and take note of Elliott's position on the other side of the room. I force my blood crusted hand into my new glove, the tight material sends shivers of pain up my arm.

"Time to stretch!" Andre announces. He herds the group into the center of the gym.

Stepping closer to Elliott, I notice dark circles clouding his eyes. He smiles gently. I avert my gaze to the mural of the two clashing purple gloves on the back wall.

I practice as much as I can with my left hand leading. Andre's lesson is more cardio heavy than last week, so I'm able to get by with minimal damage. Elliott breaks into applause when I finish more than ten push-ups without using my knees.

After practice, he approaches me. "What's up?"

His voice is raspy, like he's been screaming or smoking. Probably both. I shove my hand wraps into my backpack, trying to come up with a convincing excuse to leave.

"Hello?" he repeats.

"Hey," I say.

Elliott reaches into his bag and pulls out my clothes from the other night. I grab my jacket, which smells like lavender laundry detergent. Sweet and familiar. It smells like *him*. I rub away the moisture that surfaces on my palms.

"Thanks," I say, turning toward the door.

Elliott follows at my side. His sweat-soaked T-shirt sticks to his chest, revealing the outline of his muscles. I force myself to look away. I should be avoiding him, not ogling.

"Do you want a ride home?"

I pause. I've never seen him put so much effort into something, so shooting him down makes me feel like an asshole. But I can't trust somebody who is so clearly keeping secrets, especially when those secrets might involve Harris Price.

"No, thanks."

Finally, he takes the hint. Disappointment flickers across his face. He leaves the parking lot of Midtown Ring without another word. Even through the music in my headphones, I hear the revving from the engine as he speeds past.

*

It's midnight by the time I finish the rest of my homework. Reaching for the glass of water on my nightstand, I notice a sudden flash of movement outside of my bedroom window. I peek through the curtains.

Buzzed hair. Strong shoulders. A black backpack hanging across his body.

*Elliott.*

Dressed in basketball shorts and a black tank top, he scurries down the sidewalk. Twice, he glances behind him, as if someone might be following, but the street is empty. He ducks his head as he nears my house. I inch away from the window and listen.

"I'm on my way," he tells someone on the phone. He lowers his voice to a whisper when he passes beneath my window. "Let's get this over with."

My stomach drops.

I shouldn't do what I'm about to do.

But I can't help myself.

Tiptoeing out of my bedroom, I rush down the staircase and escape through the back door. Elliott jogs toward the train station—the same direction as Harris's house. I have to run to keep up with him, but I remain in the shadows so as not to reveal myself.

Elliott enters the station and heads toward the east platform. *Where is he going that he can't drive to? He's never without his car.* I linger behind him for a few moments before swiping my pass. The rational part of my brain screams to go back home, to quit being a total creep before Elliott notices, but I keep moving. If Elliott and Harris are planning something, I have to know. I can't lie in wait like a sitting duck.

Dr. Taylor would call this paranoia.

The train arrives. I slide into a train car three down from Elliott's. He exits at the station closest to Midtown Ring and takes the exact set of turns that would get him there.

He makes his way to the back entrance of the gym. Apart from a few scattered cars in the parking lot, the building appears abandoned.

*Nobody is here.*

He must be letting off some steam. And I'm the obsessed girl who followed him. I let out a frustrated sigh and turn around, flushing red with shame.

Then I hear screaming.

At first, the sound is so faint that I think I might have hallucinated it. But when I turn my ear toward the gym, the noise swells. The screaming is from more than one distinct voice—none of which sound like Elliott's. As I edge closer to the building, I hear conversations, yelling, and applause.

*What the hell?*

Accepting that Elliott will know that I followed him and never want to speak to me again, I swallow my pride and knock on the door of Midtown Ring. A few seconds of silence pass before a stranger shouts from behind the door.

"Go around back!"

I follow his instructions. Behind the dumpsters, a sliver of light bleeds out from a cracked door. The man throws it open and exposes a sight through the doorway that makes my jaw drop.

Midtown Ring is packed with people.

Most are older men, but there are others scattered in the corners. Men and women in their late twenties and thirties. The collective screaming of the crowd is deafening. Everyone inside of the gym is engrossed in something on the opposite side of the room. I slip through the door, standing on my toes to get a better view, but I can't make out much from this distance.

I snake through the crowd. A tall, bearded man next to me holds up his hand and screams.

"Take him down!"

Someone pushes me forward. I stumble into a group of onlookers, and they push back, moving me against my will toward the front of the crowd. By the time I regain my balance, I've made it to the outskirts of the boxing ring.

Two men are in the middle, walking in slow, taunting circles around each other. They stare hungrily at their opponent as if the other is unsuspecting prey. There are no boxing gloves. No mouthguards. And blood. Blood everywhere. Puddles of it are smeared across the floor, dark red, a sharp contrast to the white tile.

I stare, mouth agape, as the bigger man pins the other down with his knee. He holds him down, choking him, until someone from the crowd rushes in to break the two apart. The audience erupts into screams. Some are excited, victorious, others furious. I slide my bandaged hand over my mouth to cover the sound of my own shriek.

Atlanta has a fight club.

And I'm standing in the middle of it.

I don't have time to process what I'm seeing before the ring clears out for a new set of contestants. From the left side of the crowd rises a competitor whose tattoos I recognize.

Elliott. He comes nose to nose with a man twice his size in the center of the ring. The room fades into perfect silence. As onlookers thirst with anticipation, my dinner threatens to resurface.

The sound of a piercing whistle earns a cheer from the crowd. Abruptly, the bigger man throws a punch straight into Elliott's jaw, knocking him off of his feet.

"Don't get too close, sweetheart," warns someone behind me whose breath reeks of vodka. I inch away.

I can't look away from Elliott. He recovers easily from the impact, pulling himself off of the blood-soaked floor with ease. Although his competitor is twice his size, Elliott outsmarts him: he knees him in the abdomen then punches him in the side of the head. The man drops to the floor. Elliott uses his body weight to keep him there. A glimpse into the guy's mouth, open and drooling, tells me he's unconscious.

"Winner!"

The crowd erupts into applause. Elliott stands, brushes dirt off his bare knees, and turns to face the adoring audience. His right eye is bruised and swollen. Blood trickles out of his nostrils. A person in the crowd passes Elliott a wad of bills, then escorts him out of the ring. Elliott pockets the cash in his gray shorts, now stained from the other man's blood.

The random bruises. The strange phone call. His undeniable talent at the gym.

It all makes sense, now.

There must be at least a hundred people packed into the building. Onlookers smile flirtatiously at Elliott. He waves to the crowd, bouncing on his toes as he does with what I imagine must be the purest rush of adrenaline humanly possible.

That's when his eyes meet mine.

The color drains from his face as he realizes I'm there.

His mouth forms my name, but I don't stay to listen.

# CHAPTER EIGHT

**A FIGHT CLUB.**

Not a movie set, not a hallucination, and not a nightmare.

What I saw was real, so real that I can still taste the sweaty air on my tongue during the train ride home. He's insane. Absolutely, undeniably crazy. I am *not* the only person in this town who needs therapy.

I spend the rest of the night replaying through every interaction that Elliott and I have ever had, noticing pieces of the truth within each memory. The mysterious phone call must have been about the fight club. In the early morning, I comb through the darkest parts of the internet, but I find nothing except weirdly specific biographical facts about Brad Pitt and Edward Norton. *Fight Club* was apparently a pretty popular movie back in the 90's. When I finally get to sleep, my dreams are plagued with violence.

My phone vibrating wakes me up from my restless night of sleep. I answer the call.

"I'm outside."

It's Gemma, and she sounds like she's been waiting for a while. Cursing under my breath, I glance at the time on the screen: 8:00 a.m. I should've been up thirty minutes ago.

"Give me five," I grumble.

I tie my hair into a bun, pop a Prozac, then toss my backpack across my shoulder. The pocket of the green sweatshirt that I fell asleep in hides my injured hand, so I don't bother changing out of it.

Gemma's lips part when she takes in the sight of me. "You look . . . tired."

That's her nice way of saying that I look like absolute crap. I pluck some hair from my bun to frame my face, but I can tell from her displeased expression that it doesn't help.

"I fell asleep doing homework," I lie.

I still haven't processed what I witnessed last night.

Elliott will want to talk, maybe try to explain it away or swear me to secrecy, but I don't know if I want an explanation. The blood on the floor of the gym was a warning for me to stay as far away from him as possible.

"Nishi's mom found out she went to Alex's party and took away her phone."

"What?" I ask. "How did she know?"

"Tracked her. I'm so glad my parents don't understand technology."

My dad could probably figure out how to track my phone if he wanted to, but he's never been the type of parent to breathe down my neck. Only recently have I had a reason to go behind his back.

As Gemma and I pass by Elliott's house, I gulp. His car isn't parked in the driveway, which means he must already be at school.

"Why doesn't Elliott walk to class like the rest of us?" Gemma asks. "He lives two seconds away."

"As if he'd be caught dead doing that. Such a waste of gas."

"I guess it's hard to care when you're made of money."

Gemma's parents own a grocery store on the corner, but they've been slowly losing customers ever since a bigger chain went up down the street. Most of Atlanta's small businesses are suffering a similar fate.

"How is your mom doing?" I ask.

"Fine. Still trying to set me up with Jeremy Toh. I finally told her he's in rehab."

*At least he's not part of a fight club.*

"Now who will you say you're with when you're actually out with Nishi?"

"My best friend, who will lie to my mom if she calls to confirm."

"Genius."

As we approach the entrance to the school, my thumbs twiddle within the pocket of my sweatshirt. Elliott won't mention what I saw in front of everyone, but he might try to poison my lunch or run me over with his car.

"See you at lunch," I say, taking a step through the door.

None of my worries come to fruition because Elliott isn't at school. A few of his girlfriends stare longingly at his empty desk while Mr. Ruse lectures about eighteenth-century poets. At lunch, Elliott's still nowhere to be found.

*Maybe he's hurt.*

Anything might have happened after I left Midtown Ring last night. *Did he fight more?* Visuals of Elliott's limbs twisted in unnatural poses fill me with dread.

"You okay?" Gemma questions.

"Do you have Elliott's number?" The words come out before I can stop them.

"What for? Nudes?" she teases.

"No!" Blush paints my cheeks. "I want to check in, okay?"

Gemma texts me his contact number, and I send him a message. After a few minutes pass with no answer, I assume I'm never getting one.

By lunch time the next day, Elliott still hasn't returned to school. I send another text that goes unanswered, and the anxious pit in my stomach grows substantially. I force myself to swallow down a bite of turkey sandwich, but images of his body decomposing in the Midtown Ring dumpster make the task difficult.

"Did you get your phone back?" I ask Nishi, trying to distract myself.

Nishi shakes her head. Gemma pouts, "Lame."

"I'm never sneaking out again," says Nishi.

"Oh, you'll sneak out again. You just won't get caught."

Gemma leans into Nishi's shoulder. As she does, she glances toward Elliott's usual spot. "Still no sign of him?"

"Nope," I reply.

"Maybe you should check in."

"How? He won't answer my texts."

She waves me off as if the answer is obvious. "Why don't you knock on his door? You do live next door, don't you?"

Honestly, it doesn't sound like the worst idea in the world, but what if Elliott were to answer? He would be even angrier with me for following him around again. Then I can add *stalker* to my list of nicknames.

"Fine." I resign. "If he misses another day, I'll go to his house."

Elliott's car is still missing from the parking lot by the time the school day ends. I half expect to find it in the lot outside of Midtown, but all the spots are empty except for Andre's truck and a few coffee shop patrons.

The gym is eerie after what I witnessed Monday night. There's nothing left to imply that anyone was ever here after hours, not even a single new scratch on the floor of the ring.

Elliott was the only person I recognized, but there were too many faces to have possibly seen them all. *What if someone else from practice was there?* Glancing around the room, I narrow my gaze on Riley and Sofía, but neither of them pay me any attention.

I focus on the cardio and bag routines that Andre assigns the class. Even after these last few weeks of practice, I'm so much stronger than I was. The bag moves farther each time I throw a punch, and with every wide swing, I breathe a little easier.

"Careful."

Sofía interrupts my movements. My right hand, the one still coated in bloodied bandages, trembles inside my boxing glove. Fire rages from my fingers through my wrist. I didn't realize I was using it.

"Thanks," I whisper before collapsing onto one of the benches.

Without Elliott's snarky comments, Midtown Ring is quiet. I keep expecting to hear his applause when someone lands a complicated move, but I'm greeted with nothing but silence. It's a lot easier to focus without him watching me, but considering the state of my hand, I'm not sure if that's such a good thing.

"I've registered all of us for a competition," Andre announces toward the end of the evening. "Next weekend, in Savannah."

The group cheers and high-fives each other. I slip away from the crowd. I can't compete. I can barely throw a cross without falling on my face. Swallowing the sour disappointment in my throat, I turn my back to the group, but Andre catches my arm before I make it to the door.

"You'll be ready to compete in the next beginners tournament," he states. "I'll make sure of it. Let Savannah be a learning experience. Okay?"

I'm only a newbie. It wouldn't make sense to go up against someone with twice the amount of experience, but I still crave the challenge of an opponent. I can pick and choose what happens to the bag, unlike my thoughts and reactions to anxiety, but right now my opponent is an immovable object. I want something—or someone—I can knock out.

"Okay," I agree. "I'll be ready."

And I will be. I promise myself that I'll at least try to commit to getting good enough to fight, if not for my own sake, for my father's and Dr. Taylor's.

Elliott still hasn't answered my texts by the time I get home from Midtown, and the silence is maddening. I just need one word, one reaction or emoji to prove to me that he's at least alive. I check his Instagram feed, but there are no updates.

Tossing my phone onto the counter, I sit on the bathroom floor and peel the stained bandages off my hand. The injury is more gruesome than before. On top of the healing cuts on my knuckles from the glass is a range of purple bruises. Dried blood and scabs fill the gaps between the sliced-up pieces of skin. I run my hand under the shower water to wash away some of the red. The heat seeps into my wounds, creating a ripple effect of pain.

I catch a glimpse of my reflection in the mirror.

*Behind me, a face appears so close to my hair that she may as well be touching it. My mom. A fuzzy outline. A version of her with wrinkles and graying hair that I never got to see, but it's her.*

I stop moving. My hand burns. But with every sting, the details of her face become less blurry. I don't dare turn around—she's not there, not actually there, she can't be there, *but if she was, and I tried to look at her, she would disappear again*—and I don't want her to disappear.

I can't think. The pain is too much. In one quick movement, I pull my hand out of the sink. My skin blazes red, the cuts throbbing.

"Shit!"

I slab on Neosporin and wrap my skin in a fresh layer of bandages. Behind me, the bathroom is empty. No footprints, no blurred outlines of my mom, or weird apparitions. I wonder if this is what Dr. Taylor calls derealization. My mom fell into a spiral of it for days at a time. She told Dad and I that she didn't feel real. I never fully got what that meant until now. Medicine helped Mom sometimes, but Dr. Taylor will notice if I double up on my Prozac without asking. Maybe I just need more sleep. I grab a bottle of melatonin from downstairs and store it in my bedroom for later.

Dad makes it home before sunset. He cooks a mountain of pasta that makes my stomach growl. I shove down half the bowl before speaking.

"You mentioned that Damon King wasn't really around a lot?"

My dad lifts his head at the sound of Damon's name. I can't read his expression, but he doesn't seem particularly excited to be discussing Elliott's father.

"Yeah. Why?"

"Did he leave town often? Like, to take the kids camping for the week?"

Dad chuckles, apparently amused by the question.

"Never. When you were young, your mom tried to invite Elliott with us on a weekend to the Smokies. Damon wouldn't even consider it."

When I spent the night at Elliott's, I asked him why his house was deserted.

He told me that his family was away on a camping trip.

\*

Two tall, white columns hold up the roof of the King house. The old Southern architecture, now refurbished, attracts tourists and photographers on occasion. All of the houses in our neighborhood have unique features, but Elliott's stands out from the rest. The columns resemble what I imagine one might design for a throne room, the towering rose bushes guarding a palace fit for kings.

It's Thursday and Elliott didn't show up to school again, so, after some convincing from Gemma and Nishi, I decided to act on my promise to pay his house a visit. The only car parked, a silver Range Rover, doesn't belong to him, but I knock anyway.

Nobody answers.

As I'm turning to leave, I'm greeted by a face remarkably similar to Elliott's. The boy in the doorway is about my age, with blonde hair, blue eyes, and a pointed chin. A few freckles line the top of his cheeks and nose.

"Um, hi," I stutter. "I was wondering if Elliott is home?"

The boy smiles curiously. He seems friendly enough.

"He's on his way back right now. Do you want to wait inside?"

*Phew. Elliott's okay. Not dead. That's all I needed to know.*

"It's okay—"

He interrupts, "I insist."

He steps out of the way, leaving room for me to enter the house that I've become a little too familiar with. He holds out his hand, and I shake with my left. His grip is unusually tight.

"I'm Luke."

Luke King, Elliott's brother. The one that everyone tried to hook up with last year before he graduated. I've been so caught up in Elliott's drama, I forgot his brother existed.

"Rose," I utter.

Luke guides me to the kitchen. I take a seat at the end of the table, in the same chair I sat in when I ate pancakes last weekend. Elliott's brother crosses the kitchen. He has a commanding presence, an aura to him that radiates power and domination, but not in quite the same way as Elliott. I can't put my finger on it. He pours two cups of water and passes one to me. I take a sip, trying to wash down my nerves.

"So, how do you guys know each other?" Luke inquires, rhythmically tapping his fingers against the marble tabletop. He takes the seat across from me. His posture is rigid, as if he might spring out of his chair at any second. It puts my anxiety into overdrive.

"We're in the same English class. I'm helping him with a paper."

"Is his writing that unbearable?"

I laugh awkwardly. "Not unbearable. He just needs some help with grammar."

Luke presses on. "Is he paying you?"

"No."

"So, he's fucking you, then?"

I spit out my drink. Luke's face remains perfectly serious. The sound of the front door opening startles both of us.

"Excuse me," barks Luke. He exits the kitchen abruptly.

I remain frozen in place, unsure of what to do. Something feels wrong. I shouldn't have come here without Elliott knowing. From across the house, Luke shouts, "We have company!" Elliott, Luke, and Damon King enter the kitchen before I can make a run for it. The first thing I notice is the skin around Elliott's right eye. It's a gruesome purple color, swollen and puffy to the point where his vision must be constricted. His upper lip is split and scabbed.

No wonder he hasn't been at school.

Elliott stares me down, probably trying to figure out exactly why I'm sitting in his kitchen. Damon King towers over both of his children. He shares the same piercing features as Elliott and Luke—triangular chin, blue irises, and muscular arms. The only difference is his hair, a caramel brown rather than blonde.

"You're Doris Berman's daughter, aren't you? Rosalyn?" Damon asks.

The sound of my mom's name on his lips makes my heart skip a beat.

"Yes," I respond. "I go by Rose. I'm here to help Elliott with his essay."

Elliott plays along with the lie. "Right. Did you want to go to—"

Damon cuts him off, "Would you like to stay for dinner?"

Judging by the tone of his voice, I don't think I'm allowed to say no.

"Elliott's never brought a girl home," Damon continues. "You must be pretty special."

He walks over to the dining table and pulls food out of a bag that I now recognize to be from Simone's. Elliott grabs a few plates from the cabinet, dishes clashing together. Each of the men takes a seat: Elliott across from me, Luke to my right, and Damon at the head of the table. Luke scoops a mountain of orange chicken onto his plate. I wait for everybody else to take their turn before doing the same.

As I reach for the serving spoon, Elliott catches my eye with his. The swelling is worse up close. He parts his lips, as if to whisper something to me, but his voice catches in his throat when Damon speaks.

"Is this food okay with you?" he asks.

I grin. "Of course. Simone's is the best in town."

"I actually gave them some money to start up. I'm a proud investor in local businesses."

Lawyer and investor. No wonder he lives in a mansion.

"My law firm has a lot of work opportunities available for next year. Maybe you can join us since you're such an impressive writer?"

"Rose will be busy with college," Elliott interrupts.

"But I'm mainly applying locally."

Elliott glares at me.

"Can't say the same, can you?" Damon asks his son. There's no compassion in his voice.

"Nope," Elliott replies.

Luke chews on his food like it's popcorn, and we're the movie. Elliott stands up from his chair. I drop my fork at the screeching sound of wood sliding against tile.

"Thanks for dinner," Elliott says to nobody in particular. "Rose, are you ready to study?"

I exhale. "Definitely. Thanks for dinner, Mr. King."

"You can call me Damon."

I pick up my plate, but before I can step away from the table, Luke lunges. His hand wraps around my right wrist, and he hardens his grip, preventing me from moving. His long, tattered fingers dig into the bandages hidden beneath my flannel, and I wince at the pressure on my open wound. *What the hell?*

"You've hardly eaten anything," Luke hisses.

Elliott is at my side in a second. His shoulders stiffen, eyebrows tensing into a straight line as he demands, "Let go of her."

Despite Elliott's threatening tone, Luke doesn't release me. Damon, unbothered, picks up his plate, walks it to the sink, turns on the faucet and begins scrubbing. Luke's pale hand slides up from my wrist to my forearm. The cloth of my shirt moves with him, revealing the bloody cloth dangling around my skin. Elliott's eyes widen.

He's across the room in an instant. He slams his brother into the wall, elbow pressed against Luke's throat. I jump backward. Both of their movements slow. Everyone falls into perfect stillness, and everything is quiet, except for the sound of water rushing from the sink and the pounding in my ears.

The suspense is broken by Luke's sudden fit of laughter. It's a loud, guttural noise that sounds more animal than human.

"You're totally hung up on her." He marvels, grinning at his brother. "I don't believe it."

Elliott spits against Luke's cheek. The weight of Luke's words takes a moment to register, and when they finally do, I don't know how to react.

"Are you done?" Elliott hisses.

To my surprise, Luke nods. He relaxes against the wall. Elliott releases his elbow and takes a slow step away from his brother. The picture frame behind Luke crashes onto the tile.

Glass spills in all directions of the room, but Elliott doesn't flinch. He opens his mouth, but I'm already out the front door.

Elliott follows at my heels. "What happened to your hand?" he asks.

He reaches for my hand, but I jerk my arm away.

"Seriously? You're asking about *that*?" I exclaim in disbelief. "Tell me what the hell just happened in there!"

Elliott pauses. He looks toward the front door. Nobody follows. "I'll explain," he starts, ". . . but not here. Come on."

He moves toward the black convertible, now parked at the bottom of the driveway. The clouds above his head are dark, and a boom of thunder shakes the neighborhood. It will be pouring any second now.

I freeze.

If I get into the car with him, I'm going to learn something that I'm not sure I want to know.

*He's bad news. You've met the man who raised him. You know how wrong this is.*

I think back to the moments during practice where he took extra time to teach me something even when Andre hadn't asked him to. His tone was patient and compassionate, a sharp contrast to what I heard from his family tonight. As much as it terrifies me, there's something about Elliott that I can't shake. His brother might be an empty shell, but he's far from it.

Elliott turns the key in the ignition, and I buckle up.

"Why did you come over?" he asks.

"You weren't at school, and you never texted me back."

"Well you shouldn't have shown up at my house."

I roll my eyes, but he keeps talking. "Or followed me the other night. What the hell was that?"

"Really?" I snap. "If you're going to act like a child, then let me out of the car."

The veins in Elliott's hand threaten to pop. He swings the steering wheel, the car reversing with a screech out of the driveway.

"Luke won't touch you again," he mutters, this time more to himself than me.

He lets out a shaky breath and speeds through a red light. Ahead of us is the parking lot of Midtown Ring. Elliott pulls the convertible into a spot close to the front, then grabs a silver key from the cupholder. I follow him. The key unlocks the back door to the gym.

He's at one of the punching bags in an instant, throwing his fist into the hard material with enough force to shake the ground beneath our feet. The scabs on his knuckles bleed as skin comes into contact with leather.

"Elliott," I say, in the calmest tone I can muster. "Stop."

He chuckles and it reminds me of Luke. Again, he raises his fist, but I grab his wrist midair, stopping his movements. Beads of sweat drip down his forehead as he rotates his body toward mine, chest heaving from the weight of his tattered breaths. We're standing close enough that I can see every detail of the tiny broken blood vessels surrounding his right eye.

We breathe in the same few inches of air for what feels like an eternity, until Elliott drops his arm back to his side. My fingers remain wrapped around his wrist.

"What happened?" Elliott whispers, examining my battered hand.

"I punched the mirror in my bedroom." If I expect the truth from Elliott, he deserves the same from me. "I'm sure you know what happened last year."

"I haven't heard it from you," he replies.

I tell him about that day in March, only months away from the end of junior year, when I had the worst panic attack of my life. One second, I was presenting in front of the class, and the next, I was surrounded by a group of EMT's. They told me I lashed out when my calculus teacher tried to help me. They told me that I forgot my own name, my identity. It was a miracle that I came back to myself when I did. That was the day the *Psycho* nickname started, courtesy of Harris Price, who was sitting in the front row when it all happened.

"My mother had severe panic attacks, too," I say, finishing the story. He softens, which makes the next part easier to get out. "She killed herself. That's why I was so surprised when your dad brought her up."

A frustrated sigh escapes his lips. "My father has a talent of bringing up the one thing you don't want to hear."

"He's not the first one to ask. All I've wanted since that day was to go back to normal. Boxing helps. I like being in charge of my own strength."

"You're not going to be able to keep practicing if you don't get this looked at, Rose."

Elliott leads me to a bench in the back corner of the room. Carefully, he peels the bandage off my hand. My skin stings as the sticky cloth breaks away from it. Most of the cuts are swollen and irritated. It's infected.

"There might be glass stuck in there."

"Elliott—" I start.

"It's not going to heal itself."

"I—"

"You need a doctor. I'll take you tomorrow."

"Elliott," I say again, louder this time.

He finally stops talking. I wish I could sit here and play out this fantasy, ignore everything else that happened and let myself feel for him what I think I'm starting to. But I can't. Not if he's not willing to tell me the truth about what I discovered the other night, or whatever just went down in his kitchen.

"You need to tell me what's going on," I assert. "What did I walk into on Monday?"

He tenses. "I think you already know the answer to that."

As insane as the idea of a real-life fight club is, I can't help but feel relieved that it wasn't all in my head.

"Then tell me why," I demand. "Why are you doing it?"

He doesn't answer.

I point to the bruise on his lip. "Is that from Monday?"

Again, he doesn't reply.

"Your father?"

"Rose," he says. "I can't."

The despair on his face is enough to confirm my suspicions about Damon, but I still have no answers to the rest of my questions. I clench my jaw.

"Then take me home."

"What?"

I stand up from my spot on the bench, tossing the bloodied bandage into the garbage. "If you're not going to give me any answers, I'm not going to keep asking for them. Take me home."

Elliott opens his mouth like he might argue, then shuts it just as quickly. He guides me out of the gym without another word. We drive back to our neighborhood in silence; the only sound is the humming of the radio. I don't know what would make Elliott feel as if he can't trust *me*, the girl that nobody would believe regardless of the circumstances. The rejection stings more than I care to admit.

"Go to the doctor," Elliott suggests. "For your hand."

I get out of the car without replying.

I want to run upstairs to my bedroom and lock the door. I want to hit something, but I can't even punch the air before my dad notices me walk in.

"Where have you been?" he asks.

I bottle up my anger and force my feet toward the kitchen. He passes me a bowl of rice and beans, but I don't tell him I've already eaten.

"I went to Elliott's house to help him with an essay. You were right about Damon being unapproachable. He told me I look like Mom."

My dad freezes, putting the spoon in his hand back onto the table.

"You spoke with him?"

"Yeah. Only for a few minutes."

My wrist throbs from the spot that Luke grabbed. After shoving a few spoonfuls of food into my mouth, I slip out of the kitchen and lock myself in my bathroom. The yellow skin of my arm is something out of a horror movie. My stomach grumbles at the sickening color. I don't want to appease Elliott, but I know that he's right. I pick up my phone and dial the receptionist at Grady Hospital.

"I need to make an appointment."

# CHAPTER NINE

## "IT'S POETRY DAY, EVERYONE!"

Mr. Ruse is dressed in a theatrical red suit and round glasses. I snicker. Elliott does too, but I pretend not to hear him. He finally returned to school with a halfway healed face, resulting in a flood of confused whispers.

"Our lesson today is a bit different than what we've been doing so far. I want everyone to spend this time writing poetry instead of reading it."

A few students groan, Elliott included.

"You won't have to read it out loud; however, this is a graded assignment, so you'll need to actually try. And yes, if you plagiarize Dr. Seuss, I will know."

It's been a long time since I've put words on a page. Ruse plays orchestral music through his laptop speaker, but that doesn't stop one of Elliott's girlfriends from talking over it. As class comes to an end, I finish with something that I'm at least somewhat proud of.

A fighter
With battered fists, slamming against concrete.
He bleeds, wishing
Could he be
A lover?

"Where were you this morning?" I ask Gemma after school.

She skips up to me with a goofy grin plastered across her face.

"I went to get coffee with Nishi. She's officially my girlfriend!"

I hug her, both of us squealing like mice. She's practically glowing, and for a moment, I forget about everything else.

"I need to spend more time with Nishi," I confess. "I'm sorry I haven't been around. Things got crazy all of a sudden."

Gemma lowers her voice. "Don't worry. I want you to focus on yourself, okay?"

"Why don't you set up something with Nishi soon so I can hang out with her?"

She beams. "I'm on it."

The train ride to the hospital passes by too quickly. I've been dreading this appointment all day. This section of the hospital, where they took my mother in a last attempt to save her life, makes me feel like I've been locked in a cage. One step through the front entrance and the claustrophobia is overwhelming. I half-smile at the receptionist.

"Do you have an appointment?" she asks.

"Yes, Rosalyn Berman. I called last night."

She passes me a pile of paperwork on a clipboard. A girl, about twelve years old, stumbles through the door to the office. She's holding hands with her mother. She reminds me of my younger self with her uncontrollable wavy hair and goofy smile. There's a red stain across the neckline of her tank top. Blood. It drips from a spot in her mouth where an adult tooth should be. I smell the salt from the wound in the air. I clench the clipboard, hand shaking as I fill in the underlined gaps on the page.

"Rosalyn Berman?"

A blonde nurse calls my name. "I'm Cassandra. Follow me back."

She guides me to an electronic scale, and the number that it settles on is lower than it should be.

"Are you okay?" she asks. "You're sweating."

"Sorry. I get nervous in hospitals."

"Nothing to be nervous about."

She guides me to an empty room, and I sit down on the tan bed, the sheet of paper underneath my thighs crinkling as I do. Cassandra asks a few questions about my health history, then gets up to check the state of my hand. The cuts are more green than yellow. A few spots bleed as Cassandra peels the gauze from the sealed wound.

"Well, this is definitely infected." She observes.

*No shit.*

"We'll prescribe you with some antibiotics that should help."

I let out a breath of relief when she doesn't tell me that my hand needs to be chopped off. She glosses over sections of the skin with her gloved finger. I shudder when she reaches a spot in the bottom right corner of my palm. She presses on it again, and I wince.

"I think there's something lodged in your skin here."

"Glass," I whisper. "I thought I got it all out."

"Let me get a doctor."

Cassandra returns a moment later with a bearded man at her side. He introduces himself as Dr. Kilmer, then opens up a drawer across the room, revealing a collection of sharp medical supplies. He grabs a pair of silver tweezers and inches toward my bed. As Dr. Kilmer presses against the cut, the same salty smell from earlier fills the room.

"Are you okay?" Dr. Kilmer asks.

"Can you smell that?" I sniff the air. "The blood?"

The young girl and her mom looked so much alike. I never took much notice as a child, but now every time that I look in the mirror, the similarities between my mother and I are all that I can see.

I look like her. I talk like her. At what point will I die like her?

If Dr. Kilmer answers my question, I'm not awake to hear it.

*

"Rosalyn?"

My eyes shoot open. The stark white walls of the hospital room remind me of where I am and how I got here. Dr. Kilmer and Cassandra blink with concern as they take in the expression of terror on my face.

My father is between them.

"Dad?" I murmur.

He steps closer. I can smell his cologne from across the room. "Are you okay?" he asks.

"Yes," I lie. My voice is hoarse.

Even though he's probably pissed I didn't tell him I was coming, I'm relieved he's here. Cassandra helps me sit up. There's a machine positioned next to the bed.

"How did you get here?" I ask my father.

"The doctor called. You wrote my phone number down on the paperwork."

"Oh," I huff. "Right."

My bangs fall into my eyes. I wipe the hair away with my right hand, which is now wrapped in a clean set of bandages. The piercing pain has subsided, replaced by a dull ache.

"We removed the rest of the glass while you were out," Dr. Kilmer reports. "We put in some stitches, so you'll need to be careful not to break them."

"How long was I out for?"

"You woke up after about ten minutes, but then we gave you some laughing gas to relax you. You don't remember?"

"I remember."

I don't.

"Your dad told me that you have a history of anxiety," Cassandra adds, pulling up a chair in front of the bed. My dad droops a hand across my shoulder and squeezes gently. This room is feeling more and more like the same one they took my mother into.

"I need to know if this wound was self-inflicted."

"What?" I say. "No. It was an accident. I threw my water bottle, and it shattered my mirror, and when I went to clean up the pieces, I cut myself."

She looks doubtful.

"I'm not saying that I don't believe you. I just want to make sure that you're in a good place, physically and mentally."

My dislike for her grows with every word.

"I am," I state, as calmly as possible. "I've been taking Prozac and meeting with a therapist. I'm fine."

"He's reported her as stable," my dad affirms.

Cassandra scribbles something down on the stack of paperwork. She asks my father for Dr. Taylor's phone number, and I make a mental note to act extra cheerful at my next appointment.

"Rose, would you mind stepping outside for a moment so I can talk to your father alone?"

As if I can say "no." I hate that they're allowed to talk about me as if my opinion isn't relevant. My eighteenth birthday can't come soon enough.

Leaning against the wall in the hallway, I notice the young girl from earlier walking in my direction. She's dressed in a new, clean tank top. The blood around her mouth is gone. When she sees me she smiles, less a front tooth, and I return the gesture.

Cassandra and my father join me outside of the room.

"I recommend you talk with your therapist as soon as possible so he can evaluate you. Your dad and I agree that if an incident like this happens again, more intensive steps will need to be taken," she says.

*Screw that. I'm not going to inpatient.*

"I understand."

My dad appears more afraid than angry, but I can sense from his rigid posture that he's about to explode. We walk to the parking lot in silence.

My phone vibrates. I check it, half hoping for a text from Elliott, but it's Gemma asking how the checkup went. My father opens the passenger door of the white Honda. In the safety of the car, I feel comfortable enough to speak.

"Didn't you have work tonight?"

"I got the night off."

Code for: he ditched work abruptly. I lean my head into my hand. If my dad loses his job, we'll have no income. Most of his savings went to paying for my mom's care and now my therapy.

"Well, I have no plans if you want to do something," I suggest.

"Like what?"

"*Star Wars* marathon?"

We have them a lot, complete with Yoda Soda and Blue Milk, but we've never made it through more than two movies before at least one of us falls asleep. My dad nods. Turning the key in the ignition, he pauses.

"Rose. Why did you hide this from me?"

This is it—the moment that will make or break my excuse. If he learns the truth, I may be going back to the hospital.

"I was afraid of the bill," I whisper, tucking my hair behind my ear. "I thought if it healed on its own, you wouldn't have to pay for anything."

He sighs, a loud, sorrowful sound that breaks my heart.

"You can't be afraid to ask for my help with something like this. We can afford it. I need you to believe me."

"I'm trying. I just wish you had some help sometimes."

"I know," he says. "I do, too. But this is how it is, and we have to accept that. We're going to be okay."

"Dad?"

He turns to me with his round face and warm smile, and it takes all of my willpower not to spill all of the gory details from the last two days.

"I love you," I whisper.

"Love you too, kiddo."

We bicker back and forth about which *Star Wars* movie to watch for the remainder of the drive. We spend the rest of the night sitting together on the couch, joking around and eating more sugar than we should. I feel like a kid again, so much so that I almost forget about everything else that's been going on.

Almost.

The next morning, my dad volunteers to drive me to therapy. Rain sprinkles against the windows as our car snakes through the neighborhood. There are no cars parked in Elliott's driveway, which means he must be out with his family.

"What happened to your hand?" Dr. Taylor asks as I step into his office. Of course, it's the first thing he wants to discuss. My dad must've texted him about my trip to the hospital.

"It was an accident," I lie, "but everyone is convinced that it wasn't."

"What makes you say that?"

"The doctor that I saw gave me the 'we're monitoring you' speech. And my dad won't stay more than ten feet away from me at all times."

He frowns. "I'm sure they want what's best for you."

There's a new picture hanging in the corner of Dr. Taylor's office, a stick-figure drawing of a family. The man on the right of the page has a pair of glasses and gray speckled hair like Dr. Taylor.

"Do you have children?" I ask, feeling guilty that I never have before.

He peeks at the drawing and smiles. "My wife and I adopted a five-year-old boy last year. He thought my office could use some more color."

"He's right," I affirm, pointing to the array of dark wood that sucks all of the natural light out of the room.

Dr. Taylor chuckles. "I'll be sure to let him know you agree."

Outside, the rain tapping against the window turns from a sprinkle to a pour. The steady sound is soothing. Dr. Taylor relaxes, too, letting his hands hang freely from the chair.

"Have you thought about the incident at school recently?"

"Sometimes," I confess. "I try not to."

Truthfully, I think about it all the time, even when I'd rather not. That day in calculus has been fresh in my mind ever since I told Elliott about it. Fragments of the repressed memory keep showing up in my dreams.

"Why not?"

"It's not really something I want to dwell on."

He doesn't look away from me, even as I seal my lips. Soon enough he's going to start analyzing my breathing patterns for inconsistencies.

"What about boxing? Are you still enjoying it?"

"There's a tournament next weekend in Savannah. I'm not allowed to compete yet, but I think I want to try once I'm good enough."

I pause, fingers rubbing against the scratches in the arm rest.

"This sounds weird, but I wish my mom could have tried it. It grounds me. Makes me remember who I am, where I am."

Dr. Taylor nods, brushing away a loose piece of silver hair. "That may be true, but everyone has a different way of staying grounded. What works for you might not have helped her. The important thing is that you've found *your* outlet."

Selfishly, a part of me is grateful that I've found my niche, something that belongs only to me and not her. We share so many similarities that sometimes I want to celebrate the differences. The smell of sterilization from the hallway seeps into the office. I crinkle my nose.

"I hate this hospital," I groan. "Every time I come here, all I can think about is her. I see her face in the walls, and I hear her voice. Sometimes she just . . . screams."

"What does that sound like?"

The sound has plagued me ever since the first time I heard it. A constant ringing in my ears, reminding me of my own fate.

"Like she's trapped in a cage. Like her only escape is dying."

# CHAPTER TEN

**MONDAY AFTERNOON, I SHOW UP TO BOXING A FEW MINUTES EARLY TO TRY** and avoid an awkward conversation with Elliott. Andre meets me at the front door. I reach to turn the doorknob, but he stops me.

"What happened to your hand?" he asks.

I decided not to hide the injury, since punching with my right hand might break the stitches. "I hurt it on glass."

"You should give it time to heal. Hit with your left."

The gym smells like a combination of sweat and bleach, which has strangely become comforting over these last few weeks. The door swings open again, and I recognize the sound of the heavy footsteps. Elliott nods approvingly at my fresh bandages.

Andre makes me practice solo because of the injury. I perfect my left-handed crosses even though it feels unnatural. I channel every ounce of energy I have into nailing the routine. My mind goes blank of anything and everything that isn't boxing. I practice the same move over and over again until I can't feel my arm anymore, and even then, I don't stop.

"Keep that up, and you'll be competing in no time," Riley remarks. He passes me my water bottle.

I drain what's left of it and continue. Occasionally, Elliott opens his mouth like he might say something, then shuts it. By the time class ends, I'm the last one in the gym except for Andre. He corrects my posture on my hook, then waits patiently in the corner until I can't find the strength to keep moving.

"Let's start some private lessons after Savannah," he suggests on our way out the door.

I stop walking. Private lessons with Andre are exactly what I need to improve enough to compete, but after my hospital visit, I can't ask my dad to pay for anything else.

"That sounds great, but we're struggling to pay for practice as is," I say.

Andre shakes his head. "I'm volunteering. You motivate me, kid."

To his surprise and my own, I pull Andre in for a hug. He relaxes against me, patting my back like my father does. He smells like moss and oak trees, which is fitting for the person who has kept me grounded.

"Thank you," I whisper.

*

"What the hell happened?" Gemma asks, narrowing her gaze on my injury.

I give her the same bullshit story I gave Dr. Taylor. She grabs my hand and inspects it carefully. As she runs her index finger across my arm, I let out a dramatic moan of pain. She drops my hand, and I burst out laughing.

"I'm messing with you. It doesn't hurt that bad."

Gemma slams her shoulder into mine.

"Did that?" she retorts.

We hurry to school, pausing at the entrance to say our goodbyes. I pass the time in my morning classes by sketching flowers in my notebooks. In English, Elliott falls asleep and snores. Mr. Ruse wakes him up by throwing a ruler at his head. The girls crowding his desk do the same three things every day: smirk, giggle, and ask questions with no real answer. Considering none of them get any further with him than the day before, I wonder why they keep trying.

When the bell rings, I'm the first out the door. Elliott rises out of his chair and lingers closely behind me.

"Berman!"

I pause. The voice is like a foghorn. Harris Price. He lurks on the other side of the hallway, leaning casually against the cinderblock wall. He isn't wearing his football jersey today; instead, he's dressed in a blue varsity jacket and sweatpants. My flight instinct kicks in, and I start in the opposite direction. He calls out again, but this time he chooses a new word.

"Psycho!"

I freeze. My fingernails dig into the bottom of my palm. A few of the students around slow down their walk, watching as the quarterback makes his way toward me.

"What do you want?" I ask.

"I saw you at Alex's party," he states. "I tried to say hello."

"I was busy."

From the other side of the hall, I notice Elliott approaching. He steps in front of me, and as he does, my racing pulse steadies.

"Is everything okay?" Elliott asks, glaring at Harris.

The crowd of onlookers grows in size. I slide closer to Elliott.

"Everything's fine," Harris responds. "It's been a while, King."

"It has," Elliott grumbles.

Harris grows bored with him quickly. He turns his attention back on me, piercing eyes drifting over my face and my chest. I squeeze the sides of my jacket together to cover my tank top.

"Are you busy this weekend, Rosalyn?" Harris questions.

I growl, "Yes."

Harris grins, the anger in my voice only encouraging him. His gaze flickers between Elliott and I, and amusement spreads across his rugged features.

"Yeah?" Harris probes. "Doing what?"

I open my mouth to respond, but Elliott beats me to it.

"Me."

I choke. A hushed whisper falls upon the crowd of spectators. Harris shuffles back a step.

"Nice bluff," he says. "I'll believe it when I see it."

He sounds unimpressed, but I can tell by the shakiness in his voice that he's not so sure. The quarterback stomps down the hallway. I get the feeling that he's still not satisfied.

"Let's go to lunch," Elliott whispers.

The moment is over in an instant, and yet I feel like I've been standing here for years. I swallow my pride and follow him out of the hallway. He doesn't take me to the cafeteria, though. Instead, we head straight through the front door out of the school. My mind clears in the fresh air, and the realization of what he just said slaps me across the face.

"You won't answer any of my questions, and now you're implying that you're sleeping with me?" I spit.

Elliott's eyes widen. "You're mad?"

"Yes!"

Across the parking lot, a teacher spots us and scowls. Elliott doesn't lower his voice.

"I didn't think that would piss you off!" he shouts. "I thought I was helping you!"

"I don't need your help." A few lessons with Andre and I won't need a protector. "You can tell me the truth about whatever the hell you're involved in, or you can leave me alone. And by alone, I mean *alone*. No more stepping into my drama. I'd rather face Harris myself."

Elliott inches backward, running his hand through his short hair. Finally, he says, "There's a fight tonight. Come with me."

I pause. I wasn't expecting him to offer, and now that he has, I'm not sure what to do.

"Fine," I say, because I can't think of something better.

"Fine," he repeats. "I'll pick you up at midnight."

He turns back toward the school, then pauses.

"Is it really that bad if everyone thinks we're together?"

I gulp. Lying to piss off Harris was understandable, but I didn't think there was a sliver of truth to it.

Did he?

The idea both excites and terrifies me. Elliott's loud and impulsive, the opposite of the type of person I would ever want to date, but for a second, I allow myself to imagine the two of us together. And it's kind of beautiful.

"I didn't say it was bad," I whisper.

Elliott lingers for another moment, lips curling into a gentle half-smile, before going back inside. I count to three, then follow behind him. Gemma and Nishi's jaws are on the floor when I walk into the cafeteria. Word travels way too fast within the walls of this school. Preparing myself for an assault of questions, I take a seat.

Gemma goes first. "You really didn't tell me that you're seeing Elliott?"

God, this is a disaster. My skull pounds as the adrenaline coursing through my veins slows its course.

"I didn't think I was," I say, hiding my face in my hands. "I'm so confused."

"He likes you," Gemma counters. I throw my hand over her mouth to quiet her, but she keeps talking. "If you're hoping for my approval, I like him. If I wasn't a lesbian, I'd probably jump his bones."

Nishi laughs at the sudden rush of color in my cheeks. I sink into my chair and wish that I could disappear, but by the end of lunch, I'm apparently more popular than ever. Everyone I pass has my name on their lips.

The stares and whispers continue throughout the rest of the day. During my walk to last period, I spot Maddy in the hallway. She glares. I consider saying something, but by the time that I decide on what, she's already gone.

\*

Elliott's car pulls into my driveway a few minutes past midnight.

My lips part at the sound of the revving engine. I wasn't sure if he would actually show. He parks the black BMW and smirks through the car window. I creep down the stairs, then pause at the back door, waiting to hear if I woke up my father. The house remains quiet and still.

My palms dampen with sweat as I slide into the passenger's seat of Elliott's convertible.

"Morning," he says, smiling wryly.

In the darkness, I can barely make out the details of his face. Shadows cover the blue in his eyes, making him look more like Luke than usual.

"You're not going to laugh at my joke?"

"It wasn't funny," I reply.

He puts the car into drive and coasts in the direction of the gym.

"Are you fighting tonight?" I ask.

He shakes his head *no.*

"Good. I don't really want to see you get your ass kicked again."

"I won!"

It's 12:15 a.m. when we arrive at Midtown, but it feels later. Elliott parks across the street. The cold nighttime air and incoming storm clouds make the hair on my arms stand up.

Elliott pauses before getting out of the car. His cheeks are stripped of color. "Keep your head down," he says.

"Are you nervous?"

He nods. "Yeah."

I guess we really are being honest with each other. We jog across the street to the back of the gym as it starts to pour. Elliott stops before the doorway and faces me. He tucks his hands into the pockets of his soaked basketball shorts.

"Ready?"

"No," I declare before Elliott throws open the door.

The gym is crawling with people. An older man greets Elliott by name as soon as he steps inside. Strangers pat his shoulders and cheer, clearing a path for us all the way to the ring. Two men are circling each other in the center of it. The taller of the two lurches forward, grabbing the other's wrists with his hands.

"Foul!"

The fighter lets go. Elliott points to a guy in a ball cap standing on the right side of the ring.

"That's Jacob," Elliott says. "He refs on occasion."

"Since when are there fouls in illegal fighting?"

"There has to be some rules; otherwise, everyone would end up dead."

I pause. "Has anyone ever—"

"Elliott!"

I recognize the voice. Andre. His mouth falls open when he registers my face. I glance at Elliott, but he just shrugs. *Oops,* his expression seems to say. *Forgot to mention that one.*

"Rose," Andre stammers.

"Um, hi."

Logically, it makes perfect sense for Andre to be involved since he owns the gym, but I can't see it. He's so . . . patient. He doesn't have a mean bone in his body. Why would a person like him come to a place like this?

We both stifle nods, not daring to say anything else.

"Shitty lineup tonight," Andre tells Elliott. "Can you fill in next?"

"Against?"

He points to a scrawny, acne-ridden boy in the corner. He's half Elliott's size and shaking like a leaf.

"You want him breathing after?" Elliott sneers.

I elbow him. "You said you weren't competing."

"Not much of a competition," chuckles Andre. "Guys like him show up all the time. They want to prove something, but they end up on the floor."

The boy is almost the same height as me. He seems like someone I could spar with without me ending up a bloody mess. "Well if that's the case, I could take him on," I say, only half joking.

129

Elliott cranes his neck.

"What?" I mutter defensively. "You said anyone is allowed to fight in these matches."

"You have no experience. You'd get your ass kicked."

"Isn't that how you learn?"

"No," he responds shortly. "Not happening."

I steal another glance at Elliott's opponent. He looks prepared to throw himself off a ledge without bothering to look down first.

"Fine," I concede. "Another time."

"Rose—"

"Match is up," Andre interrupts. "Are you in?"

Elliott doesn't give me the chance to oppose. He takes off his jacket, revealing a blank tank top that shows off his tattoos. His muscles protrude through the thin material. He's always been a bigger guy, but I never noticed exactly how hulkish before.

Elliott and the scrawny boy meet each other in the middle of the ring. Around us, the people of the crowd lick their lips, thirsty for action. The boy lurches forward, startling Elliott as he lands a cross punch that slams into his abdomen. Elliott hits back harder. As the kid crashes to the ground, he grabs a hold of Elliott's ankle and pulls him down with him. The boy climbs on top of Elliott and throws his fist into his nose, but Elliott gets the upper hand without much struggle. He pins him to the floor. Elliott raises his fist, stopping only when the boy lets out a petrified scream.

"Stop!" the boy shouts.

The referee, Jacob, inches toward the ring, but Elliott doesn't need to be told twice. He stands up. Blue eyes stare regretfully at the damage he's caused. He's made an absolute mess of this boy without even trying.

As soon as the first person in the crowd cheers, Elliott's guilt transforms into a victorious smile. He waves to the adoring faces without missing a beat. A middle-aged man dressed in an outfit much too fancy for a mostly abandoned boxing gym passes him an envelope. Elliott slips it into the pocket of his shorts before stepping away from the ring.

"Your nose is a mess," I observe. "You need a doctor."

Bouncing on his toes, his pupils shoot across all directions of the room. He's high off of pure adrenaline. At least, I hope that's all it is.

"I'm not going to a doctor."

"Then come home with me."

Elliott blinks. I raise my brows, challenging him to protest, but he doesn't. He takes his car keys out of his pocket and leads me through the crowd. A woman holds the door open for us, while others sigh and pout at the sight of Elliott leaving.

The King nickname is appropriate. We may as well be royalty here.

"You're hurt," I declare, crossing the street and climbing into the BMW. Blood trickles from his forehead and nostrils. "You said you wouldn't fight and now you're bleeding."

Elliott laughs. He starts the car without putting on his seatbelt.

"I'm fine. Barely a scratch."

"You're deranged," I respond. "More than me, I think."

The convertible races down the empty roads. Elliot parks at his house since my father's car is in my driveway. If he catches me sneaking a boy into my room, I'll be grounded for life—and probably the afterlife, too.

"Be quiet," I whisper, guiding Elliott to the back door.

Elliott rests his index finger over his mouth. He follows me up to my bathroom, pausing in terror every time the staircase creaks. We make it to the top without my father stirring. I point toward the edge of the bathtub, trying to distract his wandering eyes from the clothes and trinkets scattered across the floor.

"Sit."

He does. I grab a pink washcloth and soak it through with warm water. I can feel Elliott's curious stare on my back as I move.

"I saw the way you looked at that boy when the match was over," I whisper.

"What?"

He builds a wall around himself, deflecting my statement with ease, but I press on. "You looked at him like you hated yourself."

"You're digging," he scoffs.

"I'm not."

He taps his fingers against his skinned kneecaps.

"It's not a bad thing," I add. "I would be afraid if you didn't feel guilty."

He's coated in so many bruises and scratches that I'm not even sure where to start. I decide on the blood dripping from his forehead since it needs the most immediate care. The cut isn't too deep, just a nail scratch, and the bleeding stops with a small amount of pressure. Elliott doesn't wince.

"Freshman year, I got involved with some stuff," he begins. "You name the drug; I was taking it."

Elliott has always been a partier. I'm pretty sure Gemma bought alcohol from him on more than one occasion sophomore year.

"I spent everything I had on drugs and drink, so I stole some of my father's money. He noticed."

He grimaces at the memory, reconfirming my suspicion that his bruises have to be from something other than fighting at Midtown—Damon's hand.

"I had to find a way to pay him back. That's when I met Andre, and he introduced me to The Ring."

I still can't believe that Andre was there tonight. All of this— The Ring, Elliott's father, Andre's involvement—feels like something I would've made up in a hallucination or a nightmare. None of it should exist. But the remains of the fresh blood from Elliott's nose and the trembling in his voice are enough for me to know that it's real. Blood this dark can't be faked.

"I got my ass kicked the first time, obviously. I begged Andre to give me another chance. I couldn't go home without the money. He let me, and I won."

I don't want to know what would've happened if he hadn't.

"My dad wanted to know where I got the money from. So, I told him about what I did."

I move the washcloth so I can see his face in its entirety. His bushy eyebrows and rounded lips are shadowed by bruises. His breathing is heavy and uneven; he smells like salt and violence and bad decisions, but I don't care.

"He told me to keep going."

Rage boils the blood in my veins at the thought of Damon encouraging his own child to risk his life. Elliott pulls out an envelope from his pocket. It's filled to the brim with money.

I gasp. "How much is that?"

Elliott cringes, as if biting down on something sour. "Doesn't matter. It all goes to my father."

I run my fingers across the green paper. All the bills are hundreds. There's enough in the envelope to cover at least the cost of my stitches and another month's worth of boxing lessons. No wonder his family has so much money.

"You didn't have to hide this from me," I say.

He shakes his head. "There's more. More than I can tell you in one night. There are layers to all of this. People in higher places that my dad is working with."

"But you want to get out?"

"I'm not sure," he admits. "It's kind of nice to have something I'm good at."

He's good at a lot of things. Saving Gemma. Telling jokes. Assisting Andre at the gym. Biology, considering he's in the advanced class and nobody talks about it. And helping me, reminding me how strong and capable I am.

"Oh," is all I say, because I'm not sure how to put all of that into words without revealing how much I've been watching him.

Gradually, I move the washcloth from his face down to the neckline of his tank. His fingers wrap around the bottom of his shirt, and he pulls it over his head, exposing his bare, battered chest. I hold my breath.

He watches steadily as I clean the remains of blood and dirt off his skin. Like the rest of his body, his chest is covered in black ink. I lock onto the detailed image of an anatomical heart on his ribs. Each line is intricately connected; the crimson blood stains make the design more realistic.

"Rose?" Elliott asks softly, bringing me out of my daze.

"Sorry," I mutter. "I like your tattoos. They seem meaningful."

He pulls up his pant leg, exposing the skin around his ankle. The word "fuck" is etched into his ankle in blue ink. I cover my hand with my mouth to keep my dad from hearing my laughter.

Elliott points to the anatomical heart. "This used to be a slice of pizza until I got it covered up."

"Somehow, I'm not surprised."

He sticks out his tongue. "Whatever."

Silence fills the space between the two of us. My hands absentmindedly dab at the cuts on his chest.

"I should get home," he mumbles. "Thanks for your help."

"Of course."

There's so much more I want to say. But I don't. And Elliott doesn't. He takes his tank with him as he slips out of my bathroom. Haltingly, I pick myself up from the floor.

If not for the stained washcloth on the counter, I could convince myself that this night never happened. That Elliott is someone I dreamt up, the ghost of a person who I might be starting to feel something real for.

But it did happen. And now I can't get him out of my head.

# CHAPTER ELEVEN

**FOR THE FIRST TIME IN OVER A YEAR, I WEAR A SKIRT TO SCHOOL.**

The cold, smooth satin material hugs my hips. Chills run up my legs from the breeze, but I'm so nervous that I sweat. As wrong as it feels to admit, I wore this skirt for one person, and that person isn't me. Gemma grins from ear to ear when she spots me.

"Don't," I say, before she can even open her mouth.

I make it to Mr. Ruse's classroom before Elliott. Some people stare. *Ugh. Too obvious?* Fighting the urge to sprint into the girls' locker room and change into my P.E. uniform, I droop my jacket over my bare legs to hide the goose bumps. I can practically hear every feminist that ever lived rolling over in their graves.

Two minutes before the bell, Elliott slips through the door of Mr. Ruse's classroom. His injuries look much less gruesome than last night, though that's partly thanks to the navy blue beanie covering the scrape on his forehead. He smiles when he notices me, and I smile back. I open my mouth to say something, but before I can get a single word out, he turns his chair to face Maddy.

I'm an idiot. Why did I think that things between us might be radically different now? He's still Elliott King, and I'm still *Psycho*. Not exactly in the running for most likely to get together.

"Hey."

Elliott lurks next to the door after class. Maddy is halfway down the hallway, and there aren't any other girls beside him.

"Hey," I respond.

"You want a ride later?"

One second he's ignoring me, and the next, he's offering to drive me to practice. I want to slam my head into the wall.

"Sure," I reply.

"Sweet. Meet me in the lot after last period."

I nod. During lunch, Gemma and Nishi pester me with questions about Elliott, none of which I have answers to.

"I ran into him last night," I lie. "I went to the gym to practice alone, and he was there. We talked about his family and his tattoos. I thought maybe . . ."

My voice trails off. Elliott slipped out of the bathroom before anything happened between us. "But nope. Nothing. And today he's still all over Maddy."

"There's a simple solution to this problem," Nishi states. "You have to play hard to get."

"But I'm not hard to get. I'm literally the least hard to get person at this school."

"Who cares? Just don't let him know that he has so much power over you. He'll be crawling at your feet in no time."

I lower my head. "I already agreed to let him drive me to boxing."

"Act like hot guys take you to practice every day."

Nishi's right. Elliott gets anything and everyone he wants. I don't want to be the girl fawning over his every word.

I bite into the apple in my hand. "You make it sound so easy."

"Hey, you're a good actress," Gemma counters. "Remember middle school theater?"

She has a point. At this point, I can lie as easily as I tell the truth.

"Fine," I concede. "I'll try."

When school ends, Elliott's waiting inside of his convertible. Following Nishi's advice, I smile as I sit down, but I don't say anything. Neither of us speak as he drives out of the parking lot. After only a minute, the awkwardness becomes too unbearable to stand.

"Nice weather outside," I whisper.

*Really, Rose? You may as well jump out of the car.*

Elliott taps his scabbed fingers against the steering wheel. "Yep."

When we arrive at the gym, Andre greets both of us with a knowing smile. I fight the urge to pull him aside and demand he answer all my lingering questions. For starters, why the hell create an underground fighting ring in the first place?

I wrap only my left hand, dressing it in my pink boxing glove. The gym is spotless, floors sparkling from what I can only imagine took hours of work and at least a gallon of bleach. As usual, I'm partnered with Elliott. I begin to exercise with my left hand, but then I position myself so I'm leading with my right.

"No," Elliott declares. "You'll hurt yourself."

I grumble, annoyed. "It's going to get weak. I can't fight with one hand."

"I didn't know you had plans to fight anyone."

"Well, you made it look so fun."

My voice drips with sarcasm, but Elliott still shoots me a death glare.

After a few rounds of jabs and stretches, Andre breaks us up into sparring partners. To my surprise, he pairs me with

Sofía and Elliott with Riley. Approaching Sofía with caution, I remind her of my injured hand before she can accidentally (or purposefully) break it.

"How did it happen?" she asks.

"I punched a mirror," I admit since I don't have to worry about Sofia reporting me to Dr. Taylor. "It was a shitty day."

She's the first person that I've ever sparred with, and after only one round, my confidence is destroyed. She's too fast for me to keep up with and strategic in a way that only someone with years of training could be. Her glove clashes into mine. I pause, heaving, to reach for my mouthguard.

"You know, you're not too bad at this," she says. "But you'll never improve if you don't believe you can."

"You don't think I want to get better?"

"I didn't say that. I said you want to get better, but you're convinced you can't. You keep stepping backwards so I won't hit you. That's not how you improve."

"Sorry," I stammer.

"Don't apologize," she replies, unflinching. "Take a hit. You'll feel better."

And I do. Many. By the time Andre ends practice, I've been punched in the forearm, shoulder, and abdomen more times than I can count. But Sofía was right. After so much falling on my face, my only option is to get back on my feet and try again. I almost tied a round before I tripped on my own shoelace and landed butt first on the floor.

"You're brave for going against Sofía," Elliott comments, joining me on the bench after practice ends. "Your first sparring partner is a professional."

"Trust me, I know." I moan, stretching out my sore arm.

I gulp down my entire bottle of water, choking on the last sip, which makes Elliott laugh. *I'm really not doing the best job of playing hard to get.*

"I want to remind everyone about the competition in Savannah this weekend. If any of you aren't going to be able to make it, please let me know by tonight," Andre announces.

*Crap.* I completely forgot to ask my dad.

Elliott glances at me. "Are you going?"

"Hopefully. You?"

"Yeah."

Swinging my backpack across my shoulder, I leave the gym. Elliott follows a few paces behind. The sun sinks beneath the horizon, lighting up the sky in gold and orange hues.

"Want a ride home?"

He's not making this easy.

"No, thanks."

He pulls a cigarette out of his pocket and lights up. He speaks through a mouthful of smoke, "There's a match coming up. You should come."

The way he emphasizes *match* clues me into the fact that it's not a legal one.

I straighten my spine. "Where is it?"

"Savannah."

"Like . . . the competition?"

Elliott smirks. He takes another hit of the cigarette, blowing out the puff of smoke in one fluid motion.

"Andre's clever. This one will be big. People will travel from far away for it."

If Elliott doesn't classify the fights at Midtown Ring as big, then I'm not sure I want to find out the scale of this one. I picture the usual crowd at Disney World crammed inside of a large gym.

"Oh," I murmur. "Well, I'll let you know what my dad says."

He nods, then turns toward his car, clouds of tobacco smoke following his broad footsteps. As his convertible exits the parking lot, the remnants of the orange sunset fade into darkness. I spend the train ride home trying to come up with the best strategy to convince my dad to let me go to Savannah. I decide on a combination of flattery and begging.

My father is standing over the stove when I get home. The house smells like broccoli and cheese. I turn my nose, holding in a gag. Even though I've told him a thousand times that I hate broccoli, he cooks it anyway. Mom remembered those things—never him.

"Hi," he says as I step into the kitchen. "Are you hungry?"

"My coach signed us up for a boxing competition next weekend in Savannah. We would leave Friday, so I'd have to miss a day of school, and we'll get back Sunday. Andre already booked hotels. I don't even have to pay anything," I blurt out, tripping over my own words.

*So much for strategy.*

My dad puts down the spatula. He inspects my injured hand. I know what he's thinking—letting me go anywhere alone is a bad idea. Considering there's an underground fight club in Savannah, his instincts are right.

"I'm only an alternate, so I won't be competing," I plead. "I want to go to support everyone, and Andre thinks it will be a great learning experience."

I wish my name was on the lineup, but Andre is right. I need more preparation before I can fight in any sort of tournament.

This weekend could be the learning experience that I've been waiting for. I don't want to miss it.

"Rose, I don't want you to feel like you're jailed, but it's hard for me to know that you're safe when you're so far away."

This is a big ask. I haven't been allowed to spend much time away from home since my mother died. And after my hand injury disaster, I doubt my father wants to make an exception. He runs his hand through his curls and lets out a sigh that destroys any sliver of hope I had left.

"I know," I respond, defeated. I take a seat at the dinner table.

My dad sits down next to me. "You have to text me every few hours with updates. Get your homework done early. And I want Andre's number, just in case."

"Yes!" I shriek, standing back up and wrapping my arms around his body. I squeeze, practically lifting him off of the chair as I do.

"Damn!" he exclaims. "You are getting stronger."

I flex my biceps with a giggle. We discuss more details of the competition over dinner. I text Elliott to let him know about my dad agreeing.

**ELLIOTT: Cool. I'll drive.**

Four hours alone in a car with Elliott. The opposite of distancing myself from him. Gemma and Nishi might kill me, but I can't bring myself to care. This road trip is the perfect excuse to ask him the questions that I've been sitting on.

"Rose?" my dad interrupts. "Are you okay?"

I snap out of it. This is probably one of the only times that my zoning out has nothing to do with anxiety. As much as it kills me to do, I pull out my phone from beneath the table and hold it up to him.

"I was texting Elliott," I admit. "Hence the distraction."

His face turns as red as a tomato. My father is the last person in the world that ever wants to discuss boys. I think he'd rather me wrestle an alligator than go out on a date.

"Well, then," he states. "That's . . . good."

My poor dad. I wish my mom were here to let him know that everything was going to be fine. I would tell her all about Elliott over one of the small tables at Simone's Chinese Restaurant. She would've adored him. She had a soft spot for people who needed it most.

*

The next two days pass by in a blur. On Thursday night, I pack a bag with clothes for every possible occasion, because who's to say there won't be a ballroom dance after the underground fight club?

I'm hardly able to sleep, kept awake by imagining a thousand different scenarios of how this weekend will play out. I'm deep into a version where Elliott's car breaks down when my alarm goes off. As nervous as I am for this trip, I've been looking forward to it ever since Andre first brought it up.

I throw myself out of bed and start getting ready. Twenty minutes later, Elliott texts me to let me know that he's on the way. I tuck the front of my black T-shirt into a pair of high waisted blue jeans. Then, I grab my backpack and head downstairs. My dad passes me a granola bar and a banana.

"I'll text you when we get there," I say.

"Be safe, Rose. Call me if you need anything at all."

"Will do. Love you!"

I plant a kiss on his cheek. Elliott's convertible revs from outside. He's right on time. My father peers out the front door, taking in the sight of the BMW with a disapproving frown.

"Is he a safe driver?"

*Nope.*

"Yes. I'll be fine. Please don't embarrass me."

He hesitates, and I know that it's taking every bit of his willpower to let me exit the front door. I inch my way toward it, and to my surprise, my father remains in the kitchen.

"Morning," Elliott yawns.

We're wearing almost the same thing. His black V-neck sticks tightly to his chest.

"Nice outfit," I tease.

I toss my backpack on the floor of the passenger's seat and grab the aux cord without asking permission. I've been working on a playlist ever since my dad approved the trip. I don't know anything about Elliott's music taste apart from the horrible stuff he blasts when he drives by my window, so I chose a variety of artists from Frank Ocean to Florence and the Machine.

"The best part of all of this was getting out of school. I was supposed to give a presentation in history today," I say.

"You have Dr. Jules?"

I nod, and Elliott groans. "Hate her. She failed me twice."

"Twice? Wouldn't the school hold you back for that?"

"Not if you pay them enough."

He relaxes against the driver's seat, unafraid despite the hours of alone time ahead of us. Meanwhile, I might explode from anxiety at any given second.

"So, we're friends now, right?"

I contemplate his question. "I know your darkest secret but not your favorite color. Does that make me a friend?"

"Blue," he answers with a smirk. "What's yours?"

"Purple."

Not exactly the conversation that I was hoping we would have, but I'll take anything at this point.

"What's your favorite book?" he asks.

I have to think about the answer to that one. I've read so many in the last few months that the titles blend together. The escape from reality that books offer kept me relatively sane after my mom died.

"Probably *On the Road*. What about you?"

"*The Things They Carried*," he replies. No hesitation.

"I haven't read it."

He half smiles. "It doesn't feel like a book."

I make a mental note to get my hands on a copy. Elliott turns onto the highway that leads out of Atlanta, and I silently pray that nothing crashes and burns while I'm gone. I want to focus on learning from the competition; maybe even have some actual fun. God knows I need it.

"Are you into any sports apart from boxing?"

"My dad made me join the swim team when I was kid," Elliott responds. "I sucked. Kept feeling like I was going to drown even though I could swim. I'm kind of terrified of water."

"What about your mom? Did she have any say?"

It's a delicate topic, I know. Elliott hasn't spoken a word about her to me. He pulls out a cigarette from the package in the cupholder and holds it up against the lighter, smoke covering the frown on his lips.

"Drugs. My dad got custody when I was young."

I think back to the line of cocaine on the table at Elliott's party. He told me the other night that drugs were what got him into fighting in the first place. It's strange that he would try something that ruined his life so much already.

"Where is she now?"

"Last I heard, somewhere in Florida with a new boyfriend."

He takes a hit of the cigarette. The smoke floats out of the window and into the morning air.

"Have you ever been to Savannah?" Elliott asks.

I tell him the story of the one time that I went for my tenth birthday. I begged my parents to take me after learning that one of the most haunted cities in America was only a few hours away from our house. My dad thought I was mad for wanting to go, but my mom was thrilled. We spent most of the trip trying to photograph ghosts. My mom was convinced that we had seen a few by the end of the trip.

"Do you think you did?"

"At the time, yeah. But now I think she was probably imagining shit."

"You haven't told me much about her," he prompts.

I rub some of the sweat on my palms onto my jeans. Talking about my mom is never easy, even when the questions are innocent. I always learn something new about her when I do. Those discoveries are rarely good.

"She had anxiety like me, but it became more severe as I got older. She started feeling . . . disconnected. Talking nonsense or locking herself in her room for hours staring into space. We took her to an inpatient psychiatric facility during my freshman year. She was only there for a week until she escaped."

Elliott throws the remainder of the cigarette out the window. His grip on the wheel hardens.

"I found her at home," I whisper.

Most of that day is still a blur, but I remember an empty pill bottle and ambulance sirens as EMTs rushed her to the hospital, only to report hours later that they weren't able to save her.

"How the hell did she get out of the facility?"

It's the million-dollar question that my dad and I still haven't gotten an answer to. At first, I put all my energy into hating her caretakers, drawing up elaborate revenge plans where I would storm their houses or get them fired. But Dr. Taylor talked me off the ledge. "Rose, *giving them your energy won't change the past. What's done is done. Your mom would want you to focus on healing.*"

I shrink into the seat. "No idea. I try not to think about it."

Elliott turns down the music as we merge into the lane that leads to Savannah. The sky above us is clear, but there are patches of dark clouds ahead.

"What did she like to do?" Elliott asks.

I grin, grateful for the question. "She was a writer. A really good one. She loved gardening, but the plants usually didn't make it more than a month."

My dad and I joked that she couldn't keep anything alive.

"What about the rest of your family?" Elliott continues. "Grandparents?"

"I see my grandparents on my mom's side sometimes, but they're all the way in Maine. My dad's family doesn't speak to us anymore. My dad's Baptist, but he knew raising me Jewish was important to my mom, so he tried—well, he's trying his best. They don't really approve."

"My family isn't much of anything," Elliott says. "I don't know about my mother's parents. My father's are dead."

I stare out the window, entertained by the colors of the changing leaves on the trees. We talk about little things that feel like big things to me. Elliott has a story to tell about any topic I bring up, but usually it involves drugs or alcohol of some kind. I honestly don't know how he's managed to stay alive this long.

"You did *what?*"

"The opportunity was there, so I had to take it," Elliott states.

"You partied with Conor McGregor?"

He presses a finger to my lips, shushing me. The clash of his skin against mine is unexpected but tender and comfortable. I smile through the touch.

"This is classified information, Rose. If you tell a single soul, he'll come after you."

I burst out laughing. Elliott leans his head against the back of his seat, the convertible coasting through the Savannah city limits sign. By the time we arrive at our hotel, I feel like I know Elliott better than I did before, yet I still have a thousand more questions prepared. I'm tempted to bring up the fight club, but I hold off. I'm sure most of my questions—and some that I don't even know I have yet—will be answered this weekend.

The hotel, a shining example of old Southern architecture, is only a few streets away from the Savannah River. With its Colonial style windows and columned doorway, it's straight out of the eighteenth century.

"You made it!" Andre declares, meeting us outside of the hotel entrance. "Everyone's here except for Max. Stomach flu."

*Yikes.* I hop out of the car, grateful to stretch my legs. Andre passes us both a set of keys.

"Rose, you're rooming with Sofía. Elliott, you'll be with Riley."

*Sofía. Great.*

With a huff, I lug both of my bags out of the trunk.

The interior of the hotel is stunning. Antiques and old paintings line the walls, and the ceiling is painted a royal gold. When I arrive at my room on the fourteenth floor, Sofía is seated on the bed closest to the window. The wallpaper, an unappealing floral pattern, is peeling in several sections. The furniture is a deep, imperial red. It smells like cheap wilderness scented air freshener.

"Are you going out with us tonight?" Sofía inquires.

Glancing in the mirror on the wall, I don't appear a day over seventeen.

"I doubt I can get into any bars."

"Mierda. I completely forgot," she mutters. "We could try to sneak you in?"

"It's alright. Not worth getting everyone in trouble."

We sink back into silence as I unpack my suitcase, placing my gloves and hand wraps onto the desk so I don't forget them tomorrow. Then, I pick out the cutest outfit I brought with me: a forest green T-shirt dress and white combat boots. The dress brings out some of my few curves.

Sofía smirks mischievously. "Estás buena. You'll definitely get in with that outfit on."

She's not the type to throw around compliments, so I take her word for it. I carefully braid my hair down my back, then pull out a few stray pieces to frame the round shape of my face. Sofía adorns a pair of black baggy jeans and a silky red tank top. She looks glamorous, the opposite of how she's usually dressed at Midtown. We meet up with the rest of the group in the lobby. Tourists buzz around the hotel, chit-chatting about their plans for the night. Riley has a drink in his hand.

Elliott's lips part when I approach him, scanning my body up and down.

Andre chuckles at Elliott's surprised expression. "You look great, Rose," he states, breaking the silence between Elliott and myself. I thank him.

"Yeah," Elliott agrees. "You do."

Andre calls the group together. It's weird to see everyone dressed in non-athletic clothes. Riley's wearing a red button up, and Andre is sporting plaid pants and a fitted T-shirt.

"I want us all to have fun tonight, but keep in mind that we have to be up at six in the morning. I don't want any of you hungover. Got it?"

Spoken like a true coach. I nod, even though I have no intention of staying out late or drinking.

"Aye, captain," Riley says, saluting Andre.

"There's a strip of bars down the street," Andre continues. "I say we hang out there?"

Everyone escapes out of the revolving door. I skip to Elliott's side.

"I can't get into any bars. Neither can you, right?"

He pauses, confused.

"What?" I raise an eyebrow. "You can?"

He opens his wallet and passes me a Connecticut driver's license with his picture on it. The date of his birthday is printed in a bigger font than the rest of the ID. I've done better work in Microsoft.

"Nobody will ever believe that's real."

"You'd be surprised."

"Well, real or not, I don't have one," I murmur. "Can you tell the rest of the group I'm sick, and I'll head back upstairs?"

"I'm not leaving you alone in that shitty room all night," he says, as if I've suggested something totally nonsensical. "Why don't we go spot some ghosts?"

All of a sudden, I'm a child again, believing my mother's stories about hauntings and spirits. Elliott lights up at the innocent smile plastered across my face.

"Really?" I exclaim.

"We're here. Why not?"

We wave goodbye to the rest of the group before wandering in the direction of the harbor. The streets are alive with children licking ice-cream cones and parents snapping photographs.

"I haven't seen the harbor in the daytime," I tell Elliott.

During my family trip, we were always hopping from one place to the next, never actually stopping to take in the views. Anything that kept her mind distracted was my mother's idea of a perfect vacation.

"We'll come back tomorrow," Elliott demands. "You have to see the colors."

I don't argue. One of the promises that I made after my mother's death was that I would try and see everything that she never got the chance to.

"There's a cemetery nearby," Elliott states, pointing down at a map of the area he grabbed from the hotel lobby. Bonaventure Cemetery. We're only a block away. "Want to go?" he asks.

I nod. We leave the harbor behind us and snake down one of the cobblestone alleyways, following a few steps behind a ghost tour. Some of the headstones scattered throughout Bonaventure are twice my height. One in particular stands out. My father took a picture of the inscription on the stone.

"I've been here before." I realize.

Two security guards approach, informing us to be quick since the cemetery is closing in half an hour.

"Not a problem," I reply. "I know where to go."

I lead Elliott to a stained glass crypt positioned at the bottom of the hill. The exact details are hard to make out, but the streetlamps are bright enough to illuminate the biggest words on the headstone. Elliott's bruised lip curls as he reads it out loud.

"Rosalyn Berman. Died in 1825. Beloved daughter and friend. You were reincarnated?"

"I was so surprised to find somebody with my name here," I recall. "It was one of the first times I really thought about death."

Walking to the side of the structure, I pause in view of the stained glass design. The image of a cross surrounded by several wilting roses stares back at me.

"I think about death all the time now."

Elliott takes a step closer. He tucks his hands into the pockets of his black skinny jeans.

"What do you mean?"

I take a seat on the curb. "There was a version of myself that I liked a lot more than who I am now. I've been trying to go back to her."

The Rose who existed before my mother's death had less fear. She was careless and impulsive and compassionate to a fault. Now, I can't do anything without hesitating. I'm afraid of everything, it seems like.

Elliott pulls a cigarette out of his pocket. His sharp jaw turns as he stares down at me. "You shouldn't let yourself get stuck in the past. Shit happens and it changes you. You can be the person you want to be right now."

"But I don't know how to get unstuck. Every time I see an old picture of myself, I remember how much happier I was, and I can't let it go."

"Let's bury her then," he suggests. "The old you. So that perfect life doesn't haunt you anymore. Start a clean slate."

Elliott steps up to the structure, lighting the cigarette in his hand as he moves. I stand and follow at his side.

"Pretend this tomb is yours. The old you. What do you want it to say?" he questions.

"Here lies Rosalyn Berman, so pale we mistook her for a vampire."

He rolls his eyes. "I'm serious."

Elliott takes my hand, holding the cigarette in the other, and slips his fingers in between mine. His skin is warm. I inhale a sharp breath as he applies steady pressure to my palms.

"Tell me what you're thinking," says Elliott.

*Nothing now, except for your hand on mine.*

"I wish I didn't feel like I'm on the edge of losing it all the time," I admit. "I miss the person I was when I was here with my mother."

Elliott releases my hand and kneels down to the ground. He puts out the cigarette on the ground, then passes me a handful of dirt. Some of it escapes through the cracks between my fingers, unraveling right in front of me. I sprinkle the remainder on top of the grave.

"Here's to burying who I was and appreciating who I am now," I whisper, this time more to myself than Elliott.

He nods approvingly. I remain still for a long, quiet moment. The wind rushes through my hair, slipping through the thin material of my dress, but I'm not cold.

Elliott doesn't take my hand again, but he doesn't need to. I can stand on my own.

"You should go find the rest of the group," I suggest. "I think I'll go back to the room for the night."

"Are you sure?"

"I want to be alone, if that's okay."

He guides me back down the main road, tourists and families laughing with each other as they pass us by. Elliott stops at the doorway to the hotel. He looks older and more intimidating in the darkness, but I still feel comfortable next to him.

"Call me if you need anything."

"Thanks." He turns in the direction of the strip of bars down the street as I slip back inside of the lobby. Without Sofía around to make fun of it, the vintage décor is spooky. I take one of the portraits down from the wall and turn it facedown on the table so the man in the frame isn't watching me.

I can't get Mom out of my head.

An image of Doris Berman is plastered there, frozen in time like the man in the portrait. She isn't afraid, or tired, or suffering. She's the person I grew up loving, who loved me more than I ever could have known.

I spent weeks after her death regretting every rude comment I ever made. I shunned myself for not appreciating her more while she was around. But she must have known that I loved her. I'm not that good of a liar, even now.

She didn't kill herself because of me. I've been trying to come to terms with that truth every day since I found her body in the bathroom. Blaming myself rather than her invisible illness was so much easier, especially when acknowledging that illness meant accepting that I might be suffering from it, too.

Tears well in the corner of my eyes. Sometimes, I cry when I crave the warmth of her arms around me, comforting me, promising me everything will be fine. That longing has vanished. Right now, I feel her next to me. She's inside every crevice and corner of this town. She's the ghost we were chasing.

"I love you," I whisper, holding onto the hope that she might be listening.

# CHAPTER TWELVE

**THE BOOMING SOUND OF NIRVANA'S *COME AS YOU ARE* PLAYING THROUGH MY** iPhone startles me awake. Across the room, Sofía springs up from her bed. She glares in my direction.

"Can you turn that damn thing off?"

"Sorry," I say, blindly pressing buttons on my phone until the music stops.

My head is throbbing. I fell asleep before Sofía came back, but judging by her loud yawn, that wasn't until the early morning. Forcing myself out of my cocoon of blankets, I saunter to the bathroom. The reflection that greets me is less than attractive. A few red pimples line the bottom of my chin. My hair is a frizzy, uncontrollable mess. I throw it into a ponytail.

Sofía's already dressed in a matching pair of purple sweatpants and a crop top by the time I step out of the bathroom. I slip into a pair of gray athletic shorts. Even though I'm sure I'll sweat it off throughout the day, I cover up my chin with a layer of concealer.

"How was your night?" I ask as we leave the dingy room.

She smirks. "Your boyfriend was a lot of fun. Bought us all shots."

"Not my boyfriend."

She ignores me. We get into the elevator with a man who's totally a professional bodybuilder. His biceps are the size of my head. I'm suddenly grateful that I'm not competing today.

Elliott is bouncing back and forth on his toes when he notices Sofía and I enter the lobby. He smiles his lopsided grin and I return the favor. Andre brushes past me with a box of donuts sent straight from heaven.

"Take your pick, and then we're headed out."

I grab one with pink icing and sprinkles. Elliott takes two, biting back and forth between them.

"You've got icing on your face," he states, brushing his finger against the corner of my lips.

A tiny bit of pink comes off my skin. Elliott licks the icing off of his finger. I watch him closely, heartbeat racing.

"I heard you were the life of the party last night," I say.

He winks. "You should've been there. I'm tons of fun."

"No fake ID, remember?"

"We'll have to fix that when we get home."

We. The word rolls off his tongue with ease.

Andre piles us into the shuttle bus outside. A few others from the hotel join, including the gigantic man from the elevator. Fortunately, the rest of his team isn't quite as intimidating. Despite its old architecture, the city feels young in the morning sunlight. The convention center, with its gray stone exterior, looks more like a medieval castle than an event venue.

We huddle outside the entrance. Andre passes out copies of the schedule. Over twenty teams are listed to compete over the next two days.

"The rounds are split between men and women," he explains. "The last few matches of today will determine who competes in the finals tomorrow."

The first bout is scheduled to begin in a little over an hour. Midtown Ring is listed first to compete in the men's category.

Andre volunteers without any opposition from the rest of the group.

"Going first is bad luck," Elliott whispers in my ear.

"Andre doesn't need luck," I protest. "He'll be fine."

Inside, the walls are towering, complete with huge windows that fill the place with natural light. Friends and family members of competitors swarm the open hallways. Vendors sell event T-shirts and snacks at booths across the arena. Elliott sighs, unimpressed.

"How many of these competitions have you been to?" I ask him.

"More than enough."

I wonder how many of these faces I'll spot at the other match tonight. My stomach twists thinking about a place this size filled with spectators watching people get bloodied up. I thought the crowd at Midtown was impressive; if half of the people here show up to the ring tonight, the audience will be at least three times the size of Midtown.

Andre leads us into a small room with "Midtown Ring" scribbled on a piece of paper on the door. There are a few tables scattered around the room with water bottles and snacks. Riley takes a seat in the corner. Andre, Elliott, and Sofía sit on the floor and stretch. I examine the schedule again. Midtown Ring is registered to compete in a women's match directly following the men. Sofía is the only female fighting from our group, so she'll be competing.

I approach her with caution. "You're after Andre?"

She nods. Her face is stoic. I'm convinced she doesn't feel fear.

"Better be. Made me submit twice as many forms as the dudes. Including a freaking pregnancy test."

"What?"

"Female matches require it. You can't fight if you're pregnant."

"Wow," I mouth, "I never even thought about that."

I spend the rest of the hour discussing the differences in the matches with Sofía. Fifteen minutes to nine, a bearded man opens the door to the room to inform us that it's time to go to the arena. Elliott stays close to Andre as we start down the hallway. They whisper back and forth to each other. I lean in, but the noise of the crowd drowns out their conversation.

The arena is massive. The two boxing rings in the center of the room put the Midtown one to shame. The blue floor is spotless, untouched by a single drop of blood or sweat. Spectators fill the bleachers, and a camera captures footage that's projected onto a billboard-sized screen. The bearded man leads us to an empty row of seats close to the ropes.

"Good luck," I tell Andre, followed by a chorus of support from the rest of the group.

Andre's competitor enters from a room on the opposite side of the arena. He has blonde hair, pale skin, and soulless eyes. The two of them are total opposites except for their protective headgear.

"Andre's got this," Elliott reassures the group. "He's taken down people bigger than that."

As the men meet in the ring, the crowd around us erupts into applause. I sink into the aisle seat, craning my neck to get a better view.

The announcer's voice booms through a gigantic speaker. "Good morning, Savannah! Welcome to the National Southeast Amateur Boxing Tournament! This is our first round of the day, so I hope you all are ready for some action. I know I am."

Sofía pumps her fist into the air, cheering as Andre places his mouthguard around his teeth.

"From Atlanta, Georgia's Midtown Ring, we have Andre Castillo competing!"

His smile, usually patient and kind, is vicious and unrelenting beneath the harsh fluorescent lights. The crowd loves it.

"From Asheville, North Carolina's Mountain Fitness, we have George Durham!"

The blonde man holds his red glove up into the air. Andre and George distance themselves into separate corners of the ring.

Then, the referee blows the whistle. The bout begins.

Elliott drops one of his hands across mine.

My heart stops beating.

I wrap my fingers around his and squeeze. Andre and George circle each other in slow, taunting movements. At exactly the same time, both men lurch forward, but Andre is the first to raise his fist. George ducks, escaping Andre's hook just in time, but Andre doesn't hesitate to make another move. This time, George isn't fast enough. His body whips around from the force of the hit, blonde hair flying in different directions as he stumbles to the ground. Andre lands two more punches to the shoulders.

The referee starts counting. When George doesn't rise from the floor, a whistle blows, signaling Andre's victory in the first round. I throw myself out of my seat and cheer, but the celebration is short lived. The whistle sounds again. Andre is quicker on his feet in the next two rounds.

"Midtown Ring wins the bout!"

We cheer. Andre crashes into an empty seat, sweat dripping from his head to his toes. The same man who led us from the break room interrupts our celebration to inform Andre that we're up next for the women's match. Sofía's dressed in what looks like a piece of medieval armor for her breasts and groin.

Sofía's opponent is a redhead identical to her in weight and height. They circle each other, occasionally throwing punches that I don't think are intended to land. It's more a test of strategy than brute force.

Sofía's shoulders tense. I lean forward, standing out of my seat. Sofía's opponent raises her glove, slamming her fist into Sofía's ribs. She gasps at the impact but stays on her feet. She throws a jab and hits the girl's stomach.

"Foul!" shouts the ref.

The first round is over before it starts and Sofía is pissed. She shakes out her hands at her sides and gets into position as the bell signals the next round. This time, she's on the offense. She lands a cross and a jab. Her opponent returns with equal force, a punch to the shoulder and arms. But Sofía doesn't fall. I watch, enthralled, as they go back and forth trading blows but, neither will give in.

At the end, Sofía and her opponent wait in the center of the ring for the ref to announce the results.

"Winner!" He announces as he raises the redhead's glove.

Sofía's head falls. "Shit," I utter.

We rise to greet her, but she doesn't allow any of us near her before leaving the arena entirely.

"Let her go," Andre coaxes.

I follow her into the hallway. She glares at me, but I don't leave.

"Hey. Are you okay?"

She hisses, "I'm fine."

"You don't seem fine."

Sofía lets out a dramatic sigh, running her hand through her thick mess of brown hair. Her chest heaves with tiredness, breathing spattered from her injured ribs. She curses under her breath, "Mierda! I should've won. I had that!"

"It happens."

"Not to me."

I inch closer to her, noticing how tired she looks.

"My boyfriend broke up with me on Friday," she confesses. "I'm not thinking straight."

"And you still showed up to this? You're strong."

"No entiendes. He's a crappy person. He shouldn't be distracting me."

"I know the feeling," I say. "I started boxing because of a bad guy at my school. I did this to get stronger, but every time I see him, it's like I forget everything I've learned."

Sofía frowns. She brushes her hand against my arm. I never thought I'd open up to her, but oddly enough, she reminds me a bit of my mother.

"I'm sorry that happened to you."

"Women like you get me through," I say. "Look at you. Even after a breakup, you're kicking ass."

Her muscles are well-defined; her glistening skin and heavy breathing make her look like the goddess Athena.

She wraps her hand around my arm, feeling the muscle. There's more there than ever before. "Keep practicing," she says. "And stay away from boys."

A blush creeps into my cheeks.

"Does that include Elliott?"

A mischievous grin edges the corner of her lip. "Ah. So, I was right." She leans into my ear. "He's an exception. He knows how hard you hit."

The rest of the group approaches from inside of the arena. Elliott raises an eyebrow at the two of us standing so close. I shoot him a look as if to say, tell you later.

"Let's go to lunch," suggests Andre, gathering us into one big circle. "We're off the roster for the rest of the day, but we can watch a few more matches after we eat. Okay?"

Everyone agrees. We walk to a café next to the convention center and fill one of the empty tables.

Andre addresses the group. "Tomorrow, Riley will fight. If he wins, then it's Elliott's turn."

Elliott will be the final competitor if we make it to the end. Selfishly, I hope we do so I can watch him spar in circumstances that won't result in his possible death.

"Excited?" I muse.

He leans into his chair. "Sure."

I take a bite of my turkey sandwich. "How did you get into boxing?" I ask Andre.

"I grew up in the Bronx. A group of us would hang out at the rec center on the weekends and practice. It was fun and therapeutic since most of us had family issues. I always knew that I wanted to pass it on. When I fell in love with a woman from Atlanta, I moved down here to be with her. It didn't last, but I liked the city enough that I decided to stick around and open the gym."

"I, for one, am glad you did," says Riley, scooping a handful of chips into his mouth.

Glad is an understatement. Boxing has helped me feel more connected to the people around me, my city, and my own brain. I feel like I'm a part of something bigger than high school.

The group of us slip into small talk until lunch ends. At 2:00 p.m., we make our way back into the convention center to watch a few more bouts. I pay close attention to the women's matches, noting moves I want Andre to teach me.

"We can head out," Riley states, after another hour. "Day's over."

There are a few more matches left, but nothing that we need to be around for now that Sofía is off the roster. As we leave the convention center, Elliott pulls me aside.

"Want to go down to the river?" he suggests.

The sun is still up, which means I'll finally see the water in the daylight. I nod. When the bus arrives back at the hotel, I rush up the elevator and change into something more presentable: black jeans and a red flannel.

"We're going exploring," Elliott tells Andre, who's seated at the bar next to Riley.

Andre warns, "Be back before dark."

My stomach drops. In the midst of the chaos of the competition, I somehow forgot all about the *other* match tonight, half the reason I wanted to go on this trip in the first place.

"Ready?" Elliott asks, snapping me out of it.

"Yep."

I follow him out of the lobby. He was right about the water being beautiful. In the light, the small waves are icy cold and stunningly blue. The color mirrors Elliott's eyes. His shoulders relax as he watches the water. It's nice to see him so peaceful for a change.

"What time are we supposed to get there tonight?" I question.

"Eleven, I think. Do you still want to go?"

"Of course."

He bites down on his bottom lip. His skin turns slightly green. "You look sick."

He shakes his hands out at his sides. "I guess I'm afraid of what you're going to see. It's not pretty."

"I don't care."

"You will."

I try to picture Elliott, all bloodied up and teeming with rage. But when I study him now, he's compassionate and merciful. Two sides of the same coin, but neither can exist without the other. He's not a monster, even if he thinks he is.

We stand in silence at the edge of the harbor until the sun disappears behind the horizon.

\*

A few hours after dinner, Andre, Elliott, and I slip inside the back door to the convention center. All of the spectators from today's competition went home for the night, so the building is empty. Our footsteps echo through the lofty rafters. Elliott keeps my pace as we snake through a maze of hallways. A few stragglers follow behind us.

We arrive at a metal door. Andre grips the doorknob and opens it.

The screams are deafening.

A vast crowd of people are gathered inside of the arena. Their mouths water at the sight of fresh meat. Elliott waves and flashes a winning smile. They whistle and applaud. He holds the attention of the crowd without even trying.

"Lots of adoring fans," I scoff.

His lips turn into a smug smile. "Jealous?"

"Confused, actually. Why do they care so much about a seventeen-year-old?"

"Isn't that why you're here? To find out?"

Without warning, Elliott grabs my hand. I smile, cheeks flushing, and I don't let go.

The three of us walk to the center of the arena where a fight has already begun. Neither of the men in the middle are wearing boxing gloves or any other protective gear. One of them throws the other into the standing crowd of spectators. They scream with morbid enthusiasm as the man smears blood onto the shirt of someone in the audience.

"This is insane," I whisper.

Elliott watches me closely, squeezing my hand. His purple bruises clash with my untainted skin, the colors mixing together like a watercolor painting. I wonder if he sees it, too.

"Are you okay?" he asks.

I snap out of it. Not the time or place to contemplate if Elliott might have feelings for me. "Yeah."

Two women take the place of the men in the ring. This is the first time I've watched a woman fight in this type of match. I straighten my back, snaking through the crowd to get a better angle. They shove each other around like they're weightless; the arm of one of the girls twists savagely as she crashes into the floor. A sliver of white bone breaks through her skin. I gag, a knot twisting in my gut.

"Are you sure you want to do this?" I ask Elliott.

His grip on my hand tightens, but it doesn't do much to stop the bile from rising in my throat. I swallow it down.

"I don't really have a choice."

As if on cue, his name is called. Elliott moves to break away from me, and I recognize the same expression on his face that he wore during his last underground fight, a look of terror mixed with excitement that he so vehemently denied.

I squeeze his hand with all the strength that I can muster before he's forced to let go. I'm not sure if I can watch what's about to happen. The crowd quiets when Elliott enters the ring. My gaze drifts to the other side of the room where Elliott's competitor will come from. After an eternity of waiting, nobody shows. The audience murmurs impatiently.

"What's happening?" I ask Andre.

He shakes his head, equally confused. Then, the arena breaks into a hushed whisper as the makeshift referee leads someone that I recognize to the ring. Even from this distance, his blue, monstrous eyes are piercing.

Luke. Elliott's brother.

# CHAPTER THIRTEEN

**ANDRE PALES AT THE SIGHT OF LUKE KING.**

I've never seen my coach so afraid. I shiver. Luke is an animal. He'll tear his brother to shreds without thinking twice.

"Luke told Elliott he had a surprise coming," Andre grumbles. "I didn't think that involved him following us to Savannah."

I try to catch Elliott's attention, but he won't turn away from his brother. The audience quiets. The profiles of the two boys are practically identical. Everyone in this room must know that they're related.

Elliott's hands tremble behind his back, a miniscule movement that wouldn't be noticeable to anyone who wasn't searching for it. He's perfected the art of masking his emotions for the crowd. He takes one step toward his brother, and Luke grins wickedly.

They meet in the center of the ring. Luke's mouth is moving, but I can't make out what he's saying over the noise of the mob.

"He'll be fine," Andre reassures me. "He's fought worse than Luke."

I don't believe him, but I don't have a moment to argue before the whistle blows.

I want to look anywhere else but the ring, but I can't. The tension between Elliott and Luke, the anticipation of the crowd, and the murderous hunger in both of their expressions is utterly transfixing. Those who came here for a show are about to get one.

Elliott throws the first punch. Luke dodges him without a moment's hesitation, as if he predicted the move—after all, Luke's probably the one who taught Elliott to fight in the first place.

There's an earsplitting sound as skin comes in contact with skin. I gasp. Blood pours out of Elliott's nostrils and drips onto the floor. He grips his nose with one hand and punches with the other. This time, he strikes Luke's shoulder, but Luke barely stumbles. He grabs a hold of Elliott's shirt and pushes his younger brother to his knees.

I lunge. Andre grips the collar of my shirt, holding me in place.

Luke slams his knee into Elliott's stomach. He falls onto his back with a sharp wheeze.

"He's hurting him," I plead with Andre.

Luke kicks Elliott again. Elliott curls onto his side, covering his stomach with his knees.

"Please," I beg.

Andre glances between me, Luke, and Elliott. Elliott lets out a moan that echoes throughout the arena. The crowd hushes, wincing at the pained sound.

To my surprise, Andre lets go of my shirt.

I don't hesitate. I sprint through the crowd, pushing people out of my way, and dive into the center of the ring. Luke, recognizing my face, breaks into a fit of hysterical laughter.

I swing my fist into the side of his jaw.

He freezes. A piercing pain explodes throughout my knuckles, but I'm too distracted by my proximity to Elliott's brother to care. Luke brushes his fingers against the spot on his cheek where I hit him.

Suddenly, Luke grabs my right wrist. He yanks me forward, and I gasp at the searing pain of my stitches ripping open.

"Was that fun?" he hisses.

We're standing only inches apart, and from this close, I can see the deadness in his eyes, the total absence of love or care. I clench my jaw. I won't give him the satisfaction of an answer to his question.

From the floor, Elliott groans before forcing himself to his feet.

"Go," he begs, meeting my gaze.

I try to turn around, but Luke won't release my wrist.

"Your girlfriend is feisty," he says. "I like her."

Elliott spits a mouthful of blood onto Luke's cheek. The older boy lets go of me and grabs Elliott's T-shirt with both of his hands. They stand, nose to nose, lungs heaving with the same tattered breaths. The heat of the burning rage between them is blinding.

"You look like Dad right now, with your brows all furrowed like that," Luke sneers, curling his lips.

"Fuck you," Elliott scoffs.

"When you brought her to dinner, I honestly thought it wouldn't last, but you always    do the unexpected. You have a thing for crazy girls?"

"Elliott," I whisper, inching closer to him. "He's trying to piss you off. Let's go."

"Go?" Luke roars. "But we just started! Hit me."

Elliott stiffens. Luke lifts his hands into a mock surrender.

"Hit me," he begs his brother. "I want you to."

"This is ridiculous," I interrupt. "Come on, Elliott."

He seems to actually hear me this time. The muscles in his face relax. Elliott shuffles in the direction of the exit right before he turns around and punches Luke in the face. The audience erupts. Luke chuckles, imploring Elliott to keep hitting him. Elliott's knee slams into his brother's stomach, and Luke coughs up a fistful of blood.

"Elliott," I repeat. "Stop. You don't want to do this."

Luke's ruthless smile doesn't falter. He *wants* this. He wants Elliott to lash out, to do something that he can't take back. I wrap my fingers around Elliott's arm and pull with everything that I have.

"Stop!" I scream. "It's over! You won!"

Again, Elliott kicks Luke in the stomach. Luke topples onto his back, laughing uncontrollably through bloody wheezes.

"Please, Elliott." I whisper. "You're scaring me."

He pauses.

His bloody lips part. Slowly, he puts his foot down that was going for another kick. His adoring audience breaks into applause when Luke doesn't get back up. I glare at them as Elliott drags me out of the arena.

We stop once we reach the empty hallway.

"What the hell was that?" Elliott exclaims.

I clench my jaw. *He's mad at me?*

"He was hurting you!" I retort.

"He's my brother!"

I laugh neurotically. It sounds eerily similar to Luke's.

"So, in your family you beat the shit out of each other? How was I supposed to know that?"

Elliott stares, bewildered.

"I'm not going to stand by and watch you get your ass kicked, even if Luke's the one responsible," I continue, "Okay? I'm not. And if you don't like that then—"

Elliott stops my words when he presses his lips to mine.

I gasp at the sudden, all-consuming warmth of Elliott's kiss. His hand wraps around the back of my neck, and he pulls me against him. I breathe in the taste of the salt and blood on his tongue. Every muscle in my body relaxes into perfect stillness.

I wanted this. I didn't realize how badly until now.

Elliott melts into me, holding me close as we both pull away to take a breath. His eyes widen as he realizes what he's done.

"Shit," he mutters. "Sorry—"

I don't give him the chance to finish his apology. I kiss him back, harder this time, and wrap my hands into his sweat soaked T-shirt. The blood from his nose drips down my face, but I don't care. We stand enveloped in each other for an eternity until both of us have to breathe again. And even then, I wish it didn't have to end.

Elliott smiles weakly. He would almost look innocent if not for the battle scars dispersed across his body. "Please never punch my brother again."

I grin. It was reckless and impulsive and stupid, but I would do it a thousand times over if it meant kissing him. His fingers slide from the back of my neck all the way to my uninjured hand. He holds it steady, and I relax.

"You're a mess," I observe.

Elliott smirks. He uses his thumb to clean a trail of blood off of my lip.

"So are you."

Behind him, the door to the arena opens. Luke hobbles out, clutching his stomach and wincing with every step. Damon King lurks at his side. Elliott curses under his breath when he notices his father. I should've guessed that he might be here watching, but seeing him in the flesh makes me shiver.

Damon proudly holds up a pile of cash in his hands. "Good show," he proclaims. "The crowd liked it."

Damon admires me like I'm some sort of a trophy; a possession that he's only now decided is valuable enough to keep around. He steps closer.

"They liked you, too."

Elliott growls, but Damon ignores him, greeting me with a knowing smile.

"Your cut, sweetheart." Against my will, he slides some of the cash into my jean pockets. I swallow down a lump in my throat.

He smiles when he says, "Welcome to the family."

# CHAPTER FOURTEEN

**THE HOTEL BAR IS EMPTY.**

Nobody bothered to check my ID, so I ordered an old fashioned even though I have no intention of drinking it. Andre and Elliott sit on either side of me. They gulp down their drinks as if the alcohol is water. Elliott holds a bag of ice on his nose, courtesy of the hotel clerk who panicked at the sight of his bloodied-up face. I tried to clean him up after Damon and Luke finally left us alone, but we didn't have much time before the convention hallway filled with guests going home for the night. Apparently, none of the other fights compared to the one between brothers.

"Are you sure he doesn't need a doctor?" I ask Andre for the third time.

"It's not broken."

"Are you sure?"

"Rose," he barks. "I'm sure."

I sigh, frustrated. The cloudy bruise on the bridge of Elliott's nose is darkening by the minute. Beneath the bar counter, our fingers are intertwined. He hasn't moved his hand away since our kiss.

Elliott King *kissed* me. I can still feel his lips against mine. I've only kissed one other person in my life, and that was Gemma, so this is brand new territory. Elliott's rough, all angles and ridges, but kissing him was soft. Safe.

*Maybe he's exceptional because he's kissed half the school.*
I swallow some of my drink.

Andre says, "I still can't believe you did that."

"I still can't believe you let her," Elliott replies.

Stepping into the fight was careless and impulsive, but it might have saved Elliott's life.

No lesson learned.

Orange lights brighten the empty tables across the bar. The two bartenders watch us, checking their watches impatiently. It's almost two in the morning. They'll be closing soon. But with the heat of adrenaline still pumping through my veins, I feel like doing anything but sleeping.

"Do you think your family went back home?" I ask Elliott.

"Hopefully," Elliott murmurs, pressing ice to his nose.

We spoke with them for a minute or two after Damon showed up. When Elliott asked why he didn't tell him that his brother was coming, his dad responded that it would make for "better entertainment."

"Please promise me that you won't agree to anything my dad suggests."

He sounds desperate. The last thing I expected when I stepped into the ring was to earn the admiration of Damon King.

"You think he would want me to fight?" I ask, tilting my chin.

"Maybe," Andre butts in. "There's not a lot of women in this sport. People would pay extra—"

Elliott interrupts, "It doesn't matter."

He meets my eyes with a pleading stare, which puts me even more on edge. Elliott is not the type to beg for what he wants.

"Promise me," he implores.

He doesn't have to ask again. I would be a fool to involve myself any further in this. I'm risking everything I've built: my college plans, my father's trust, by attending the bare-knuckle match tonight.

"I promise. Trust me, I want to keep all my limbs on my body."

Andre chuckles and finishes off his vodka soda.

"Do you ever fight in these?" I ask him.

"Sometimes. The men upstairs prefer that I stay on the sidelines. They want me to keep the Atlanta branch running, not dying in a ditch somewhere."

"You both keep mentioning the people above us like they're some sort of mythical creatures," I scoff, taking another small sip of whiskey. "Who are they?"

"Don't know," Elliott admits. "We've only met a few but never the bosses."

"There's not a single person in charge," Andre adds. "Most regions have their own hierarchies. Like the Northeast, for example. There are a few people there who oversee all of the New York, Pennsylvania, and Massachusetts rings. I met one, once. Scary lady."

"So, if the police want to make an arrest, who would they go for?" I ponder, narrowing my gaze on Andre. "You?"

Elliott and Andre laugh. They glance at each other as if recalling a private memory.

"We don't really have to worry about the police, if you know what I mean." Andre says.

Elliott leans into my ear. "The police are in on it."

He catches the glass when it falls out of my hand. I should have assumed given the amount of people in the arena tonight that the police at least knew something about The Ring. There's no way a secret this big could stay a secret.

"He's right," confirms Andre. "A lot of them show up to make bets."

I grimace. "That's so messed up."

From behind the bar, one of the staff members informs us that they're closing for the night. I slide my empty glass across the counter.

"What time do we have to get up tomorrow?"

Andre glances at his watch, then wearily back to me. "Four hours from now."

Elliott and I groan. Andre pays our tab then leads us back into the lobby.

"Sleep well," he yawns, turning the corner toward his room. My eyelids grow heavy with exhaustion as the adrenaline leaves my system. Elliott and I saunter into the elevator. He leans against the wall, squeezing the bag of ice in the hand that isn't holding mine.

"Are you okay?" I question.

"No."

His stare flickers between our intertwined fingers and my face, as if he's trying to figure out how this possibly could have happened. I can't read his expression, but he's not happy. I pull my hand away.

"My father," he sighs, frowning at the loss of touch. He's cold and distant again.

"There's nothing that he could possibly say that would make me want to be a part of this," I state. "Trust me."

"I do. It's him I don't trust."

The elevator stops at my floor.

"We'll talk about this later. Get some rest," Elliott suggests.

I don't argue. The tiredness has hit, turning my brain to mush. I move the bag of ice, which is now just a puddle of cold water, back to his nose.

I whisper, "You too."

He nods. The elevator door closes, and he disappears upstairs. Without his hand on mine, I feel like something is missing, like a part of me has been stripped away without my permission. I tip toe into my room and turn on the shower. Sofía is snoring by the time I get out.

For the next few hours, I barely sleep, kept awake imagining the feeling of Elliott's lips on mine. My alarm goes off right as I slip into a dream. A harsh cramp eats away at my stomach. I let out a hushed moan. I shouldn't have drank so much.

Across the room, Sofía pops out of bed. She's downstairs by the time I get up. I stumble into the bathroom and plop down onto the toilet. There's a small stain of blood on my underwear.

"Shit," I grumble.

Of course, I haven't had my period in weeks, and now that I have a long day ahead it shows up. Luckily, I spot a box of tampons on the ground that Sofía brought. I shove a few into my bag before making my way to the elevator. Elliott stares me down from the corner of the lobby. He's dressed in a pair of sweatpants and a long-sleeved jacket that hides most of the evidence from yesterday.

Everything that happened last night comes flooding back in a wave.

The kiss.

He wanted to kiss me, and he did. I kissed *him*. And it felt like heaven.

He starts in my direction. I push away a piece of hair from my face.

"Hey," Elliott says with a smirk.

He's holding a plate of scrambled eggs from the buffet. The injury on his nose is already healing.

"Hi," I respond.

"Muffin?"

I nod eagerly, then scarf down half of it in one bite. We join the rest of the group around Andre.

"If we get through this morning match, we'll be in the finals," he explains. He turns to Riley. "You're up first."

I high five Riley, who's nervously rubbing the back of his neck. Andre shoves a croissant into his mouth before herding the group of us out to the shuttle bus. I steal the seat next to Elliott and notice a layer of concealer across his nose. No wonder the injury looked so much better.

"Did you sleep?" I ask him.

"Nope."

Instead of going to the break room, we walk straight into the arena to watch Riley's fight. He's a bundle of nerves, but I'm not sure why. Strength and confidence radiate off of him when he spars, sometimes even more than Elliott. He's going to be fine. He pulls his locs into a bun atop his head and salutes us goodbye before entering the ring.

Riley barely wins the first round, but he finds his confidence again during the second and third. We rush him as he exits the ring, and in true Riley fashion, he credits all his success to us.

"You're up next," I inform Elliott.

He shrugs, not displaying the slightest bit of apprehension. The semifinals will take place at noon, two hours from now. We make our way back to the break room to wait it out.

"Every single one of you has impressed me this weekend. It's been incredibly rewarding to watch," Andre says, "Rose, your moral support is unmatched."

I smile not knowing if he is referring to my stint last night with Luke or my cheering during the tournament. Either way,

I'm not sitting on the sidelines for our next competition. I don't care how many private lessons it takes.

"How are you?" I ask Sofía, who has barely spoken since this morning.

"Better. Ready to go home."

I couldn't agree more. This trip has been exciting but exhausting. I miss my own bed. At 11:30 a.m., Andre gathers everyone to stretch. Elliott sits on the floor next to me, half attempting to touch his toes.

"You nervous?"

"Nope," he replies, straight-faced.

The same bearded man from yesterday escorts us back to the arena. Elliott remains at my side.

"Good luck," I whisper.

For a second, I consider kissing him, but that idea vanishes when I remember that we still haven't talked about what happened. He fist-bumps Andre before making his way into the ring.

# CHAPTER FIFTEEN

**"LOOKS LIKE AN EVEN MATCH," ANDRE OBSERVES.**

Elliott is smaller and younger than his competitor, but I know he's smarter. His strategy combined with his unshakable confidence should guarantee him this win. Every team gathers in the arena to watch how the weekend will end.

"For our final bout today, we have Elliott King from Midtown Ring versus Jameson Meyer from Sweat Shop Boxing!"

The referee starts the match.

Elliott steps forward to swing, but his movements are surprisingly slow. Jameson dodges him easily. Elliott jabs and hits nothing but air. His lips part in surprise when his glove returns back to his side, untouched. I'm not surprised when he takes a hit to the shoulder. I expect the impact to startle him enough to at least wake him up, but then Elliott gets hit again.

And again.

Jameson's black glove hits his arm, his chest, and then his stomach.

Elliott stumbles to the floor.

"Well shit," Andre shudders.

I don't take my eyes off Elliott. Fortunately, the referee calls the round before Jameson can cause any more damage. Elliott stays on the ground, unmoving, as the whistle blows. Andre and a medic rush into the ring to help him.

"Is it over?" I ask Riley.

Andre whispers something to the medic. After a moment of deliberation, the referee blows the whistle, signaling the end of the match. Elliott forfeits. Sofía breaks into a round of applause when he stumbles back to the group.

"Nice one, King. You really showed them."

Elliott shoots her a glare but says nothing. She's right. He blew it.

"At least we'll get a head start on traffic," mourns Andre. "Come on. Let's head out."

At the hotel, the five of us grab our bags from the concierge and make our way to the parking lot. Elliott drags his feet across the gravel. Once we're both seated inside of his convertible, I face him. There are more bruises on his face than clear patches of skin.

"You threw the bout."

He sighs. "It wasn't on purpose. I can't stop thinking about what my dad said. He saw you fight. He liked it."

He bites down on his lip, tears welling.

"Elliott," I plead. "You and I both know I'm nowhere near as good as I'd need to be to hold my own in a fight. You have years of practice, I have weeks. That would be insane."

"I know," he cuts me off. "But my father isn't one to take sanity into consideration."

"I—"

He shakes his head. "Everywhere I turn, he's there. If you're part of my life, he's going to be a part of yours, too. It isn't fair."

I slip my index finger under his chin and push, forcing him to look at me.

"I'm not afraid of him."

Elliott smiles weakly before I press my lips to his. The feeling raises the hair on my arms. I sink into him, pulling him closer, embracing the comfort of his touch.

"I don't want to be anyone's entertainment," Elliott professes between breaths. "I don't."

"Then quit?"

He shakes his head. "It's not that easy."

I pause, hoping he'll finally tell me more, but he remains silent. I continue, "You deserve better, Elliott. We'll find a way to get you out."

Even though I have no plan, Elliott nods like he believes me. He lights a cigarette, takes a puff, then turns the keys in the ignition. He seems lighter, as if the weight of tackling this problem alone has been lifted off his shoulders.

We leave the windows down for most of the ride home. The gentle breeze rushes through my curls. Elliott turns the music up, blasting Florence and the Machine out of the stereo.

"How would you feel about me telling Gemma about all of this?"

At first, he looks slightly horrified. He drums his fingers against the steering wheel until horror morphs into reluctant acceptance. "I don't think there's anything I could do to stop you."

"She's good at keeping secrets."

Gemma keeps all of the gory details of my past to herself, even when she would have benefitted from adding to the gossip.

"I was always terrified that somebody might find out," mutters Elliott, glancing at his bruised nose in the car mirror. "Every time I thought about telling someone, I talked myself out of it."

"Probably because it's stupid and illegal," I muse. "Who would you have told?"

"I don't know. Maddy?"

"I think she'd be into it," I joke even though it hurts.

"Yeah?"

"Hot guys beating each other up is every girl's wet dream."

He smirks mischievously. "Is it yours?"

I hit him with my elbow. My dad sends a text to let me know he won't be home until dinner time, so I ask Elliott to drop me off at Gemma's. But when his car pulls into her driveway, I wish the ride didn't have to end.

"I'll see you at school tomorrow?" I say.

"Sure."

He watches expectantly as I lean in close to him. Instead of a kiss, I whisper into his ear.

"About that dream." I bite down on my lip before continuing, savoring the sweet moment of closeness. "It could be."

He grins as I step out of the car. I can't even get in one knock on Gemma's door before she answers.

"Hi," she says, watching as Elliott's convertible speeds away.

I beam. "Hi."

We make our way inside her small cottage-style house. Blue couches, eccentric decorations. It reminds me of a vacation beach home. Gemma's mom smiles from the kitchen. Mrs. Shao is the closest I've had to a mother since mine died, though she's way too overbearing.

"Gemma told me you went boxing this weekend. Are you crazy?"

"Mom!" Gemma shrieks.

"I was extra safe," I reassure her. "Don't worry."

Mrs. Shao nods apprehensively, pouring me an ice-cold glass of lemonade. I down it. We chitchat about school until Gemma finds an opportunity to drag me upstairs. She locks her bedroom door behind us as she inspects me. I notice the injury at the exact same time that she does; my right wrist has a bruise the size of an orange from when Luke grabbed me. My bandage, coated in dry blood, has almost completely fallen off.

*Crap. I need to go back to Dr. Kilmer before it gets infected again.*

"Jesus," Gemma yelps, running her finger lightly over my wrist. "How did that even happen? They're allowed to grab you like that?"

"Not exactly."

I take a deep breath and sit down on her bed. "I need to tell you something."

"I'm listening."

I swallow. Telling Gemma about Elliott's secret was a lot easier in theory. "Elliott's . . . part of something."

She tilts her chin. "Like what? A brothel?"

"Oh my god, no!"

"Well, you're being super vague!"

"Sorry," I reply, cheeks flushing. "The tournament in Savannah was fun, yeah, but that's not really why we went. Elliott and my coach from the gym are involved in something."

I'm not making any sense. There aren't words to describe what I witnessed this weekend, but I can't turn back now.

"Something . . . underground."

Gemma perks up. "Like *Fight Club*?"

It sounds insane, but I guess she's right. I nod and her mouth drops open in surprise.

"Oh my god. Did somebody hurt you? Did you get in a fight?"

I shake my head, shushing her. "No. Elliott's brother showed up, and I got in the middle of it."

That only scares her more. Her concerned frown mirrors my father's—a clear reminder that I can *never* let him find out about any of this. Maybe telling Gemma was a bad idea.

"Holy shit, Rose! What if he gets caught?"

"I don't know," I reply, truthfully. "He keeps mentioning how there's 'more to all of this than I know.'" I pull out the wad of money that's been loitering in my pocket since last night and toss it onto the bed. Gemma eyes it suspiciously. "This is a small cut. It's five hundred dollars."

Gemma holds up one of the bills to the light.

"It's real," I assure her.

"This is like . . . blood money."

"I think they treat it more like gambling. People bet on who they think will win."

She stares at the money in disbelief. "They bet this much on Elliott?"

"More than that."

Suddenly, Gemma wraps her arms around my shoulders and pulls me in for a hug. I exhale, relieved, as I relax against her.

"I'm glad you told me," she says, inching away to face me again. "But I don't think it's a good idea for you to be involved."

There's no way that I can abandon Elliott after everything we went through this weekend. "It's a little too late," I respond. "We bonded on the way there, talked about our parents and stuff. He likes to read, and he's scared of swimming."

"Seriously?"

"And . . . we kissed."

She shrieks. I shush her, then proceed with the story of Elliott's fight with Luke. Gemma listens intently like I'm describing the next season of *The Bachelor*.

"You and Elliott King getting together wasn't on my bingo card."

"No shit," I groan, collapsing against her bed.

She lies down beside me, both of us contemplating the total madness that is my life now. Who would've thought one party could lead to all of this?

"Thanks for not thinking I've totally lost it," I say.

Gemma laughs. "Oh, I think you're certifiable."

# CHAPTER SIXTEEN

**"HOW WAS IT?"**

My father's waiting in the kitchen when I get home for dinner. Gemma's mom offered to cook, but I wanted to get home and bathe; I smell like sweat and nicotine from Elliott's car. The pride on my dad's face makes all the pain and confusion of this weekend worth it.

"Awesome! I'll tell you everything after I shower."

The hot water eases my sore muscles. I throw on a sweatshirt that covers my fingertips, hiding the sight of my tattered knuckles and fresh bruises. My dad presents a gigantic plate of pasta, which I devour in a few bites.

"We did really well. I got to watch Sofía in the women's match. It was badass."

I tell him all about the hotel and our walk around the harbor. I don't mention the fight. Or the bartender serving me alcohol.

"I was thinking . . ." I start, swirling my fork around the plate, "that this could be a great story for my college applications."

Dad blinks. He's been avoiding the college conversation for months now. He says he isn't sure if I'm ready, but I'm running out of ways to prove myself to him. He chews and swallows without speaking.

"I have to apply soon," I add.

"We'll talk about it with Dr. Taylor. Alright?"

"Alright," I concede.

Not an enthusiastic yes, but not a no, either.

My phone vibrates with a text from Andre saying that he's called off practice tomorrow. *Thank god. I think my hand might fall off if I were to try to spar.* My phone lights up with another text, but this one is from Elliott.

**ELLIOTT: Want a ride to school tomorrow?**

I fight a smile. The thought of Elliott driving me to school in front of all of our classmates is oddly satisfying.

**ROSE: You're asking for trouble.**
**ELLIOTT: Pick you up at 7:30.**

"Who's texting you?"

My dad peers between me and my phone.

"Elliott," I confess. "He's giving me a ride to school tomorrow."

He puts down his fork. "Is that something I need to know more about?"

"Nope," I reply.

*Not yet.*

I finish off the plate of food before heading upstairs. The exhaustion of the weekend's events catches up to me, and I sleep harder than I have in weeks.

Until I see her again.

She's in my dream, not my reality, though the two have become less discernible.

She grabs my injured hand and squeezes. *It's obvious she's trying to tell me something, but her mouth doesn't move. Mine won't move, either. I stare into her eyes, unblinking, and she looks back with urgency, her grip on my wrist tightening until I can feel my blood pumping, the pressure enough to explode my veins—*

My alarm goes off. I pick up my phone and find a text from Elliott that he's on his way. Stumbling out of bed, I throw on my favorite pair of black jeans and an oversized Pink Floyd sweatshirt. I pause when I grab my backpack.

My hand injury is worse; I must have been touching it in my sleep because two of the scabs are ripped off and bleeding. My skin is inflamed, and the open stitches are straight out of a slasher movie. I sigh, moving down my sleeves so Gemma won't notice. She's on my porch, coffee in hand, when I step outside.

"Elliott's picking us up," I announce.

We don't have time to discuss details before Elliott's convertible pulls into the driveway. He's dressed in a black, long-sleeved shirt that hides the bruises scattered across his arms. Cigarette smoke escapes from his battered lips.

"I love this," says Gemma, sliding into the back seat. "Not sweaty from walking and arriving in style? We're doing this every day."

"Not asking, just stating," Elliott teases. "Typical."

I reach for the radio and turn up the volume. *About a Girl* blasts from the speakers.

"Cobain at eight in the morning?" Elliott asks.

"Rose is weird," Gemma answers before I have the chance.

"You know, you're actually the first one to ever tell me that."

Nishi is already waiting for us in the parking lot. She's dressed in denim overalls and a floral top that matches Gemma's style more than her own. As we get closer, I realize it actually is Gemma's shirt. I turn to my best friend, and she winks.

Students swarm Elliott's usual parking spot. He stops the car and faces us.

"Are you sure about this?" I ask him.

He shrugs. "People talk. Don't listen."

Gemma is the first one to leave the BMW. A few girls lurking around the lot stare and whisper amongst themselves. Then, Elliott follows. He winks as he slides his bag across his shoulder, tossing the remains of the cigarette underneath his boot.

My turn.

I inhale a shaky breath before opening the door. Students, some I know, some I don't, watch us like hawks. The whispers turn into buzzing when they realize it's me.

"I feel like a celebrity." Gemma sounds awestruck.

Nishi crosses the parking lot. She grabs Gemma's hand. I peek at Elliott's destroyed knuckles. He grins slyly and takes my hand in his. The lump in my throat vanishes with the touch of his skin.

The attention is suffocating.

"... *weird sex.*"

"... *must be desperate.*"

"... *kinda hot?*"

We make it inside, but the conversations only get louder. Gemma and Nishi take a turn toward the art room. Elliott remains at my side, his grip on my hand unbreakable.

"See you at lunch?" I ask Gemma.

"If you're still alive by then," she replies, glancing at a brunette flaring her nostrils at me from across the hallway.

My grip on my backpack straps tightens. Elliott walks me to my first class, even though the bell ringing signals that he'll be late for his.

"Thanks for the ride," I say.

He grins. "I had fun."

He lets go of me, adjusting the collar on his shirt to hide a bruise on the back of his neck. I watch as he disappears down the hallway before stepping into history class.

The stares are louder than the whispers. Throughout my morning classes, everyone watches me, even though I purposely bury my face in a book.

"Her and King? I don't believe you."

"No joke," adds another voice. "He drove her to school this morning."

In English, Elliott's usual crowd isn't surrounding his desk. He sits alone, scrolling mindlessly through his phone.

"We're free writing today," Mr. Ruse announces.

He projects a list of writing prompts onto the whiteboard. I scribble nonsense throughout the hour, unable to focus on anything except Elliott occasionally turning toward me. When the bell rings, he's already seated on top of my desk. Maddy glares from her spot in the doorway. She grinds her teeth before turning around.

"What'd you write about?" Elliott asks, helping me pack my notebooks into my bag.

"Impending doom. You?"

"Pizza."

The cafeteria reeks of cheese and marinara sauce. Burnt meatball subs line the tables of the room. Elliott grimaces. I clutch my paper bag with my dad's leftover pasta.

"Gross. I hate Meatball Monday," he says. "Where do you sit?"

"Don't you think we have the school riled up enough for one day?"

"Nope."

He's insane. Mind boggling insane.

"You're digging your own grave."

"Good," he says. "The deeper the better."

I take him to the round table in the far corner of the room. Gemma and Nishi grin from ear to ear as we approach. Elliott slides into one of the empty blue chairs.

"What's up?" he inquires, drumming his fingers on the table.

"Watching the drama unfold," Gemma replies, glancing around the room at our ever-growing audience. "Do you think enough people are staring?"

Elliott lifts his hand into the air and shows off his middle finger to the crowd. I slam his hand down onto the table.

"Well Elliott, if you're going to sit at our table, we have to know more about you," chirps Gemma. She leans in close. "Does pineapple belong on pizza?"

Her tone is deadly serious. Elliott runs his hand through his buzzed hair, scratching the triangle tattoo behind his ear, as he contemplates the question.

"Plead the fifth. Never tried it."

"Good," Gemma growls. "Keep it that way."

I chuckle. Gemma fixes a piece of my hair, patting down the loose curl until it sticks. I finish my leftovers and slide Elliott a granola bar. He eats the entire thing in one bite.

Gemma asks Elliott, "So, is Rose any good at boxing?"

He beams. "She's one of the best newbies I've met. With some more training, she'll be a pro."

My face is burning. "Andre volunteered to give me some private lessons."

Elliott perks up. "Why practice with him when I'm right here?"

"Damn," Nishi proclaims. She looks at Gemma as if to say *are you hearing this?*

I face Elliott. "I'm not sure I trust you to teach me how to fight by the rules."

He half smiles. "Rules were made to be broken."

I open my mouth, then shut it. We spend the next twenty minutes discussing classes, homework, and the other drama that Elliott is somehow always in the middle of.

"Rose told me about your secret," Gemma says in the middle of a conversation about Elliott's time at Midtown Ring. I freeze. Elliott pales as he glances between the three of us. Gemma, realizing what she's implied, rushes her words.

"You like to read."

Elliott's back to himself in an instant, playing off her statement as if it's exactly what he expected her to say. "And? I'm not that much of a caveman."

"Well then, I guess you don't remember making me do all the work on that *Great Gatsby* group project last year because you told me you were illiterate."

"Figure of speech," Elliott retorts. "I knew we'd fail if I took the lead. I was doing the group a favor."

The bell rings, signaling the end of the lunch period. I throw away my trash and snake through the crowd. Gemma pulls me aside before I reach the classroom door.

She lowers her voice. "You really thought I was going to bring that up?"

"No," I respond. "Maybe. I don't know."

"I wouldn't, Rose. You can trust me."

I know she's right, but it's impossible not to be on edge about Elliott's secret. If anyone at school found out, he could be expelled or arrested.

Apart from the stares and whispers, the rest of the day is uneventful. Gemma and I walk home after school noticing that Elliott's car is gone from the lot. Since Andre canceled practice, I have the rest of the night to catch up on homework. I send Andre a text when I get home.

**ROSE: Hey. It's Rose from Midtown. Do you still want to set up private lessons?**

He replies immediately.

**ANDRE: Def. Let's do next week.**

I let out an excited shout. Seconds later, my dad throws open the door to my bedroom. He pants, "Are you okay?"

"Sorry," I laugh, passing him my phone.

He reads Andre's text, then shakes his head. "You're serious about this?"

I don't get his hesitation. Boxing is a grounding exercise, a coping mechanism. It's something to do that isn't a pile of homework, something I *want* to do, even if it hurts sometimes. And it's a hell of a lot more effective than talk therapy.

"Dr. Taylor's been monitoring my progress, and you agreed to let me practice, so why is this now a problem?"

"It's not a problem, Rosalyn. I'm being cautious."

*Other teenagers can play a sport without caution.*

I sigh.

"I thought you were glad that I found something I like."

"I am! The private lessons are generous. I want you to take Andre up on the offer. But you have to be okay with letting go if it becomes too much."

"I'll take things slow," I reassure him. "But boxing is helping me. I can feel it."

He nods. I know he wants the best for me, but sometimes we're on totally different wavelengths.

"I'm proud of you, Rose. Your mom would be, too."

I smile, chuckling under my breath at the thought of my mom attending one of my practices. She hated anything violent, but she would've been proud of me for pursuing something that I love.

"Love you," I say, both to my father and my mom, who I hope can hear me.

"Love you too, kiddo."

On the way out the door, he pauses. There's a spark of hope in his eyes that gives me hope, too.

"Let's work on those college applications soon."

\*

"Michael Wall just asked me to prom," Gemma announces after school ends on Tuesday. "In October. Who does that?"

I snort. Most of our school knows that Gemma is gay, especially now that she's been spending so much time with Nishi. Still, guys ask her out all the time, either convinced that they might be able to turn her or too stupid to realize that she's not attracted to them.

"You're a heartbreaker," I sneer.

"No, I'm a lesbian." The sun outside illuminates Gemma in a halo. She tucks her hands into the pockets of her lavender sweatshirt. The red dye in her hair has almost faded completely.

"Well, I hope you told him *no*," I say. "And don't tell him that I'm available."

"You're available?"

*Elliott.* I turn around as he approaches, an excited skip in his step.

"Andre texted," he says. "He's sick, so I'm taking his place training you tonight."

He smiles mischievously. Elliott and I alone inside of Midtown Ring. The thought makes my palms sweat.

"Make sure to get a good hit in," Gemma adds with a wink. Elliott drops his jaw in mock surprise. He sizes her up, lifting his hands into fists.

"Maybe you should train with us?"

Gemma and I break into a fit of laughter. Gemma and boxing don't belong in the same sentence.

"I'm sure that I would look great in gloves, but there's no way in hell I'm letting anyone near my face," she says.

She giggles, then waves goodbye as she leaves the parking lot. I face Elliott. "I didn't think you wanted to help me be a better fighter. Remember the million times last weekend you made me swear I wouldn't get involved in all the craziness?"

He snorts, as if I've suggested something totally out of left field. "I'm not training you for bare knuckle. You say you want to be a better boxer, right?"

I nod.

"Then let me help you."

We arrive at Midtown Ring in record time thanks to Elliott's reckless driving. The gym is empty. Every footstep echoes from the high walls. Tossing my backpack to the floor, I wrap only my left hand. The broken stitches on my right are a cruel reminder of this past weekend.

"Let's warm up," Elliott instructs.

He plays rock music out of his phone speaker. I stretch to touch my toes, then jump in place to get my blood flowing.

Positioning myself in front of the heavy bag, I picture Sofía. She's exactly the type of fighter that I want to be. When she moves, she's quick and effective, always one step ahead of the person in front of her.

I exhale before swinging.

"You're doing that wrong," Elliott says.

He wraps his hand around my elbow, straightening the bend in it. His warm breath on my shoulder makes me shiver.

"Like this," he says, standing behind me, moving his hand from my elbow to my wrist.

I catch his fingers with mine. We stand still, inhaling the same few centimeters of air, until I work up the courage to turn my head toward him. In a flash, Elliott has my back pressed against the exposed brick wall.

He pins my left arm above my head. "First rule. Don't get distracted."

I lean in, tempted to close the distance, but I push my palms against his chest instead. I lift his arm, turning our bodies so he's the one standing against the wall. Elliott smirks as he realizes what I've done.

"I win," I say.

"You cheated!"

"How?"

"You distracted me."

I grab a handful of his T-shirt, pulling the material toward me before kissing him. My right hand travels from his shoulder to his neck, all the way to the back of his buzzed blonde hair. Elliott's lips move from my lips, to my chin, to my collarbone, stopping when he reaches the strap of my sports bra.

"What are you doing Friday?" he asks.

Up close, the ocean color of his eyes is hypnotizing. He's so easy to stare at. And I'm becoming less afraid to do so.

"Nothing," I answer, catching my breath. "Why?"

"There's a party at the lake. Come with me."

"I'm not really—"

"Please," he persists.

It's impossible to make a rational decision when he's standing this close. "Will Harris be there?"

He grimaces. "I don't know. Maybe. I promise—"

"It's fine. I don't want to make decisions based on him."

"He won't get near you," Elliott affirms, in a tone that I know means he's telling the truth. He won't let Harris get close to me. He proved that weeks ago.

"Do you think he thinks about what happened as often as I do?" I ask, more to myself than Elliott.

That question has lingered in my mind every day since the party. Does Harris stay awake at night thinking about what he did? Does he ever regret it?

"No," Elliott states without a semblance of doubt.

*Always truthful, even when it hurts.*

"But I think he'll get what he deserves."

The sternness in his voice shakes me to my core. I look up.

"Teach me how to fight like you did that night. I want to know how to defend myself."

Elliott opens his mouth, then closes it. After a long moment, he nods. "Okay."

I smile as I step back.

"Get into a supportive stance," he instructs. "You know how to punch, I don't have to teach you that. But one punch isn't going to stop someone as big as him. Let's say he moves forward—"

He steps closer to me and places his fingers around my left wrist. "Slam your hand back toward you. Carefully."

As my arm swings behind my waist, his grip on my wrist releases. I grin. "Nice," I say, "but that's child's play."

"Rose, I'm not going to let you mess up your hand more. We can try again another time."

"C'mon," I plead. "Teach me one more move, and I promise I'll get my hand fixed."

"Are you blackmailing me?"

"I would never," I say sarcastically.

He moves behind me. Lightly, he places his arm around my neck so that my chin meets the inner crook of his elbow. He applies slight pressure. Not enough that I feel threatened but enough to make my heart race. We're closer than before, but this is different.

"Grab my arm with both hands," he says.

Instead of fighting him off, I want to melt into his grip, his rugged chest rising and falling against my back, but I follow his instructions.

"Now tuck your chin and pull as hard as you can."

I give it my best attempt. I don't know if Elliott's going easy on me, but I'm able to escape his choke hold.

I beam. "I did it!"

He nods like he never doubted I would. "Good. Now keep practicing your jab and cross. Left hand only."

I roll my eyes, but I do what he says. I throw jabs and crosses until my arm goes limp. After another hour, we call it quits. My green tank is drenched. I toss my glove into my bag, and we turn off all of the lights. I follow Elliott outside. He locks the door to the gym behind him, slipping the key back into his pocket.

We climb into his black convertible. The first time I sat in this car feels like years ago, even though it's only been a couple of weeks. Elliott turns the car out of the parking lot and onto the main road. The sun is setting, leaves beginning to fall from the trees.

"What are you doing tonight?" I ask.

"My dad is on a work trip, so it'll just be Luke and I."

"What's that like?"

I can't picture Elliott spending any time alone with Luke without one of them actively trying to kill the other.

"We keep our distance. He's usually out anyways."

"Does he work?"

"You don't count illegal fighting as a job?" Elliott snickers. "He's a bouncer at the club on Ponce."

I gasp. I've heard rumors about the Clermont Lounge ever since I learned what a strip club was. "No way. The one with the eighty-year-old strippers?"

"That's the one."

"Wow," I say. "That's . . . something."

Elliott relaxes into the driver's seat, and I lean my head back. Basking in the light of the golden sunset, reveling in how easy this feels. Things haven't come easy for me in a long while. I used to think Elliott was the type of person that I would never be comfortable around, but now I can't imagine not being around him.

"We could hang out?" I suggest.

"I can't. I'm so behind on homework. My dad will murder me if I fail another class."

The rejection stings, but I play it off. "No problem."

He doesn't seem to notice the disappointment on my face when he drops me back home.

# CHAPTER SEVENTEEN

**"YOU'RE GOING TO THE LAKE TONIGHT, RIGHT?"** I ask Gemma on Friday.

She stops walking. "You're going?"

It was only after getting my stitches fixed yesterday that I decided that I should go. Dr. Kilmer told me all about his teenage years of partying as he tied my skin back together. My jealousy over my middle-aged doctor's youth became the motivation I needed to decide.

"Elliott invited me."

Gemma grins. "Yes, yes, a thousand times yes. I love him. What are you going to wear?"

I glance at my jeans and purple cardigan. "This?"

She scowls, shutting down the suggestion. "I'm coming over after school."

Gemma takes a sip from a steaming cup of coffee in her hand. She and Nishi have been meeting up at the cafe down the street before school every morning this week. I'm convinced they're doing it on purpose, so Elliott and I will have the drive to school alone.

Nothing has happened between us since our kiss at the gym on Tuesday. Not even a brush of hands. I'm starting to think I might die if he doesn't kiss me again soon, which, when I think about it, makes me want to slap myself.

"Rose!"

I peek around Gemma's shoulder at the sound of Elliott's scratchy voice. He's dressed in baggy jeans and a blue denim jacket that brightens his irises.

"Pick you up at eight?" he asks.

I grin. "Sounds good."

"Cool."

He doesn't linger. Gemma hits my shoulder as he walks away, and I hit her back.

After school, Gemma stays true to her promise to follow me home.

"Hi, Mr. Berman!"

My father absolutely adores Gemma, especially after learning that she was the only one who stuck around after what happened in calculus class last year.

"Gemma!" my dad exclaims, pulling her in for a hug. "How are you?"

"Better than ever. Rose is letting me take her to a party tonight."

He examines the desperate smile on my face. "You are?"

"Please," I beg. "I'll be back before eleven, and I won't leave Gemma's side."

Gemma flashes her best puppy dog eyes, and to my surprise, my father agrees.

"Thank you!" I squeal.

Gemma drags me upstairs. She tears apart my closet as I watch, not daring to step between her and the mountain of clothes.

"We need to go shopping." She holds up one of my tanks with disgust. I snatch it from her.

"Hey! I like my clothes."

She picks up an orange floral blouse that I haven't worn in years. It's the same color as a traffic cone.

"You like this?"

"Fine," I concede. "That one is bad."

Gemma holds a lacy green skirt up to my waist. It's two sizes too small for my hips.

"The last time I wore that was to my bat mitzvah."

She tosses it across the room. An hour later, Gemma finally decides on an outfit: high waisted jeans, a floral crop top and a pair of white Doc Martens. If not for the fresh bandage wrapped around my right hand, I might look like a normal seventeen-year-old.

"Now, hair and makeup."

The feeling of the brush drifting across my eyelids gives me goose bumps.

"You could really do this, you know," I say as she paints my face in foundation. "Like, as a job."

She shakes her head. "My mom would literally die before she'd let that happen."

Mrs. Shao is strict, and her daughter's career choice is of the utmost importance to her. With the family business losing money, they've been warning Gemma for months about their dependence on her.

"Have you thought about telling her about Nishi?"

Gemma stiffens. I've been out as bisexual to my father since freshman year, but Gemma doesn't have the same luxury.

"I've thought about it, yeah, but I don't want to be home-less. The worst part is that she asks me every day if I have a boyfriend yet."

"Maybe you can really slowly introduce her to the idea?" I suggest. "Like, casually bring up how hot Zendaya is?"

"Yeah," she whispers, letting out a long sigh. "I'll think about it."

She finishes my makeup and guides me to the bathroom mirror. The gold glitter brings out the green in my eyes. A tint of blush highlights the upper part of my cheek.

"It's so natural," I say, awestruck. "Thank you."

She beams. Her phone screen lights up with five texts from Nishi.

"Go," I insist. "I don't want you to be late for your date."

"I'll see you at the party?"

I nod, lingering in the mirror even after she's gone. A shaky breath rises and falls inside of my lungs when I think about seeing Elliott tonight. He's the textbook definition of a ticking time bomb. There's no predicting what might happen at the lake. I'm going to stick out like a sore thumb next to him—rumors and gossip clinging to us like glue. But staring into the mirror at a reflection I like, one where I'm strong and effortless, I'm more confident than I have been in a long while.

Tonight, I am beautiful. Tonight, I'm unstoppable.

Right on time, Elliott's car pulls to the front of my house. He has a tiny razor cut on his chin. The nick destroys his perfect facade, but I like the flaw.

"Hey," he says. "Ready?"

"Sure."

I buckle my seatbelt before Elliott takes off down the street, instantly coasting over the speed limit. He lights a cigarette and dangles it between his lips.

"Most of the football team is going tonight."

He means Harris will be there. My foot taps anxiously against the floor of the car.

"He won't go near you." Elliott's voice is stern.

"What about Maddy?"

"What about her?"

"Is she going to be there?"

He holds the cigarette out the window. "Probably."

*Great.*

We turn onto an unmarked dirt road. A few cars follow behind us, some of which I recognize from the Dekalb parking lot. Elliott takes a sharp right turn, and the lake house comes into view, illuminated by headlights. The house is three stories, towering as high as the oak trees around it. Fairy lights and the golden glow of a bonfire light our path. Elliott parks in a patch of gravel on the side of the house. Next to his car, a group of freshmen sit in the back of a blue Ford truck, chugging beer and laughing.

"Ready?" he prompts.

"Ready as I'll ever be."

I step outside. The humid air curls my bangs into frizzy ringlets. I spot Gemma and Nishi hanging out near a beer pong table. Elliott trails behind me. He stops every other step to talk to people I don't know.

"We're about to take shots!" Gemma shouts. "You want in?"

Elliott grabs the shot glass from Gemma's hand without hesitating.

I freeze. The last time I took a shot was the night of Elliott's party. Harris could be lurking anywhere, watching me from the shadows.

"Rose?" Gemma questions.

I pick up a glass before I can overthink it. A few other senior girls hanging around the table join us. We clink our glasses and down the vodka, which tastes like straight rubbing alcohol. I wince as the liquid burns my throat.

A long-haired boy, dressed in an oversized tie-dyed sweatshirt, approaches Gemma. His face is littered with piercings.

"Beer pong?" he suggests.

Gemma turns to face the rest of the us. Elliott gives her an enthusiastic thumbs up. Gemma, Nishi, Elliott, and I form one team. Four guys I don't recognize from school, including the one in the tie dye, challenge us from the other side of the table.

Elliott nudges me. "You're up first."

I step forward and throw the ping pong ball, expecting the worst possible outcome. To my surprise, the ball bounces once and lands in a cup. Gemma, Nishi, and Elliott applaud, and I grin from ear to ear. The long-haired boy drinks. Then, he throws the ball. It lands in a cup.

My turn to drink. The beer is weak compared to the shot. Much easier to get down.

The match is tied by the time it's my turn again. The ball hits the target. My opponent reciprocates. We both drink.

"Damn, Rose," Nishi snickers. "You're good at this."

Around me, the trees start to blur together into one giant mass of green and brown. I lean into Elliott's ear.

"I think I'm drunk."

He tilts his chin, concerned. "Good drunk or bad drunk?"

"Good," I affirm.

At least, I think it's good. I'm not so worried about running into Harris anymore, so that must be a good thing. Elliott guides our group away from the beer pong table. Around us, people from school wade in and out of the lake. The moonlight, silver and sparkling, reflects off of it.

Elliott asks, "Do you want to swim?"

I open my mouth to say no, of course not, but I pause before I do. That's not what an unstoppable person would say. An unstoppable person would jump into the lake without hesitation.

"Why not?" I respond, much to Gemma and Elliott's surprise.

I grab Gemma's hand, who grabs Nishi's and then Elliott's, then drag them all to the edge of the water. The boys in the lake have their shirts off, and most of the girls are in nothing but a bra and underwear.

"One second," I tell Gemma before pulling my shirt over my head.

She opens her mouth, watching in shock as I toss the cloth into the sand. I shiver in my purple bralette, and I debate removing my shorts, but I'm not *that* drunk. Elliott's eyes widen when I turn around, and I'm thankful it's dark outside, so he can't see me blush.

"How much did you drink again?" Gemma asks.

I shush her before dipping my toes in the lake. The frigid water sends a shiver up my spine, but it's refreshing compared to the heat of the alcohol burning inside of me. Gemma and Nishi sprint into the water holding hands and laughing hysterically.

"Come in, Rose!" she shouts.

I run in deeper toward my friends, letting the lake water consume me, and it feels like magic. Elliott wades in but stops when he's only knee-deep.

"Come on," I plead, splashing him. "It feels awesome."

He laughs but doesn't move. Oh. *Our conversation from the drive to Savannah. He told me about his miserable experience on the swim team.*

"Shit, I forgot. You don't like to swim."

"I wasn't going to let that stop you."

I splash him again. He splashes back, which makes me laugh a little too loudly. I clasp my hand over my mouth to shut myself up.

"You're definitely drunk." Elliott sounds thoroughly amused.

My gaze flickers back and forth between his eyes and the moon. Both are full, beautiful, and all consuming. Elliott reaches out and grabs my hand with his own. His skin is smooth and soft against mine beneath the cold water. His shirt, soaked through, sticks to the curves of his body. He's a marble statue in the moonlight.

Suddenly, I'm consumed by the craving that I've been suppressing all week.

I stand up, dripping lake water, and lean into him for support.

"I think we should get out of here," I say.

The words leave my mouth before I realize it. I expect Elliott to laugh at me, but he doesn't.

His lips turn into a teasing smile. "My house or yours?"

My father is at work until the morning. Nobody is home.

"Mine," I whisper.

"Are you sure?"

"Yes." I nod impatiently. "Let's go."

Elliott keeps his hand in mine as we make our way out of the water. I stumble back up to shore, shivering from the freezing air against my wet skin. I grab my floral crop top and give Gemma a thumbs up. She winks.

Halfway to the gravel parking lot, I spot a group approaching from the other side of the lake house. One of the girls has long blonde hair. Maddy. Which means the taller boy behind her is Harris.

"Ignore them," Elliot murmurs.

Maddy says my name. Harris chuckles, whispering a reply into her ear.

I stop. "Did you say something?"

The alcohol has made me braver than I am.

Maddy's thin nose turns up in annoyance. That's when I realize that Harris is holding her hand. He wraps his arm around her shoulder and pulls her close.

Harris and Maddy? Even after she watched what he did to me?

She smiles a cruel, manipulative grin that makes my stomach turn.

"I didn't know you were invited," she states.

"Elliott invited me."

She glances up at Elliott, pursing her plump lips. He crosses his arms against his chest without leaving the spot at my side.

"Rose Berman is really the reason why you haven't been texting me back?"

Elliott grits his teeth. "Don't, Maddy."

Maddy walks up to me. Her words drip with venom, "I know Elliott's a good fuck but be careful. Apparently, he'll leave you for the crazy girl."

"Yeah?" I challenge, blood boiling inside my veins. "At least he doesn't try to molest them. Or do you have selective memory?"

Harris growls. Elliott steps forward, challenging him to make a move, but he doesn't. He knows he doesn't stand a chance against Elliott.

"Let him play out his fantasy," Harris tells Maddy. "He'll screw up eventually. Then he'll be back."

The corners of his lips rise. He turns to Elliott and pulls a small bag out of his pocket. It's filled with white powder. Sweat drips down Elliott's forehead as he takes in the sight of it.

"Can't stay away for too long, can you, my friend?" Harris teases.

Elliott snarls, fingers curling into fists at his side. I wrap my hand around his wrist.

"Fuck you, Harris," I spit.

Laughing, the group walks toward the beer pong table, leaving Elliott and me alone in the darkness. He bounces up and down, like he does at the start of a match, teeming with pent-up energy.

"Let me go," he says.

"So, you can do what?"

"Kick his ass."

"Do you think that will fix anything?"

Nobody cares about what Harris Price did to me. They'll believe his word over mine. If Elliott beats him up, he'll look like the asshole. Elliott pulls out a cigarette from the pack in his pocket, lights it, and inhales the smoke in one desperate breath. He's not 100 percent convinced.

"Come on," I say, "Let's go."

He does.

Shivering in my soaking wet clothes, I blast the heat inside of the car, but it does little to help. Elliott's face is still bright red.

"Did you know they were together? Maddy and Harris?" I ask.

"They're not," he responds, shortly. "Maddy doesn't date. She doesn't even like Harris. They're probably hooking up to piss me off."

He's angry. Not the reaction I was expecting.

Elliott reverses out of the parking spot and weaves his way through the crowd of students. I'm painfully sober now, and Elliott's bad mood is contagious. I scowl through the window.

"You can drop me off," I mutter. "This was a bad idea."

The car slows down. Elliott rests his foot on the brake and turns to me. "You think because of some shit Maddy said I don't want to be your friend anymore?"

I pause. "Is that what we are? Friends?"

Elliott leans his head against the window, pressing his thumb into the button to roll it down. He takes one final hit of the cigarette before throwing the butt into the street.

"I don't know," he admits.

I don't know, either.

But I want to find out.

Elliott presses on the gas. The night sky is full of stars, darkness hiding the trees around the lake in a blanket of shadows. I hum along to the radio as we turn back on the main street. Gradually, Elliott relaxes. He smiles.

"What?" I ask.

"These parties are usually shit, but you made it fun. I'm sorry my friends had to ruin it."

His grip on the wheel hardens, but I shake my head. "It doesn't have to be ruined."

With the highway clear of traffic, we make it to my house before eleven. My father's car is nowhere in sight, thank god.

"He works nights," I explain. "He's usually back by the time the sun comes up."

"Does he sleep through the day?"

"Not always. I think he likes to be awake when I'm at school in case something happens. I honestly don't know when he sleeps sometimes."

"He's a good dad," Elliott states.

His face loses its color. He puts the car into park, staring tiredly at my house. I can't imagine how hard it must be to not feel safe in your own home.

"You know, you can pick your family."

I say the words slowly and carefully, wishing for Elliott to take away from them what I want him to. But he doesn't look at me. And when he does respond, his voice shakes.

"I look in the mirror and see my father. That's not something I can choose."

I know how it feels to not recognize your own reflection. My mother and I could have been twins. But Elliott is *nothing* like his father.

"Screw him. He's not your family. Your family is Andre and Gemma and me. The people who care about you. They're the ones who matter."

Elliott half smiles but doesn't reply. We remain still beneath the stars, both of us caught up in our own mess of thoughts until I can't take the silence anymore. I open the car door and stroll toward my house. To my relief, Elliott follows.

I lead him up the stairs and into my bedroom. He's been here once before, the first time I joined him in The Ring and I played doctor, but that day feels like eons ago now. He picks up a doll sitting on my bookshelf and inspects it with the utmost curiosity. I try to snatch it out of his hands, but he lifts it into the air where I can't reach. The crown in the doll's hair hangs on by a thread.

"That's Clara," I explain, blushing. "I got her when I was eight."

"She's cute. What's she the queen of?"

"She's the princess of Rosaville, actually."

"I like that."

Elliott, whose presence is impossible to ignore, arms three times the size of my father's, looks delicate and breakable standing in my bedroom. His eyes are rich with sadness, threatening tears at any moment.

"What if Harris was right?" His voice is dull.

"What do you mean?"

"I mess up everything in my path, and now you're right in my way. If I'm anything like my dad, I'm only going to hurt you."

Elliott studies me with nothing but innocence and compassion. So unlike his father. I wish I could show him how different they truly are.

"You can't hurt me," I state, and I know without a doubt that it's the truth. "You won't."

I move magnetically toward him, wrapping my fingers around his clenched hand. He cusps my chin and lifts it up so we're only inches from kissing. Hot blood races from my heart to my head.

"Elliott King," I start. "You're smart, kind, and strong. And you're going to get out of this town and away from your dad."

The air between us is thick, and I can smell the remains of alcohol on his breath.

"We have to come up with a plan. Maybe if I fight—"

"Elliott," I interrupt. "We can figure it out when you're thinking straight."

He's not listening to me. "But if I fight, then he'll want me to stay . . ."

"Elliott," I say again, and this time he perks up. "It's going to be okay."

He stifles a nod. He looks tired, but alert, taking in the sight of me with a patient smile. He tucks a loose curl behind my ear.

"Sorry," Elliott mutters. "I get locked in on things sometimes."

"I know." I chuckle.

His eyes drop to my bedroom floor. "I should go. It's late and—"

"No," I whisper, shaking my head. He peers back up at me, biting down on his lip as he does. He's impossibly beautiful coated in the moonlight flooding my window.

I want him. More than I care to admit.

"Kiss me."

I barely have time to get the words out before he does just that.

Our closeness warms my wet, frigid skin, and I melt into him. My hand travels from his chin to the bottom of his T-shirt. He watches me with a tender smile, leaning back to allow me to peel the damp cloth off of his skin. The hunger in his gaze, the raspy way he's breathing—it's sacrilegious.

Elliott moves slowly, cautiously even though I'm not afraid. He runs his hand through my hair, his lips inching down my neck. I hold my breath as his hand travels farther up my body. With perfect precision, Elliott lifts my shirt over my head and tosses it to the floor. He moves his fingers to my collarbone, then to my shoulder toward my bra strap. Carefully, Elliott slips one strap down my shoulder. Then the other. I unclasp the material and drop it onto the bed.

The air against my naked skin is cold, but the heat of him keeps me from shivering. The tattoos scattered across his chest belong in a gallery. I gape, frozen in place, lips curled into a smile.

"You okay?" Elliott asks.

I nod. He makes this easy.

"You're stunning," he continues.

I shake my head. Elliott lifts my chin, demanding I look at him. "You are."

Elliott watches me like I'm the only thing that's ever mattered to him. He runs his finger down my neck to my shoulders. The small, intricate movements feel like heaven, sending pulses of pleasure throughout my spine.

I've never felt this before. Closeness. Like our veins are filled with the same blood. Every move he makes, I fall into sync with. His blue eyes are limitless—full of possibilities of a future between us. His fingers drift farther down my body. I grab his hand as it nears the top of my shorts.

"Not tonight," I whisper.

Even though I can picture my first time being with Elliott, I haven't felt entirely comfortable with the idea of sex after what happened with Harris. Elliott immediately pulls his hand away. "Sorry."

"It's okay."

He whispers, "Meeting you was the best thing to happen to me in a very long time."

And I agree wordlessly, because I'm sure that he knows it from how my body leans into his. Elliott places his own T-shirt over my head. He smirks playfully as it consumes my body in one giant mess of cloth. I sink into the material. It smells like cigarettes and lavender and the salt of the ocean.

It smells like heaven.

"You should get some sleep," he suggests. His voice is husky.

"So should you."

Elliott kisses my cheek, then stands up from the bed. He buttons his jean jacket, and I frown.

"Goodnight, princess," Elliott whispers as he slips out the doorway to my bedroom.

I bury my face into my pillow so he can't see my stupid grin at the sound of the nickname.

# CHAPTER EIGHTEEN

**I DREAM ABOUT A FUTURE WITH ELLIOTT KING.**

He smiles that crooked smile I adore. He teaches me everything he knows about boxing, and when he challenges me to spar, I hold my ground. Sometimes he even lets me win. We cook dinner together like normal people, and I laugh harder than I ever have in my life.

When I wake up in the morning, my hand goes straight to my phone.

No texts. No word from Elliott at all. The only sign I have that he was here is my princess doll resting on the rug instead of her usual spot.

**ROSE: Last night was fun.**

I refresh the screen, but he doesn't type back. He must still be sleeping. I tuck my phone into the pocket of my plaid pajama pants. Downstairs, my dad shuffles through the front door as I'm putting a bagel into the toaster.

"Long night?" I question.

"Yeah. How was the party?"

"Good. I was back by eleven like I promised."

He stifles a yawn and smiles.

"Get some sleep," I suggest.

He saunters upstairs, not arguing. My stomach rumbles, desperate for a taste of something that isn't alcohol. I butter my bagel and take a bite. The carbs are heavenly. As I'm about to finish it off, there's a loud knock on the door. I jump out of my chair. The other half of my bagel falls onto the floor, and I groan as crumbs sprinkle across the room.

Elliott?

He still hasn't responded to my text. I make my way to the door and recognize the sliver of reddish black hair. Gemma. She's never awake this early on a Saturday.

"Boo!" she says, shoving a Starbucks cup into my hand. "Happy Halloween!"

I take a sip. Earl Grey, my favorite.

"What's this for?"

"I wanted to get out of my house, and you've been an exceptional friend lately. Let's hang out."

"Alright," I agree, albeit rather hesitantly.

We spend the morning in my backyard enjoying the chilly weather. Gemma paints her nails pink while I catch up on some reading for class. She hums along to Lana Del Rey playing from her phone.

"So, what happened last night? After you and Elliott left?"

Finally, the question I've been waiting for. She's probably dying for details. I don't bother trying to hide the redness in my face as I think about what happened only hours ago.

"We kissed," I confess. ". . . . And he might have taken my shirt off."

Gemma squeals. She throws the bottle of nail polish to the ground, grabs my arm, and squeezes so tightly it cuts off my circulation.

"Rosalyn King does have a good ring to it."

She giggles, smiling from ear to ear at the expression of horror on my face. "What was it like?"

"Amazing."

She lowers her voice. "Are you in love?"

I freeze. Every time I blink, I picture the mesmerized smile on Elliott's face as he worshiped my bare skin. Last night was everything I've ever wanted, and yet I still don't feel satisfied.

"I don't know," I admit. "Maybe. I need to talk to him once he's up."

She picks up her phone to change the song, then pauses. "What the hell?"

She hands me her phone. Harris posted an Instagram picture only minutes ago. The caption lists his address and a time for a Halloween party. Of the few likes that it already has, Elliott is one of them.

*So he does have his phone.*

The smile vanishes from my face in an instant. It's remarkable how quickly Elliott can change my mood. Gemma's dark eyebrows crease when she notices the change in my expression. I show her the text I sent to Elliott this morning with no response.

"Maybe we should go tonight? See what he's up to? But only if you're comfortable."

These constant ups and downs are maddening. "I'll be fine," I mutter, standing up from the grass. "Let's go. Help me find a costume."

*

Despite the dark history between us, Harris's house is more welcoming than Elliott's. Pictures of the Price family are scattered across the walls. Dirty dishes line the sink. A few students hang out around the island, talking and drinking.

I fight the urge to wipe away the stream of fake blood beneath my nose; Gemma insisted I needed it to complete my Eleven from Stranger Things costume. My dad's paint-splattered T-shirt hangs loosely off my arms. A true 80's relic. I reach for a half-empty bottle of vodka on the counter, but Gemma stops me. She's dressed as Wednesday Addams, her hair pinned into two braids. Of course, she looks perfect.

"Let's find him first, okay?" Gemma says.

Curse her and her healthy coping strategies. I huff but agree. We creep toward the living room where the bulk of the party is. The crowd is thick, full of seniors and even some college students from a campus nearby. I don't want to go anywhere near it, but I know that the center of the crowd is exactly where I'll find Elliott. I push my way through sweaty shoulders and clouds of marijuana smoke.

There's laughter in the distance. Goofy laughter from a raspy voice that belongs to Elliott. Gemma and I push through the last layer of the crowd into the middle of the room. I spot a blue velvet couch, and seated on it, two people I recognize instantly.

Out of all the scenarios I contemplated, this one never made the list.

Maddy, wearing nothing but a lacy black bra and cat ears, swings her legs across Elliott's lap, straddling him. Elliott, dressed up as a shirtless Rocky Balboa, twirls a strand of her hair with his finger. Then, he dips his chin, pulling Maddy in for a kiss that stops my heart. She wraps her hand around his head to draw him closer.

I did the same thing not even twenty-four hours ago.

I freeze. My hands tremble.

Gemma makes the first move.

She's in front of Elliott before I can process what is happening. I gasp as my best friend rips Maddy off of Elliot's lap and slaps him straight across the face. The crowd silences. Elliott's skin reddens, his fists curling, until he realizes who hit him. I watch as his expression changes from confusion to horror. He turns to me, his mouth propped open.

Someone whistles as Gemma steps away from Elliott.

"Rose," Elliott whispers.

I try to run, but the crowd is too thick. Everyone wants in on the action, and all I want is to get the hell out of it. I push someone out of the way, and as I do, Elliott's hand falls onto my shoulder. I shiver at the touch of his calloused skin.

My feet lock in place. The feeling of his skin on mine opens the floodgates of adrenaline, and it courses throughout my body. I curse my own human instincts, furious that I would allow the hands of a traitor to feel so damn good.

"What?" I spit as I face him.

Standing so close, I register the tiredness across his face. His skin is puffy and pale. He reeks of vodka and weed. There's no telling what other drugs he's abused tonight. His right eye is bruised, and I can't tell if it's makeup or the real thing.

"Please let me explain—"

I cut him off, "No."

He winces. Without offering him another chance to speak, I turn toward the front door. A group of freshmen hold up their phones and record us. I'm too exhausted to care.

"Rose!"

Elliott's voice is piercing, and my name is broken when it leaves his throat. He dives through the throng of costumes, but I'm already on my way out the door.

"I love you!"

I stop.

The crowd does, too.

Those three words rip a hole into my chest. My feet give out, and I grab onto Gemma to keep myself from collapsing.

Elliott King loves me.

I know it for a fact without even needing to see him. The pain in his voice proves it all to be true.

Tears drip down my cheek when I turn around and see him standing rigidly with his bare, bruised-up skin and bloodshot blue eyes. I want nothing more than to scream the same words back, to hold onto his admittance and treasure it. I want to melt into him and let his strength protect me from hurting. Hurt that he caused.

But I can't. I can't save him. I have to save myself instead.

"Don't," I whisper.

He lets out an agonizing sob that rips the hole in my chest further apart.

I escape the mob through the open door. Gemma follows. She keeps one hand on my back, holding tightly to the cloth of my T-shirt. Her other arm moves to wrap me in a hug. I relax against her, tears running down my cheeks.

"Please take me home," I moan.

She whispers, "Okay."

I crash into the passenger seat of Gemma's mom's car. Gemma slides the key into the ignition. She blasts warm air on my skin. It doesn't get rid of my goose bumps.

"I think I love him, too," I cry.

I wish it wasn't true. But I know that if I didn't love him, this wouldn't hurt so damn bad.

"He doesn't know what he's missing," she replies.

I know exactly what I'm missing. Elliott's gentle hands. His crooked smile. The way his laughter lights up his face. The crease on his forehead when he's frustrated. The feeling of his fingers wrapped around mine, holding me steadily in place, grounding me.

I don't think I've ever wanted or hated anything more.

"Let's go," I murmur.

Gemma puts the car into drive and speeds down the road. The music blaring from Harris's house fades with the distance. I briefly wonder if Elliott's back with Maddy, kissing her to forget about me. Maybe he's drinking, or snorting powder off the table. Or, worst of all, laughing with Harris about my stupidity.

Gemma parks in my driveway. I wipe away my tears and force my chin up. My dad's home. I don't want him to see me like this.

"Do you want me to sleep over?" she asks.

I shake my head. "No, it's okay."

"Okay," she concedes, squeezing my hand one last time within hers. I squeeze back. My breathing steadies for the first time tonight.

"Thank you," I whisper, even though it's not enough. I don't know what I would've done tonight if she hadn't been there.

"I love you, Rose. That's never going to change."

I pull myself out of the car so she can't see me start to cry again. My father perks up from the recliner at the sound of my footsteps.

"How was it?"

I open my mouth to try and come up with a convincing lie. But all my words disappear when I see him. He clears the living room in a split second and wraps his arms around me.

I let myself go. Tears rush down my chin and onto his sweatshirt.

"You're okay," he says in a hushed tone.

He doesn't ask what happened. He just stands with me until I can't hold myself up any longer. Then, he guides me upstairs to my bedroom. I pull the purple comforter up to my nose. Elliott's T-shirt rests against the pillow, and I chuck it onto the floor.

Dad disappears downstairs, then returns moments later with a steaming hot cup of chamomile tea. The warm liquid eases my raw throat.

"Thank you," I whisper.

He takes a seat on the edge of the bed, tapping his fingers against my floral sheets. The princess doll rests on the floor next to his feet. I scowl at it, cursing myself for not putting it away earlier.

"I wish your mom was here," Dad stammers. "She was better with this stuff."

I smile weakly. He's wrong. Mom would be proud of him.

"You're doing great, Dad."

He grins, brown eyes brimming with unconditional love. I place the cup of tea onto my nightstand and squeeze his hand.

"I promise I'll tell you everything tomorrow, but I don't think I can talk right now."

He nods. I finish what's left of the tea before relaxing into my pillow. My father rises from the bed, running his fingers one last time through my curls.

"Get some rest, kiddo," he says. "And call me if you need anything."

"I love you," I respond.

I hear Elliott speaking the same words in my head, his voice shattering.

He loves me.

And, exactly as Harris predicted, he ruined it.

# CHAPTER NINETEEN

**I SPEND THE FIRST MORNING OF NOVEMBER IN BED.**

The weather outside is beautiful. The sunshine calls my name. But I don't dare to venture out from my spot under the covers. I remind my dad over and over again that this is not, in fact, a depressive episode, but instead a regular teenage breakup thing. Still, he insists that I talk to Dr. Taylor. I roll out of bed not bothering to change out of my pajamas for the appointment.

The hospital is eerily quiet. I creep down the hallway, throwing open the door to Dr. Taylor's office with a scowl.

"You look . . ."

"Like hell?" I fill in his sentence. "My boyfriend cheated on me."

He raises an eyebrow. "You have a boyfriend?"

Now that I think about it, Elliott danced around the topic every time I brought it up.

"Well, no," I say. "I guess not."

I sit down in my usual spot, tapping my foot impatiently against the white tile floor. Dr. Taylor adjusts the clipboard in his hand. There's a pile of notes in front of him, all with my name scribbled on the back. A literal bible of my issues.

"What happened?"

"I walked in on him kissing another girl."

He shakes his head as if to say *boys are idiots.* "I'm sorry, Rose. You deserve a lot better. Don't you think?"

I shrug. "Does it matter? It's over now."

We slip into silence, and I realize that for the first time in a while, I don't have anything to hide. No hallucinations of my mom, no panic attacks. Just Elliott. I don't know if that's a good thing.

"How is boxing? Are you still going to class?"

"I have been, yeah. I'm supposed to have a private lesson this week, but I don't think I'm going."

"Why not?"

"I don't know. It seems like a lot right now."

"You shouldn't give up on something you love because you're hurting. You should channel your pain into something productive."

I cross my arms against my chest. The rational part of me knows that he's right, but the other part wants to crawl into bed and die. The two parts fight back and forth until the rational part gets the upper hand.

"Fine," I huff. "I'll try."

He nods approvingly.

"I don't want to talk about me anymore," I state, much to Dr. Taylor's annoyance. I focus on the crayon drawing of Dr. Taylor's family hanging on the wall. "How's your kid doing?"

He smiles. "Honestly, he's been a major pain in the ass these last few weeks."

"Ouch. You ever heard the phrase 'therapists need therapists, too'?"

He laughs. "I suppose that's how we stay in business."

He tells me more about his five-year-old son, Charlie, and how he's been searching for a sport of his own to sink his teeth into. We go back and forth debating the pros and cons of baseball. To my relief, Dr. Taylor doesn't ask me any more questions about myself or Elliott. I guess even he must know we all have our limits.

"Same time next week?" he asks as the hour comes to an end.

"You bet."

When I get home from therapy, Gemma's waiting outside my front door, peppermint hot chocolate in hand. She passes it to me. I gulp it down, letting the sweetness calm some of my leftover anger.

"How are you?" she asks.

"Fine."

I take her inside. She sits beside me at the kitchen table, watching every move I make with intense concentration. She's as bad as Dr. Taylor.

"Have you heard from him?"

I shake my head. Elliott still hasn't texted. Or called. Or done literally anything at all to show that he cares. Every time my phone lights up with a text, I convince myself it's him. It never is.

"Are you going to school tomorrow?" she asks.

I've been actively avoiding thinking about school. In only a matter of hours, Elliott will be sitting right in front of me, and I'll have to swallow my pride and pretend like nothing happened between us. I'm not sure if I'm that good of an actor.

"I have to," I sigh. "I've missed too many days already."

She rests her hand over my own. I half-smile because it's all I can muster, even though she deserves better than that.

"I'll walk with you in the morning, okay?"

"Okay."

We spend the rest of the afternoon watching black and white cartoons on my dad's old television. I fall asleep on

Gemma's shoulder, and when I wake up, she's no longer next to me. Day has turned to night. I pull myself off the couch and stroll to my bedroom, crashing face-first onto the sheets.

My sleep is dreamless, and the morning comes too quickly.

I drag myself out of my cocoon of blankets and make my way into the bathroom. I paint on a layer of concealer, but it doesn't hide the blotches across my skin. There's nothing I can do to make it look like I didn't spend the whole weekend in bed. I let my hair down in messy ringlets, bangs desperately needing a good brush.

"You sure you want to go?" asks my father, sipping coffee at the kitchen table.

He passes me a piece of toast. I take a small bite and leave the rest on the plate.

"Yeah. I'll be fine."

We both know that's far from the truth, but I can't miss another day of school. They'll hold me back a year if my absences keep up, and if there's one thing I want more than to never see Elliott again, it's to get the hell out of Dekalb High. I hug my father before meeting Gemma outside. She's dressed in a light pink dress with a floral pattern. Her cheeriness is infectious, and I smile.

"You look good," she states.

I know from the tone of her voice that she's lying, but I take the compliment. I ask about her college applications and Nishi. To my relief, she keeps talking, never stopping to ask about me. Even Gemma, queen of attention, knows how annoying it can be to have everyone worried about you.

The smell of nicotine, followed by the sound of a revving car engine, stops both of us in our tracks. Gemma grimaces as Elliott's car races down the narrow road. Maddy laughs from the passenger seat.

"He's such an asshole," barks Gemma.

"Do you think he actually likes her?"

Her cheeks turn green with disgust. "Hell no. I think she's a distraction."

I'm really, really trying not to hate Maddy. Feminism and shit, right? Plus she hooked up with him first, and there's no way she could've known that I was anything more to him than a body. Real emotions aren't exactly his thing. As the convertible turns into the parking lot, barely missing the curb, I duck my head and follow Gemma through the back entrance of the building.

Everyone stares as I walk by, which I'm sure has to do with the fact that videos from the party have been shared on at least ten Snapchat stories.

Elliott isn't in English by the time I arrive. I quietly sit at my desk and pull out the Poe anthology we're studying from my bag. He shows up five minutes late. I try to focus on Mr. Ruse, but one of my ears is tuned only to the wavelength of his voice. Everything he says, I hear. He insults poetry under his breath during Ruse's lecture. He talks to one of the girls beside him about supplying alcohol for her party.

"Rose?" Mr. Ruse asks.

*Crap. I wasn't listening.*

"What do you think is the story behind *Annabel Lee*?"

A breath of relief. I've read it a hundred times before.

"That love survives anything," I murmur. "Even death."

Ruse tilts his head.

"But, is the narrator really living in her absence?"

"No," I confess.

At least, it doesn't feel like living to me.

*

Nishi and Gemma distract me at lunch with a game of twenty questions. Every time I'm able to focus on something else for long enough to forget, Elliott laughs, and the cycle starts all over again.

I want to hit a punching bag. But Elliott has first dibs on Midtown, and there's no way in hell I'm risking seeing him there.

**ROSE: I can't make practice tonight. Private lesson tomorrow?**

**ANDRE: Sure. Meet me at 5:00.**

"Earth to Rose?" Gemma waves her hand in front of my face.

"Sorry," I say. "I was texting my coach."

"You missed Harris spilling soda down his shirt."

I glance toward the front of the room, watching with amusement as Harris curses and stands up from the table. Elliott is two seats down from him. He watches Harris with a sly smile, right hand poised at his side. I wonder if he's the one who knocked the can over.

"What are you up to tonight?" Nishi asks me.

"Suffering. What's up?"

"We're going to dinner. You want to come?"

I'm not sure that I want to punish myself by hanging out around lovebirds right now. I shake my head, mumbling something about homework and cleaning. The bell rings. I stand up from the table with a yawn. All I've done the last two days is sleep, and yet I can't wait to get back to bed.

Elliott's in his car by the time I leave school for the day. He must be heading to practice. From behind the steering wheel, his eyes meet mine, and I pause. He opens his mouth like he might try to say something, but as he does, Maddy slips into the passenger's seat.

"Let's go," says Gemma.

I don't look back toward the parking lot.

\*

Come Tuesday, I've tried to evade all thoughts of Elliott by replacing them with thoughts of boxing. Too bad the two overlap, and by the time I get to Midtown Ring, my head hurts from overthinking.

"Hey," Andre says, stepping out of his car. "I'm going to go out on a whim and guess that something happened between you and Elliott?"

"That obvious?"

"I know teenage angst when I see it. I'm glad you texted."

He unlocks the door to the gym and leads me inside. It's quiet. Remnants of sweat and shoe marks from practice yesterday are scattered across the floor. I picture Elliott at the bag in the corner before forcing myself away from it.

"There's a competition downtown in two weeks. It's a beginner's match, so you don't have to worry about getting your ass kicked. Plus, cash prizes for winners."

A cash prize? I could pay my dad back for the stitches in my hand. I perk up.

"How do I get on the roster?"

He smirks. "Already done. Let's get you ready."

Andre does not take preparation lightly. He makes me run laps around the gym to warm up. Right as my legs are ready to collapse, he moves into bag work.

"Three crosses, five jabs. Go."

My punches land, but they're not nearly as powerful as the ones I've learned to throw. The bag swings only a few inches. Andre grabs my wrist midair, stopping my movement.

"You're not focused," he declares. "Stop thinking about him."

"Trust me, I'm not doing it on purpose."

Andre doesn't let go of my arm. I face him, frustrated. "What do you want me to do?"

"This practice is for you, not Elliott. You're here because you want to be a good boxer. I recognized that drive in you the moment you first stepped through that door. So, forget about everything else and *put in the work*."

I exhale. I narrow my gaze on the punching bag, focusing on the tiny threads of material holding it together. Unconsciously, my arm swings and slams into the side of the bag. It rises into the air, almost hitting Andre.

He grins. "Great. Now do that fifty more times."

I do. I hit the bag until my knees buckle beneath me, and I crash onto the floor. The tile is cold and refreshing, and I lay flat on my back, letting the coolness revive me.

"You okay?" asks Andre.

"I'm fine," I huff. "Give me a second."

"That's enough for today. You did good, kid."

I stay on the floor for another long moment before forcing myself back to my feet. Andre hands me a bottle of water, which I finish in one giant gulp.

"Will you be at practice tomorrow?"

"Do I need to be?"

He shakes his head *no.* "Do some cardio at home if you have to skip, but I expect to see you back next week."

He's a good coach. He's never been so harsh with me before, but I know he's only doing it because he cares. We leave the gym together, my arms and legs trembling during my walk to the train. When I get home, I fall asleep to the sound of thunderstorms outside my window. Even though every part of me aches, I feel better than I have all week.

After another rude awakening courtesy of Nirvana, I get out of bed and put on an outfit that hugs my body in just the right way. After watching Elliott and Maddy drool all over each other, I think that it's time to remind him of what he's missing. The green lace tank top is tight against my chest, and my skinny jeans make my butt appear a little more round. I throw my hair into a messy bun and let my bangs rest on my forehead.

I make sure that Elliott notices me when I walk into English. Even Maddy's jaw drops.

"You look hot today," Gemma comments, meeting me in the courtyard after last period. "Any particular reason?"

"Nope."

"Okay," she says sarcastically. "Want to come over?"

We arrive at her house a few minutes later. The smell of takeout from Simone's wafts from the kitchen to the doorway. My stomach growls audibly, making both of us giggle. We shove orange chicken and spring rolls into our mouths until neither of us can take another bite. I slump into the chair. My stomach is now two sizes too big for these tight jeans.

"How's everything with Nishi?" I ask.

"I thought we agreed on no talk of romance?"

"We said no boys. Nishi's a girl. Loophole."

Nishi's been keeping her distance from the two of us after what happened with Elliott—probably trying to give me as much alone time with Gemma as possible. It's a kindness that doesn't go unnoticed.

"Things are really good," Gemma confesses. "Like so good it doesn't feel real."

She opens her mouth, then shuts it again.

"What?" I question.

Gemma buries her face into her palm. "I think she wants to have sex."

"Oh my god. Are you going to?"

There's excitement and fear in her brown eyes, but she has nothing to be afraid of.

"I want to," she admits. "But what if I mess up?"

"There's nothing that you can possibly mess up, Gemma. It'll be perfect."

I've been hearing stories about Elliott's sex life for years now. He's always the topic of some rumor involving a back of the car session or a crazy threesome. I never bothered to ask him how many of those stories were true. Maybe I should have. Might have saved me some heartbreak.

"I want to spend more time with you both," I tell Gemma. "I'm so sorry that my life got complicated right when you found the perfect girl."

"For the record, you've always been complicated. That's why we're friends."

She gets up to put away the leftovers, and I go to the bathroom. Staring into the rustic gold mirror, I look like a completely different person from when Gemma and I first met. My hair is shorter. I've lost weight. Most notably, there's something in my hazel eyes that wasn't there before. A certain darkness that I can't shake.

I turn away from the mirror and shut the door behind me.

*

Staying away from Elliott proves to be more difficult than I thought. Every time I turn the corner at school, he's somewhere in my line of sight. His voice is so loud that I can't tune out the sound. I never realized before how intertwined our lives are.

"I am so tired of hearing about weekend plans," I complain on my walk home from school on Friday. "Does anyone here talk about things other than partying?"

"Nope," Gemma replies. "It's high school. That's all we have to live for."

"I'm over it. College better be different."

"I've got bad news for you—"

"We should do something tomorrow," I interrupt. "Maybe catch a movie?"

Honestly, sitting in a dark theater alone with my thoughts on a Saturday night feels like the most depressing thing humanly possible, but Gemma's excited, so I go with it. At the theater, she picks a cheesy romance movie that results in me thinking about Elliott more than I care to admit. I do my best to pretend like it doesn't bother me, but Gemma can see right through the facade.

"I'm sorry," she moans for the fiftieth time.

"Oh my god, Gem. I'm not mad because you picked a romance."

"I didn't think it would be so . . ."

"Romantic?"

She facepalms.

"It's okay," I reassure her. "I'll watch *Saw* when I get home to flush out the images."

I do actually watch it, but the sounds of my empty house start to freak me out too much to keep it on. I yawn before making my way upstairs to my bathroom.

The darkness in my eyes has grown stronger. Their usual greenish-brown color has faded completely. I step closer to the mirror and lean in to inspect the dull, lifeless gray.

I blink.

*Mom smirks with skin so pale that it chills me.*

I let out a gasp that sounds more like a scream, tripping backward away from the mirror. My back slams into the shower curtain, and I grab the wall to stop myself from falling.

*It's happening again, it's happening again, it wasn't happening, but now it's happening again.*

When I raise my chin, all I see is myself. My face is exactly as it should be, minus the colorless shadow that won't vanish. I bite down on my lip and turn toward the doorway. The image of my mother's face blending with mine stays plastered in my brain, unfading.

*No more mirrors*, I decide. *No more reflections.*

# CHAPTER TWENTY

LIKE HE DOES EVERY SUNDAY MORNING, DAD IS SIPPING COFFEE FROM HIS recliner when I finally stumble downstairs. He must have forgotten to shave last night because his thick beard makes him look ten years older than he is. It stresses me out. I hate thinking about my only parent aging.

"Can I skip therapy today?"

He puts down his World's Best Dad mug. "Why?"

Truthfully, I don't want to go because I'm afraid that Dr. Taylor will be able to see right through my bullshit. He'll notice the color fading in my eyes, and the new similarities to my mother. He'll want to fix me in ways that involve more than weekend therapy.

"I've been talking about my emotions with Gemma nonstop. I need a break."

"What do you want to do instead?"

"We could go to the pumpkin patch?"

In November, a church on the other side of town sells hundreds of leftover Halloween pumpkins for charity. Reject pumpkins. There's something sad and endearing about them. I can relate. We used to go when Mom felt up for it.

"Fine," my dad agrees, much to my surprise. "Go get dressed."

I put on an orange sweater and combat boots. The air outside is chilly, and the hair on my arms sticks up as we walk down the driveway. The leaves on the trees have fallen into tall piles.

"We should carve one," I suggest.

In years past, we bought a basket of pumpkins and never carved them. Dad didn't want Mom near a knife.

His voice drops as he recalls the memory. "Sure."

These moments without Mom are difficult for him, but despite all the hardships we've faced in the past few years, we are still a family. It's nice to remind him of that once in a while. As the car drifts down the road, I relax my head against the cracked window and inhale fresh air. It smells new, like starting over.

At the pumpkin patch, small children run around and play in the leaves. One of them stumbles into my father. His face lights up when the child laughs, and I recognize the smile on his face from when I was young. Before everything fell apart.

I drop to my knees in the dirt. I pick out a giant, ugly pumpkin with brown spots across the sides and hold it up proudly to my father.

He chuckles. "Really? That one?"

"Don't be rude!"

He takes the pumpkin to the counter to purchase. Much to my father's amusement, I keep it in my lap throughout the entire car ride home. He parks the car in the driveway, and I hop out, pumpkin in hand. Dad puts down a pile of newspaper to protect the garage floor from pumpkin guts.

"What should we carve?" I ask.

He sizes up the hideous fruit. "Something beautiful. Like a flower?"

I smile. "Sure. I'll grab some knives."

Walking back into the kitchen, I pause in front of the last drawer. Next to the one that used to hold our medications, before dad locked them all up in the upstairs bathroom.

*She probably took the pill bottle from this very same drawer.*

I still don't know what my father did with that bottle after the ambulance arrived. I remember it falling from her lifeless hand when the EMTs picked her up off of the bathroom floor. They were delicate with her. I thought she might be alive. Hoped. Prayed. The bottle hit the floor with a little clink, heard by no one else but me. Why was I fixated on that damn bottle?

"Rose? You good?"

The screaming in my head silences.

"Yes," I pant. I carry a handful of knives into the garage. "You take the lead."

I sit down, playing music from my phone while I watch him work away at the reject pumpkin.

"So, colleges. Where are you thinking of applying?"

I pause, putting down the pile of seeds in my hand.

"Georgia State has a good creative writing program."

"Remember when you were a kid, and all you would talk about was school in New York City? You used to dress up like Miranda Priestly."

We both laugh as we recall the nights that I spent in my mother's pearls and hoop earrings. Of course, I've thought about applying to out-of-state schools, but there's no way we could ever afford it.

"You're saying that you want me to go to NYU?" I joke.

"It could be a good experience. You should apply."

His serious tone catches me off guard.

"Really?"

"You may as well try, Rose. I don't want you to limit yourself. If you get in somewhere you love, we'll figure it out."

I can't prevent the smile on my face. I honestly wouldn't mind staying in Atlanta, but the idea of moving somewhere I've never been, somewhere with new places and massive libraries and museums to explore, makes me more excited about college than I have been all year.

"I'll apply as soon as I get my updated transcript."

We spend the rest of the afternoon attempting to carve a tulip into the side of the pumpkin. When the sun finally sinks below the horizon, we take it outside. I light a candle and place it in the center of the not-so-hideous-anymore fruit. It glows, revealing the messy but beautiful image.

"I love it," I profess, staring up at my father.

He wraps his arm across my shoulder and pulls me close to him. Moments like these remind me that everything will be okay. Maybe not now. But eventually.

"I love you," he says.

He follows me up to my bedroom and tucks me in. It feels childish, but he's happy, so I don't put up a fight. He savors the small moments, too. After he leaves, I lay in bed with only one thing on my mind: I can't avoid boxing anymore.

Seeing Elliott there terrifies me, but my thoughts are scarier. I need to regain control over my brain, and one lesson a week with Andre isn't enough to cut it. For the rest of the night, I Google other gyms around the city. None of them compare to the location and cost of Midtown Ring. Defeated, I put my phone back on the nightstand.

Ten minutes later, my alarm goes off.

"Screw Mondays," I mumble, falling face-first out of bed.

The day passes slowly as usual. I linger in the hallway after the final bell, watching as he leaves the building. A pair of boxing gloves peek out of the top of his bag. I slip through the crowd of students outside, carefully avoiding Elliott's gaze. The BMW speeds out of the parking lot in the direction of Midtown Ring. Once he turns onto the next street over, I break away from the crowd and head toward the train station.

I sit in the chair closest to the window and examine my right hand. I peel off the bandage in one fluid motion so as not to prolong the stinging. Relief floods me. The injury is healed. There's a thin red line—a scar—but apart from that, nothing to show that I ever shattered the mirror. I touch the skin with delicate fingers, and it doesn't hurt.

The train stops at the Midtown station.

I spot Elliott first. He's lurking in the opposite corner talking to Sofía. He doesn't turn around when I open the door. I crouch near the line of navy lockers and wrap both of my hands.

"Alright everyone, circle up!"

Our eyes meet.

I turn away as soon as they do, but not before seeing the shock on Elliott's face. Andre gathers the group in a circle. I stay to Elliott's right, out of his line of sight. Andre assigns stretches that are difficult for my aching muscles.

"We're going to do a partner exercise today. Rose, you'll be with Elliott."

No.

I shoot Andre a death stare, but he shrugs smugly, as if this was something he had planned all along. Elliott's face is tomato red. He walks cautiously toward me as if approaching a hissing cat. At least I'm not the only one who feels like screaming.

"Hey," I murmur.

"Hey."

Elliott's gaze remains across the room. He won't look at me.

*Good. He should be afraid.*

"Each of you give me a jab, cross, hook, cross. Your partner needs to duck at every hook. Do it five times and then alternate," Andre instructs.

I get in position to duck. Elliott throws his hook high. High enough that could never hit me, even if I didn't duck. I huff, annoyed. "You can go lower than that."

"I don't want to hit you—"

"You won't."

This time, his hook is much lower, but still nowhere near low enough.

"I'm not a baby," I grumble.

He swings. I dodge it without stumbling, just like I knew I could. Elliott seems impressed, but he tries to hide it by pursing his lips, which pisses me off even more.

"Your turn," he says.

I throw every punch within a few centimeters of his body. It's refreshing to be able to use both hands again, although my right arm is noticeably weaker. My left knuckle brushes lightly against the skin of Elliott's cheek.

"If you want to hit me, go ahead and do it."

The desolate tone of his voice stops my movements. If truth be told, I want to knock his head off of his body. I know that wouldn't fix anything, but it would feel pretty damn good. But not if he lets me. So instead, I turn away and take a spot at one of the empty punching bags and strike it until Andre calls a water break. From inside of my backpack, my phone lights up with a call from Gemma. *Weird. She never calls.*

"Rose?"

Her voice is shaking.

"Are you okay?"

She sounds like she's been crying. She asks, "Can you meet me at Simone's?"

"Yeah, of course. Be there in a few."

I can feel Elliott watching me as my stress becomes obvious. I hang up the phone and jog over to Andre. He lets me leave practice without question. As I'm almost out the door, Elliott speaks.

"Do you need a ride?"

I turn around. He sounds desperate, but I shake my head.

Sprinting to the train station, I hop on the subway car and take it down to the closest stop to my house. Gemma's sitting on the curb outside of Simone's Chinese Restaurant with her face buried in her hands. As I approach her, she moves her head slightly, revealing globs of black mascara smudged down to her cheeks.

"What happened?" I exclaim.

I sit beside her on the curb. She lets out a breath that sounds more like a sob. "My parents found out about Nishi."

I freeze. There's no way that this went over well.

"They came home from dinner early. We were on the couch. *Kissing.* My mom made her leave."

"What did she say?"

She sighs a sad, empty sound that makes tears swell in my eyes. "That's the worst part. She didn't say anything. They won't speak to me. I spent the last hour trying to talk to my mom, and she wouldn't even look at me. So, I came here."

She lets out another sob, this one louder than the previous. I wrap my arm around her shoulder and pull her close.

"Mr. Lin gave me these," she says, passing me a container of spring rolls. I can't help but laugh at the sentiment. Gemma smiles weakly.

"You're going to be okay," I promise her. "Your parents need some time to process. Were they angry?"

Gemma shakes her head. "Not angry. Disappointed."

It's not fair she has to deal with this. If only her parents could know how comfortable Gemma is around Nishi, they would understand she's nothing but a positive influence on their daughter.

"I'm so sorry, Gem."

She rests her head on my shoulder, letting the remainder of her tears drip down her cheeks and onto my skin. Her phone lights up with a call from Nishi. There're at least fifty missed calls beneath it.

Gemma moans, "She won't stop."

"You need to talk to her. She's probably worried sick."

"Do you think I should break up with her?"

"What?" I scoff. "Are you crazy?"

"Well maybe I'm bisexual, like you? Maybe I don't actually—"

"Gemma," I interrupt. "Bisexual or not, you like girls. You love Nishi. She's good for you, and she clearly cares, or she wouldn't be calling. Talk to her."

Nishi is good. She's patient and kind. They bring out the best in each other. There's no way that I'm letting my best friend lose the best thing that's ever happened to her. Gemma sniffles, then slowly nods. She dials Nishi back.

"Hey," Gemma whispers. "Can we talk?"

I don't go back to practice. Instead, I stay with Gemma on the curb of Simone's until Nishi meets us.

She turns to me and says, "Thank you. For staying with her."

"Of course."

I leave them alone; she's safe with Nishi. By the time I get home, it's dark outside. A pile of untouched homework taunts me from my desk. After an hour of struggling through it, I get a much-needed distraction: a call from Gemma.

"We talked to my parents," she chokes. "I don't know if they're going to be wearing pride flags anytime soon, but they might come around."

I exhale. Gemma's parents are traditional, but they're good people. They love her more than they'll ever admit.

As she speaks, I wander to the bathroom and pause in front of the mirror. I look exhausted—not a "haven't slept" tired, but full body tired, the kind I used to wear around in the weeks after my mom died.

*In the center of my throat, something sparkles. Silver. A necklace, one Mom used to wear with my Hebrew name inscribed. I run my fingers over the cold material. It feels refreshing.*

*And wrong. Because I don't remember putting it on.*

I move closer and realize there's no necklace at all.

*Was Mom seeing things too?* Dr. Taylor says her derealization made her feel like she wasn't fully present in reality. I didn't think that meant she was straight up hallucinating, but if I'm hallucinating, surely she was, too.

"Rose?" Gemma's voice calls through my phone speaker. I turn around and walk back to bed.

"Sorry," I say. Are you okay?"

"Yeah. I mean, I still feel like I'm going to puke. That was the most terrifying thing I've ever done. But I'm better."

"I'm proud of you," I say, smiling. "Now you won't have to hide anymore."

Gemma hangs up the phone to try and get some sleep.

I do the same, but the sleep never comes.

*

Mr. Ruse addresses the room dressed as Edgar Allan Poe. His top hat is tall enough to brush the ceiling fan. Students are crammed into all corners of the classroom; it's the last day of our poetry unit, so both English classes are combined for final presentations. Which means Harris is two rows behind me. I can feel his beady eyes staring into the back of me. I gulp, refusing to turn around.

"It's been an honor reading your work over these last few weeks. So many of you expressed your emotions in beautiful ways."

"Elliott's good at that." I know that voice. Gruff. Amused. My heart stops.

Harris is making an obvious reference to Elliott's love outburst on Saturday night. Laughter erupts from several students. I sink farther into my seat.

"What?" Elliott asks.

He turns in his desk, cheeks red with anger. He's laser focused on Harris.

Not this. Not now.

I bury my head in my hands. "Love is a powerful thing," Ruse interrupts, noticing the discomfort on Elliott's face.

Elliott is squeezing the top of his desk so hard his knuckles turn white, and the veins in his arms pop.

*Let it go,* I silently beg.

"So many great poets wrote about love," Mr. Ruse continues, but Elliott's grip on the desk doesn't loosen. "It's a feeling that never gets old, never hesitates to make itself known. Love is something to scream from the rooftops."

"I bet Psycho screams loud," Harris says.

Elliott's across the room before I can blink. He yanks Harris out of his desk, tossing him to the ground like a ragdoll, the tiles cracking beneath him. Elliott punches him in the nose. Blood pours from his face. I turn around to find Ruse, but he's nowhere to be found.

*What the hell?*

Harris cries out when Elliott raises his fist again.

"Stop!" someone yells.

Elliott's hand suspends like he's in *The Matrix*. His muscles poised to do what he does best: destroy. Mr. Ruse miraculously returns with another teacher. They both grab a hold of Elliott before he lands another blow and drag him into the hallway. The classroom door slams.

Everyone is watching me. I slide back into my chair. Maddy has her phone out, texting furiously about what I can only imagine has now become today's hottest piece of drama. It takes only a minute for Gemma to text me a string of question marks and exclamation points.

"Alright, everyone. Interruptions over." Mr. Ruse's returns, his voice shaky. His Edgar Allan Poe top hat is sideways on the floor. I feel bad for him. "Take your seats, class."

He shuts the classroom door with a quiet click, straightens his shoulders, and forces a "Who knew poetry would get everyone so worked up?"

As he continues with his lecture, I notice half the class sneaking text messages beneath their desks.

\*

Gemma and Nishi have already heard the news by the time I meet them at lunch. Elliott's noticeably absent from his usual table in the cafeteria.

"Do you think they'll suspend him?" I wonder aloud.

"He'll be lucky if he isn't expelled," replies Nishi.

Gemma shoots her a dirty look.

"Sorry," Nishi grumbles.

"It's fine. You're probably right."

Our school has a no tolerance policy for fighting. They might make an exception given the status of Elliott's father, but that possibility is slim.

**Rose: Are you ok?**

I hate that I'm texting him first, but I can't help myself.

Elliott doesn't type back. By the time school ends and the sun sets, he still hasn't responded. I toss my phone across my bed.

Dad steps into my bedroom. "I'm off to work. Do you need anything?"

"No thanks."

He turns back down the staircase. I put on a pair of headphones to block out the creaking noises of the empty house. The orchestral music helps me get through my never-ending stack of homework. Slowly but surely, I plow through the remainder of it, only stopping for a break when my pen runs out of ink.

At midnight, I finally take out my headphones. The street outside is quiet except for the sound of a revving car engine. I freeze as it drifts closer to my window. Throwing open my curtains, I watch Elliott's black BMW race down the street.

He's driving in the direction of Midtown.

That can only mean one thing.

I didn't expect Elliott to tell me about any upcoming matches, but Andre could have at least provided a warning. I thought knowing about this secret made me a part of the pack. "The family," in the words of Elliott's father. Clearly, that ended quicker than I thought.

I huff as the car speeds down the street, making a sharp right at the stop sign.

*You brought me into this, Elliott King. You don't get to walk away from me.*

*

"Rose?"

Andre shuffles backward in surprise. He's standing in the doorway of Midtown Ring, blocking my path. Behind him, hordes of people shout and cheer at the sound of a fight.

I huff. "Let me through."

"I can't. Special request."

"From who? Elliott?"

His silence confirms my suspicion.

"Seriously? He's too much of a coward to see me?"

"You said it, not me."

"Please, Andre," I plead. "Let me in."

His stern expression fades. For someone of his size and strength, he's surprisingly easy to break down.

"I'm only doing this because you're nicer than Elliott," he says. "And I think you're good for each other. Talk to him."

He steps out of my way. Most of the people in the crowd are older than usual. The expensive looking men scattered around the building don't fit in against the urban background. I scan the throng of onlookers and eventually spot Elliott's buzz-cut blonde hair. Beside him stands his father. With his scowling lips and narrow eyes, Damon's a predator ready to pounce.

This can't be good. I'm about to turn around and give up when Elliott spots me. I take a step backward, falling into the crowd, but Elliott's at my side in a second. He grabs my wrist and yanks me into the corner.

In a hushed whisper, he asks, "What the hell are you doing here?"

"I could ask you the same question."

"You need to go, Rose. My father is here. You can't let him see you."

"Why? I thought we were 'family.'"

Elliott winces, the kind of painful expression that implies he's recalling a bad memory. I lean closer to him and lower my voice. The familiar tobacco scent on his skin comforts me, and I hate that it does.

I cut to the chase. "What happened? Are you expelled?"

"No. My dad bribed them with suspension. I'll be back next week."

As angry as I am, I can't help but feel relieved. "Why is he here?"

Elliott swallows. His square jaw turns as he speaks, revealing a developing bruise on his skin. "Remember when I left your house the night of the lake?"

"Of course," I mutter. "I'm not the one who left and then kissed someone else the next day."

Elliott grimaces, ignoring my comment as he continues, "I went home to tell my dad that I'm quitting."

I pause. I remember watching Elliott leave my bedroom, but nothing after that until I saw Maddy straddling him at the party.

"Quitting?"

A scream from somewhere in the gym reminds me of exactly where we are. He's talking about The Ring. Elliott pulls me farther into the crowd, hiding my face from his father's line of sight.

"My dad blamed you. He fed me drinks and god knows what else. I was wasted from the second I left your house until I saw you the next day at the party. He wanted me to forget about quitting."

I bite down on my lip, unsure of how to respond. Sure, Elliott's particularly vulnerable to alcohol, but he still kissed Maddy in front of half the school. No substance could have forced him into that.

When he speaks again, he rushes his words.

"I'm so sorry, Rose. I know that doesn't make anything better, but I am sorry. What I did was so stupid even I can't believe that I did it. I was drunk, and Maddy was teasing me and I—"

He curses under his breath.

"Rose, when I saw you for the first time, I couldn't get you out of my head. When you showed up to boxing, I thought I had to be the luckiest person in the entire world."

"Elliott—"

"Then I saw you in my shirt when you slept at my house, and I swore to myself that I had never seen anyone so beautiful. I told myself that I would change. I wanted—I *want*—to be better for you."

He inches closer. I don't step away. I don't want to.

"When you found out about The Ring, I thought it would be over. But you saw me. I think you saw more good in me than I even knew I had."

His words are a stab to the chest. Elliott's attention flickers between me and his father lurking on the other side of the gym.

"This is my last fight, Rose. My dad wants me to compete next week against a guy who would rip me to shreds. I said no."

I choke. Damon glances in our direction.

Elliott whispers, "Please, Rose. Go."

"But—"

"If you want to talk, meet me here tomorrow at midnight. I'll tell you everything. Okay?"

Hesitantly, I nod before the sound of the announcer shouting Elliott's name echoes across the gym. I open my mouth to say something—anything—but he's gone, disappearing through the crowd to take his spot in the ring.

I don't stay to watch. I can't bear to see the person I love get hurt.

# CHAPTER TWENTY-ONE

**THE NEXT DAY AT SCHOOL, ELLIOTT'S DESK IS EMPTY.**

I need to talk to him. The problem is that even after spending all of last night replaying our conversation, I still don't know what to say. He quit the one thing he's good at, the hobby that gave him a purpose, because he thought he was protecting me. But in doing that, he ruined everything.

I don't know if I'm ready to forgive him for the lines he crossed in the process.

"Rose?"

Maddy Davis is standing over me. She reeks of rose-scented perfume and hairspray. The usual scowl on her face is gone. Instead, she looks . . . worried. She taps on my desk.

"What?" I ask, confused. She squats, so we're on the same level.

"Have you heard from him?"

*Great. She's probably going to tell everyone Elliott's suspension was somehow my fault.*

"He's suspended, but he'll be back next week."

She exhales, relieved. Maddy turns away, but as she does, she mumbles something that catches my attention.

"He thought I was you."

I lean in. "What?"

"When he was kissing me. He kept muttering shit about curly hair and princesses—whatever that means. He said your name. I thought you should know."

I gulp. "Thanks."

Maddy shrugs then disappears back to her desk. Maybe she's not as bad as I thought.

After school, I go straight to Midtown for practice, half hoping that Elliott will show up. He doesn't. Andre greets me at the bench. He inspects my outfit, a mix of athletic clothes and school clothes, then chuckles.

"Don't tell me you've forgotten about the competition next week."

"Haven't forgotten," I say, truthfully. "Just preoccupied. Let's train."

I channel all my pent-up anger and confusion into Andre's routine. I keep glancing over my shoulder, desperate to see that familiar grin of approval on Elliott's face as he watches me, but all I'm greeted with is a blank wall.

"Have you talked to him?" I ask Andre after practice ends.

"Not since yesterday. His dad drove him home after he won the match."

I'm glad he won, but I'm sure it did nothing to help his case for quitting. The stronger Elliott's talent, the less likely Damon will be to accept that he wants to stop.

"He mentioned an underground fight next week," I say, after everyone else has cleared the building. "Is that connected to the one I'm competing in?"

Andre shakes his head. "No. Different nights, different places. And before you worry, I made Elliott promise not to compete. They're flying in a guy from the Northeast with a . . . *reputation*."

I swallow nervously. "He's not competing either way. He told Damon that he's done with The Ring."

Andre raises his brows. "News to me. When did he tell him?"

"A few days ago. He said yesterday was his last fight."

Andre is Elliott's coach, and Elliott is Andre's best competitor, but Andre loves him like a son. I see it in his prideful smiles, his encouraging whispers. He wants him out of this as much as I do.

"I'll keep an eye on him," says Andre. "Make sure Damon doesn't freak out."

Turning to leave, I grab my backpack from the ground. I'm halfway out the door when Andre calls my name.

"Almost forgot."

I stop. He hands me a bag stuffed full of tissue paper. "What is this?"

"Open it."

I do. Inside, I find a brand-new pair of burgundy gloves. The quality is better than the pink ones I've been using. They're *real* boxing gloves, something a professional would wear. They're firm against my hands, but still loose enough for air to travel in and out. A perfect fit.

"Everyone pitched in," Andre explains. "A good luck gift. For your first competition. I wanted you to get used to them before next week."

I hug him. "They're perfect! Thank you."

He guides me out the door, but I don't take the gloves off until I'm seated on the train. Even then, I feel lost without them against my palms. The train speeds through spatters of rain. By the time I reach my station, the sprinkling has turned into a downpour. I'm careful to avoid any puddles, nervous that my reflection in the water might trigger another vision. Every time I see my face, I spot a new change even more drastic than the one before it. Not only are my irises becoming the color of my mother's, but the structure of my face is rounding to be more like hers, too.

Soon enough, my dad will notice.

He's not home when I arrive. I head straight for the kitchen, my stomach rumbling. Preparing a pan of carrots and broccoli to go in the oven, I replay my conversation with Maddy in my head. She couldn't have lied about the princess nickname. That's something only Elliott and I knew.

Elliott.

Before I realize it, I'm thinking about him. His gentle laugh. The way that his rough skin feels against mine. And the empty look in his eyes when he was kissing Maddy. The animalistic part of him that everyone exploits. I love him, and I hate him, and I never want to see him again, and I want to kiss him until I can't remember my own name.

**ROSE: Can we talk now?**

My finger hovers over the send button.

Elliott could ruin me. Get himself killed somehow. Drink himself to a point where he kisses someone else again.

But there are good possibilities, too. I picture him holding onto me as we walk through school, smiling at Gemma's jokes. Sleeping beside him, letting him protect me from the nightmares I've been having all week.

I hit send.

"Shit!"

Smoke drifts out of the oven. I open all the doors in the house, then fan the gray clouds to avoid triggering the fire alarm. When I'm positive the kitchen is fire-free, I check my phone again.

**ELLIOTT: My place in 5. Hurry**

I don't give myself a second to think before turning off the oven and sprinting out the front door. This is probably (definitely) a bad idea, but I don't give a shit.

Elliott's car isn't in the driveway when I arrive outside his house. In fact, there are no cars anywhere on the street. Trembling in the pouring rain, I approach the front door already pissed off. If Elliott stands me up, I swear I'm going to break his face.

I knock three times. No answer. Rain beats through my sweater.

*Screw it.* I try turning the handle.

It moves.

Cautiously, I pull open the door, half expecting someone on the other side to greet me. Nobody does. The mansion is empty. The grandfather clock in the corner booms as it strikes seven. I take a careful step inside. Then another. The door creaks shut.

"Elliott?" I mutter.

My shoes track dirt on the ground as I move toward the kitchen. When I turn the corner, I'm greeted by a member of the King family, but not the one I expected.

Damon smiles wickedly.

My heart skips. I straighten my chin, but I'm sure that it does nothing to hide the terror on my face. Dressed in a black button up and leather shoes, Damon looks like he's just returned from a business trip.

"Hello," I say, as casually as I can. "Is Elliott here?"

Damon doesn't answer. I search for some semblance of surprise on his face to see me strolling through his front door, but I find none. I scan the rest of the room for any sign of Elliott. Apart from us, the house is empty.

My gaze drifts to Damon's hands. His left is hidden in his pocket, but his right holds something rectangular with a case I recognize.

Elliott's phone.

"Rosalyn."

The sound of my full name on his tongue sends a shiver down my spine.

"Where is Elliott?" I ask.

Damon's smile widens. His dark hair falls in loose curls, enveloping his face in shadows.

"He's not home."

Sweat dampens my forehead. Damon lets go of the phone, and it falls to the floor with a crash, tiny shards of glass falling from the screen. He smiles.

"I thought it was time for a family meeting," Damon says, his tone playful.

His fingers bend into fists on the counter. The repetitive movement drives me insane with anticipation. Fresh bruises and scabs line his knuckles. It almost looks like—

"Elliott really quit." I realize. "You couldn't stop him."

Damon's grim expression confirms my suspicion. I didn't consider all the repercussions of Elliott's choice until now. Elliott is Damon's lifeblood. Sure, Luke is a good fighter, but Elliott is the one who holds the crowd. He commands the room without trying. He's a god amongst men in The Ring.

"I don't understand," I whisper, stepping backward toward the door. "You have money from your law firm. Why do you need Elliott?"

He laughs. "It's not all about the money, Rose."

As he speaks, I reach behind my back to try and grab my phone, but Damon is quick to catch on.

"I wouldn't do that," he growls.

I drop my hand. "I don't make Elliott's decisions for him. If he decided to quit—"

"He decides nothing!" The force of his words shakes the crystal chandelier, but he doesn't flinch. "The fighting is a great distraction from all the bad stuff, isn't it? You have a lot of that in your life. I remember hearing the news about Doris. I pitied the child who had to find her mother dead."

Anger blinds me. I move farther away from Damon, my fingers curling involuntarily.

"Don't talk about my mother," I hiss.

The fury in my voice only encourages him. He stops a foot in front of me and twists a loose piece of my hair around his index finger. I freeze, smelling the nicotine on his tongue, his smirk taunting.

"You're her spitting image, you know. She was quite beautiful for a mad woman."

I wince as my back hits the wall. My pulse quickens, blood pumping through my veins. I'm dizzy. "What do you want from me?"

He grins like I've finally asked the right question. "Convince Elliott to fight again."

"What?" I scoff. "I can't do that."

"Yes, you can. You know how he thinks."

"I—"

"He needs this, Rose. He's good in the Ring. We both know he has no future without it."

I clench my jaw. "You're wrong. If you paid him any attention, you'd know he's smart and determined. He could do so much good if you let him out of this."

He laughs. "He really didn't tell you everything, did he?"

"What do you mean?"

"Rose, even if I wanted him to quit, he can't. He's a pawn in a much bigger game. The family profits off him, win or lose. He's the key to their whole operation. If he walks out, they'll find him. They'll find us. They'll make sure their secret never comes out."

I swallow harshly. "You mean—"

"He quits, he dies. End of story."

A thousand-pound weight falls onto my chest. My voice is shrill. "He'll die anyways if he keeps this up."

Damon cuts me off. "This isn't a negotiation, sweetheart. If you're not going to convince him to keep fighting, I'll have to."

Damon snakes his arm around my back and grabs my phone from my hand. He dials three numbers.

I lunge.

I open my mouth to scream, but his palm is pressed against my lips. I bite down on his hand. Salty blood drips onto my teeth, but I don't pull away.

"You little bitch!" he screams, releasing me.

My survival instinct kicks in. I turn away from Damon, prepared to sprint to the front door, but someone blocks my path.

Luke. He grins with false sympathy.

He's a cement wall in the doorway. I search the area, but I don't find an escape.

"He'll know," I pant. "He'll know this was you. I'll find a way to tell him—"

Damon shakes his head, shushing me. He speaks into the phone with fake concern, "Yes, please hurry, my son's girlfriend is out of control, and I'm afraid she's going to hurt herself. It runs in the family."

"Elliott!" I cry out, the sound of his name scratching my dry throat.

Damon smirks, pleased with himself, as he gives the 911 operator the address. "Hurry."

"Elliott will never forgive you for this," I say. "He loves me."

"My son loves nothing."

When the front door opens. I know it's not Elliott coming to my rescue.

"She bit me when I tried to help her," Damon tells an EMT, pointing in my direction. Blood drips from his hand. "That's Rosalyn Berman. She's a neighbor. Recall, her mother killed herself a few years back?"

"Don't worry, Mr. King, we'll take care of it."

There's a heavy hand on my shoulder. It's warm but not comforting.

*Elliott loves me.*

*I love him.*

*I need him.*

*My father is alone.*

*I might be losing it.*

*Is this what she felt like?*

I claw, but it's no good.

"She's screaming."

"Can you hear us?"

"You got something to calm her down?"

"Grab her wrist."

"Stop fighting."

There's no more air in my lungs. I grab onto the closest object to me, one of the EMT's badges, and squeeze. It falls off their neck to the floor, and I take solace in the dented plastic. At least now there's some proof I fought, proof I didn't go down without a fight as useless as it was. *Mom. Did you try to save yourself, too?*

As I fall, I gasp. Then the world goes black.

# CHAPTER TWENTY-TWO

**I WAKE TO THE COLOR WHITE.**

White tiles. White ceilings. White sheets. White restraints.

I stare at the straps around my wrists. The pressure on my skin reminds me of the feeling of hitting a punching bag without gloves. I lay frozen, inspecting the restraints, until everything that happened in Elliott's house floods back in a wave.

The white room. The sterile smell.

I'm inside Grady Hospital.

"Glad you're awake."

I whip my head around to find a woman in a nurse's uniform watching me. She keeps her distance from my bed.

"Do you know where you are?" she asks patiently.

It's the most obvious answer in the world. I've seen this room a thousand times in the nightmares that followed my mother's death. This is the same hospital they brought her to when they tried and failed to save her life.

"Yes."

She tilts her head. "You've been here before?"

"My mother was a patient."

She studies the clipboard in her hand. "Doris Berman?"

I nod.

"You said her name in your sleep."

Of course. The spirit of her is everywhere in this building. I choke down some air to try and calm my spattered breathing. "Where's my dad?"

My voice is hoarse, my throat scratchy. I don't know how long I was screaming before the EMTs finally shut me up.

The nurse shoots me a pitiful look. "You won't be able to see him for a few days, sweetheart. We want you to focus on you."

My fingers shake. The hair on my arms lifts.

They're not letting me out.

"You okay, honey?"

"Yes," I lie through gritted teeth. "How long was I asleep for?"

Glancing at a watch on her wrist, she says, "Well, you got here on Wednesday, and it's now Friday."

Two days! I can't recall two full days. There's no way I could have possibly slept for that long.

"We gave you a sedative to keep you calm."

That's when I notice the circular bruise on my arm where a needle must have been inserted. I shiver. It takes all of my willpower not to scream the truth about what happened, but it won't do me any good. They'll never believe me over the mighty Damon King.

The nurse gestures for me to open my mouth so she can take my temperature.

"All your vitals are good. I'm going to call your doctor in."

I close my eyes, but when I do, I see Damon. He used me as a pawn in his game, just like Elliott warned me about.

Elliott. Where does he think I am? What cruel lie did Damon feed him? He probably thinks he ruined everything by admitting his feelings for me. I squeeze my hands into fists as I replay his declaration in the hallway at Harris's party. His words were everything I needed. His tearful eyes brimmed with truth.

And I stood there. Frozen. Silent. Unmoving.

"Fuck," I mutter.

"That bad?"

Surprised by the sound of a familiar voice, I look up to find a head of speckled gray hair. Dr. Taylor. His familiar smile is stronger than any sedative.

"You're my doctor?"

He nods.

"Your father is very worried," Dr. Taylor explains. "I told him that you're one of the strongest people I know. That you'll get through this."

"Thank you," I whisper.

My father. He probably blames himself. I have to get out of here if only to prove to him that none of this is his fault.

"What happened, Rose?" Dr. Taylor questions.

I hate the disappointed frown he's wearing. I don't want him to be another person I've failed. I open my mouth to spill the truth, then pause. I can't tell him about Damon without mentioning the fight club. No way he'll think it's not a hallucination. And even if he miraculously were to believe me, Elliott and everyone else involved would get into trouble. It's not my secret to tell.

Sensing my hesitation, Dr. Taylor continues, "I guess that's a big question, but that's okay. We have time to work through everything in this safe space."

"How long will I be here for?"

"As long as you need to be."

That could be days, weeks, even months. I was supposed to be competing this weekend. I was supposed to win money for my college applications that I'm finally allowed to work on.

*Was* allowed to work on.

I laugh because if I don't, I'll scream.

Dr. Taylor watches me without speaking. When there's nothing left in my system, I use the same breathing technique that he's taught me time and time again. He smiles faintly.

"You remember that?"

"Yes," I say, "of course."

This time, it actually does help. I swallow. My gaze drifts from Dr. Taylor's approving grin to the restraints around my wrists. They're getting tighter with every second that passes in this room.

"Can you take these off, please?" I plead.

He hesitates, then asks the nurse to remove them. Without the straps on my wrists, I feel like myself again.

He trusts me. Maybe more than he should.

"Your father brought some of your clothes."

He points to a bag on the ground that I didn't notice before. It's a suitcase from my house. I swallow harshly, ridding myself of the sob forming in my throat.

"Someone will come get you for lunch in a bit," Dr. Taylor says. "Will you be okay alone?"

"Yes."

"If you need anything, press that."

He points to a red button beside the bed.

"Thank you."

Dr. Taylor nods and turns to walk out the door. I rise from the bed that feels more like a slab of concrete. My legs and feet ache when they touch the floor.

The first thing I find in the duffel bag is a note. With shaking hands, I pick it up. I recognize the curves of my father's handwriting.

*You're going to be okay. I love you. - Dad*

The tears come. I crash onto the hard floor and hug the note to my chest. I choke down my sobs, begging my father to understand that all of this happened against my will.

*I was getting better.*

*Wasn't I?*

I pick myself off the floor. My messy curls fall past my shoulders in a wave. All I'm wearing is a hospital gown, and the freezing cold air makes me shiver.

The same nurse from earlier comes back into my room to guide me to lunch. I smell stale mac and cheese and sloppy joes from down the hallway. The cafeteria is filled with a mix of different people. Some adults, some are my age, and there are some even younger than me.

"You have thirty minutes," says the nurse, pausing in the doorway. "Eat."

I make my way to an empty table, preparing to sit, when a girl across the room shouts, "Hey!"

She waves me over. Next to her is another teenage girl. She doesn't smile.

"I'm Camila," the affectionate one says. Her dark hair stretches to her waist. She scoots over so that there's room for me on the bench. "You can sit with us."

I do. Camila points to her silent friend. "That's Liz."

Liz's bones protrude from her gown. She has a blonde pixie cut and freckles across her cheeks. She sits hunched over, her fork drawing circles around a half-eaten plate of food.

"What are you in for?" Liz asks. Her voice is hoarse.

I take a bite of stale cornbread. "Anxiety. You?"

"What do you think?" she retorts.

"Ignore Liz," Camila butts in. "She's a bit of a downer."

"That's cool," I respond. "Not much to be peppy about in this place."

I scarf down some of the stale contents of my plate. I'm starving. I can't remember the last time that I had anything to eat.

"Every day is pretty much the same," explains Camila. "Breakfast, lunch, and dinner. Different therapies and private time with our doctors."

Her long hair bounces as she talks. It reminds me of Gemma.

*Gemma.*

I was waiting for an update on Nishi and her parents, and now I'll never get one. I miss her so much it hurts. She must know that I never would have willingly abandoned Elliott. If he talks to her, maybe together they'll figure out what really happened. I hold onto that hope, unlikely as it is, because hope is all I have left.

"Are you from Atlanta?" Liz asks, snapping me back into reality. She heaves as if exerting every bit of strength she has to make conversation.

"Yeah. I go to Dekalb High."

She beams. "No shit. I'll be a freshman there once I get out of this place."

"Well, you won't have to worry about being the weird one."

That seems to lighten her mood. She spoons a piece of mush into her mouth. The staff members inside of the room watch her like hawks.

"What kind of stuff are you into?" Camila asks.

I think of Midtown Ring, and the competition I was training for that I won't be attending. Andre's going to be furious.

"I'm actually a boxer," I admit. "I was training for my first competition before they locked me up."

"You're like the mentally ill Rocky," Liz declares. "That's dope."

I smirk. Her and Camila keep me entertained for the rest of the meal until we're called into art therapy. I draw a very phallic flower. Liz is thoroughly amused, but Camila innocently tilts her head, confused. When the hour is up, the same nurse guides me back to my room. I wave goodbye to Camila and Liz, relieved to not be totally alone.

"When will I get my phone back?" I ask the nurse. I should have learned her name, but I forgot to ask earlier and now it seems rude.

"That's up to your doctor."

"Well how long is it usually?"

She shoots me a glare that shuts me up.

I need to find a way to get in touch with Elliott. Just one simple text to let him know that I came back for him. The nurse reaches for her keys to open the door to my room. I spot her name on her badge: Mia. I make sure to thank her using it.

As the night goes on, I wish I was pumped full of drugs again. The screaming and conversation from the other rooms is too loud to sleep through. My thoughts revert back to the same three people: my father, Elliott, and Damon King. My anger toward Damon subsides when I think about the loving embrace of my father, but picturing Elliott makes me more depressed. I stay awake until the early morning, finally falling asleep as my eyes can no longer stay open.

*

Time in the hospital passes differently than in the real world.

There aren't many clocks to be found despite my constant searching. I wake up daily to the sound of robotic beeping. I go to meals when my nurse walks me down the hallway. I meet with Dr. Taylor in the afternoons. He's progressively getting more annoyed by my lack of conversation. It's not that I don't want to talk to him. It's that I don't know what to say.

"How many days has it been?" I ask.

"You don't remember?"

"I think I do. Five, right?"

"Six, if you count the first day you got here."

Six days. That means I officially missed the boxing competition. Andre covered my registration fee, and I didn't show.

"Oh," I say.

Dr. Taylor puts down the pen in his hand. "Does that bother you?"

I hate that he can see right through me.

"That boxing competition I was training for. It was last night. I missed it."

He frowns, but I don't want his sympathy. "How does that make you feel?"

"Angry," I confess. "I let down my coach."

He shakes his head in disagreement, but it doesn't rid me of the sinking feeling in my stomach. "Once he knows what happened, he won't be upset with you. People are more understanding than you would believe."

"You don't get it," I respond, shortly. "I'm upset with myself. I wasted his time. I let both of us down."

I lean back in my usual chair. The staff agreed to let me ride the elevator upstairs to Dr. Taylor's office for our daily sessions since I'm more comfortable there. I'm glad to be somewhere familiar, even if it is still inside of the hospital.

"When can I talk to my dad?" I ask, for the millionth time this week.

"Soon," he promises. "Once it'll be beneficial."

"Why wouldn't it be beneficial?"

"Well, he's the reason why you're here, isn't he?"

My father had nothing to do with this. The EMT's told him that I had a nervous breakdown at Elliott's house. He only agreed to keep me here because he thought I needed help. He was played, just like I was. I think about his gentle smile and the sweet smell of his cologne, and I'm blinded by guilt. I don't want him stuck all alone inside of our house. I want to be beside him, watching a movie, saying I *love you*.

"No," I reply. "It's my fault I'm here. My problems, not his."

Dr. Taylor seems intrigued by this. He adjusts his glasses.

"We can work out those problems, you know. But only if you talk to me about them."

"If you want me to sit here and list out every single one of my anxieties, I will, but I doubt that will help."

"Why not?"

"Telling you won't change anything," I retort. "My mom talked. She talked endlessly about what was wrong. It didn't help her."

I used to spend hours in the car with my father waiting for Mom to get out of her psychologist appointments. We played card games to distract from the reality of the situation, but even at a young age, I knew something was wrong.

"You always compare yourself to her," Dr. Taylor observes. "Why?"

He's torturing me with these questions, forcing me to speak the obvious out loud. "I'm sitting in the same hospital she was taken to. She sat in hours of therapy in this same wing, and she still killed herself. What makes me any different?"

Dr. Taylor leans forward.

"Rosalyn," he starts, and I prepare for him to finally accept what I know to be true. He's going to tell me I've gotten worse. My brain is rotting, and there's no saving it. I sink into the chair, wishing to be anywhere else but inside of this suffocating office, when he opens his mouth again.

"You are not your mom. You do know that, don't you?"

I freeze.

"Sure, you two look similar. You both went through a lot of hardships with your mental health. But that doesn't mean your fates are intertwined. In fact, I think she's probably furious that you're so convinced of this."

"What do you mean?"

"Your mother loved you more than anything or anyone else in the world. It was clear to everyone who knew her that you were her whole life. If she had known that her death would cause you this much suffering, I think she would've made a different choice."

He's wrong. My mother was a lot of things, but never ignorant. She could read my feelings like they were her own.

"She knew how much suffering it would cause me," I shoot back. "Did she expect me to celebrate? Forget it ever happened? I'm her only child! She knew it would hurt me, and she did it anyway!"

My fingernails dig farther into the chair. The marks are deeper now than the first time I entered this room.

"No, Rose," Dr. Taylor mutters, and I despise the patronizing tone of his voice. "I read her file. She thought she was helping you. She was convinced that her existence was putting you in danger. Your safety and happiness were the only things that mattered to her. Nobody could tell her otherwise."

"That's not fair."

"No. It's not. But allowing her death to consume you, to make you think that you're doomed? That's the last thing she ever would have wanted."

"I don't think I'm her carbon copy," I confess. "But things keep happening to me that I have no control over. I'm . . . seeing things. Seeing her. Every time I look in a mirror, she's there. I'm hallucinating, Dr. Taylor."

Dr. Taylor puts down the clipboard.

"Rose, what you're feeling—*seeing*—is a manifestation of your anxiety and grief. You're a complicated seventeen-year-old girl who has been through a lot, and you're coping the best way you know how."

Elliott compared himself to his father time and time again. I thought he had tunnel vision, so consumed by his own flaws that he dug himself into a hole that he couldn't crawl out of. I was the one with the level head; the one who saw through him and knew the truth about his character.

Am I really that different?

I compare myself to my mom every day. I see her in place of myself. But could that be something as simple—as human— as grief? A coping mechanism instead of a delusion?

"Are you okay?" Dr. Taylor asks.

I don't respond. I've been afraid for so long of losing control. The whole point of boxing was to get my control back, and I did.

So why am I still so convinced that I'm on the same path as my mother?

She did pass on her anxiety disorder to me, and maybe it will get worse with time. Maybe I'll need more help than weekly therapy sessions. But like Elliott and Damon, for all that we share, we are *not* the same person.

Everything I've been through, every mistake that I've made throughout these last few years, suddenly feels insignificant.

"I'm not her," I whisper, the weight of the realization pressing down on my shoulders. I melt into the chair, feet pressing into the floor as my pulse slows for the first time since waking up in this stark white building.

"No," Dr. Taylor repeats. "You're not."

# CHAPTER TWENTY-THREE

**"YOU'RE PEPPY TODAY," SAYS LIZ AS I MEET HER AT OUR LUNCH TABLE.** The staff serves us hamburgers that are probably made from dog food. I scowl at the repulsive smell and push my tray away.

"I think I had what professionals call a breakthrough," I admit, half sarcastically.

She smiles. "Yeah? Are they letting you leave?"

Even though my conversation with Dr. Taylor was freeing, he still wasn't ready to discharge me. "Not yet," I say. "How are your sessions going?"

"My therapist isn't nearly as cool as yours," she responds. "She's a divorced middle-aged woman who seriously needs to get laid."

I chuckle, then glance around the room. Usually, we're joined by Camila at lunch, but she's nowhere to be found. Liz, noticing my confusion, announces that she left this morning.

"Really?" I gasp. "She went home?"

"Yep." Liz rolls her eyes. "Lucky bitch."

I laugh, choking on a sip of apple juice. We talk about high school and the different cliques at Dekalb. I'm sad I'll be graduating before she starts her freshman year, but I don't doubt she'll be fine on her own.

The head of staff interrupts, "Lunch is over!"

I poke the hamburger in front of me, not daring to take a single bite.

By the time I'm being shooed off to sleep, I'm so exhausted that my concrete wall of a bed is comfortable. Sleep finds me quickly. I drift into a dream untainted by my mother's screams.

A faint tapping noise on my window wakes me up in the middle of the night. I groan. This place is full of weird sounds. I shove my pillow over my head to cover my ears, but then it happens again.

And again.

Frustrated, I chuck the pillow to the floor and stand up. The tapping doesn't stop; in fact, it only gets louder. I inch closer to the sound and peek out the second-floor window, expecting to find a bird or some other confused animal.

Not a bird or a rabid squirrel. It's a person. A thick mess of hair that belongs to Elliot's brother, Luke King.

I stumble backward across the cold, tile floor.

Luke points toward the window latch. I shake my head.

"Please," he mouths.

I turn around and peer out the door to my room. Nurse Mia is camped out at the corner of the hallway watching YouTube on her phone.

I push open the latch.

Luke's pale battered hands appear on the edge of the window frame. He throws himself forward and climbs through the gap, crashing onto the floor with a pained moan. I peer out the window and find a hastily assembled stack of crates. I have to give him credit for resourcefulness.

My hands curl into fists at my side. I speak in a hushed whisper, "Give me one good reason why I shouldn't scream right now."

Luke dusts the dirt off his knees. His square jaw is tense, and he checks behind him as if he might have been followed through the tiny crack in the window.

"Elliott," he replies. "That's the reason."

I don't like his tone. My feet shuffle into a defensive position. "Why are you here?"

Luke ignores my question. "Are you in love with my brother?"

"Why does that mat—"

He cuts me off, "Just answer me."

I have nothing to lose. "Yes," I confess, surprised by how easy it is to admit. "Why?"

Luke exhales. "I know it seems like I don't give a shit about him, but I do. My dad wants him to fight tonight against a guy even *he* is afraid of."

During my last practice at Midtown, Andre mentioned a fighter with a reputation. I shudder.

Luke continues, "I know Elliott. He'll die before he loses this fight if he thinks he has nothing to live for."

I picture Elliott's bloodied, lifeless body on the floor of a dirty boxing ring and shake my head. "No," I stammer.

"You need to stop him."

I almost laugh out loud at his request, but then I remember Nurse Mia in the hallway. I lower my voice. "Do you see where I am right now? What the hell do you expect me to do?"

"Get out," Luke states, as if escaping these antiseptic walls is the simplest task in the world.

Luke, as intimidating as he is with his broad shoulders and muscular arms, looks desperate, weak, and lost. He wouldn't have come here if he didn't absolutely need to. That much is obvious.

I spit, "Why don't you tell Elliott the truth? I'm here because of you and your father. Not because of anything he did."

When Damon called the ambulance, Luke blocked my escape through the doorway, a sympathetic smile on his face. At the time, I thought it was bullshit, a trick of the mind to further twist the knife into my chest, but maybe those emotions were real.

"Elliott won't believe anything that I say," Luke implores. "Not after the things I've done."

I shake my head. "Why should I trust you after all of the pain you've caused?"

"Because I'm not my father," Luke breathes. "Neither is Elliott. He's going to die thinking that he is."

His words send a shiver up my spine. If Elliott really does believe that he's no better than his father, he won't let himself survive the fight.

I inch closer to Luke, going against every instinct inside my brain screaming at me to run.

"Okay," I concede. "I'll help."

His cunning eyes light up.

"I had a feeling you would." He looks over his shoulder and waves at someone out the window.

# CHAPTER TWENTY-FOUR

**BEFORE I CAN BLINK, LUKE'S PULLING BODIES THROUGH THE WINDOW.** I have to be hallucinating. Whatever drugs they pumped into my veins must still be in my system.

"What the hell!" is all I can say as Gemma and Nishi slide to the floor in front of me. I throw my arms around Gemma and burrow into the neck of my best friend. She feels safe. Like home.

I can't believe Luke colluded with Gemma and Nishi to break me out of here. I don't know whether to be mad at him for putting my friends at risk or grateful for his fore-thought.

Gemma pushes me away softly from my embrace, stares into my eyes and whispers, "Let's do this."

I've never felt more capable of anything in my life.

Luke takes off out of the window like a ninja. Apparently, they had everything worked out ahead of time: Luke will go early to the fight to find Elliott while Gemma and Nishi stay to break me out. Nishi smiles from behind her girlfriend; she looks like a deranged version of myself. Her hair is curled uncontrollably, a stark contrast to her usually silky-smooth hair, and a thick coat of too-pale concealer covers her naturally brown skin. Up close, she looks ridiculous but, from afar, it may actually work.

Gemma turns to me.

"Time to shed that hideous gown," she says, frowning at the blue material. She doesn't have to tell me twice. I strip down to my bra and undies and toss it to Nishi. I breathe a sigh of relief like I've emerged from the deep end. Nishi hands me her sweats, T-shirt, and black hoodie.

"We have to go," Gemma gulps. "Are you ready?"

She tries to hide her fear, but I see right through her. If she gets caught playing a role in my hospital escape, her mother will have her head on a stick.

"Ready as I'll ever be."

Gemma nods. She turns and presses a kiss to Nishi's cheek. "Go raise hell."

Nishi gives an enthusiastic thumbs up before slipping out of my room.

For a moment, everything is silent.

Then I hear the shouting as Nishi barrels through the hallway. Nurse Mia yells, "Stop her!"

"Wow," I exclaim. "She believes it's me!"

"For now," Gemma replies, "I give it ten minutes until she figures out it's not. We need to go."

I crawl through the window first, Gemma following closely behind. The crates are stacked high, and they wobble as I climb down. Gemma and I both land in a pile of leaves.

The outside air is rejuvenating. I didn't realize how much I was craving the wind in my hair. For a moment, I shut my eyes and bathe in my newfound freedom.

"There's grass in my mouth," Gemma complains, spitting onto the sidewalk.

I shush her and point toward a security officer on the other side of the building. I cover my head with the hood of the sweatshirt, and we walk nonchalantly, like we're two grandmas out for an evening stroll. We make it halfway to the parking lot before he spots us.

"Where are you two going?"

"We were visiting our sister," Gemma lies. "We're leaving."

The officer contemplates her excuse for a minute. Then, he stifles a nod and steps out of the way. Gemma guides me to the corner of the parking lot where her mother's car is parked. There's no telling what crazy excuse she had to come up with to borrow it this late. I sit in the passenger's seat, pressing my body against the cold leather with a disbelieving laugh. I can't believe I'm actually out.

"Here," Gemma says, handing me her phone. "Map that."

It's an address in a text from Luke. I paste it into her GPS, and she starts the car. The address brings up images of a local shopping mall; an abandoned one judging by the negative Yelp reviews. I show it to her.

Gemma squints. "A mall?"

For a moment, I wonder if maybe this is all part of a bigger, more elaborate setup. Luke's story could be another part of Damon's game.

"Stop," Gemma demands, interrupting my thoughts.

"What?"

"You have that look again like you're overthinking. Stop. We're going."

Defeated, I strap on my seatbelt. Gemma slams on the gas.

According to her GPS, the address is fifteen minutes away from the hospital, but Gemma gets us to Eastview Mall in seven. As we near the parking lot, I recognize the building from my childhood. My mom and I used to go shopping here at closing down sales. But there are more cars now than there were on Black Friday.

A few stragglers huddle around the side of the building, passing around a single cigarette. Three men. All with muscles as big as my head.

"This is the right place," I deduce.

Gemma pulls into a spot. She taps her fingers against the steering wheel, which puts me even more on edge.

"Go back to the hospital," I suggest. "Make sure Nishi gets out without getting into too much trouble, even if they find out that I'm missing. Just tell them . . . I'll be back. Okay?"

"'You'll be back?' What are you, *Terminator*?"

"Gem—"

"I'm going," she says.

I unbuckle my seatbelt. Adrenaline pumps like a drug throughout my body. I hate that I had to involve Nishi and Gemma in such a mess, but I wouldn't trade my newfound freedom for the world.

"Rose?" Gemma asks, her voice shaking.

"Yeah?"

She squeezes my hand. "Elliott's really lucky to have you."

My lips curl into a smile. "Love you, Gem."

"Love you, too."

I hop out of the car. Zipping up my hoodie, I lower my head as I cross the parking lot, trying to avoid drawing any attention to myself. I slip through one of the back doors without anyone stopping me.

*Not the greatest security measures for the bloodiest event of the year.*

Inside, the shopping mall is crawling with spectators. Luke was right. The fights at Midtown, even the conference in Savannah, don't compare to the size of this one. I estimate about five hundred people shoved into the building, maybe more.

I'm standing in the middle of a food court. Abandoned fast food restaurants form a circle around the makeshift boxing ring. On my right, chatting with a few men in outfits much too fancy for an underground fight, is Andre. I grab the back of his dress shirt and pull.

"You're letting him fight?" I snap.

Andre gasps. "Rose? What happened? You weren't at the competition."

"Long story," I grumble. "Why the hell is Elliott here?"

He shakes his head. "I don't control him."

"Bullshit," I counter. "You told me you would keep him out of this. You lied."

"Rose . . ."

A man dressed in a long-sleeved button up slips a pile of cash into his back pocket. He's wearing sunglasses even though it's night and we are inside. I'm not sure if I should laugh or cry.

"How much is in the pot tonight?" I ask Andre.

"It was supposed to be ten thousand, but with the amount of people here . . ." Andre trails off, scanning the perimeter of the room. "I'd say maybe fifteen or more."

*Shit. The more money involved, the hungrier the audience will be for fresh blood.*

I press on. "Where's Elliott?"

"He's—"

Andre is silenced by the deafening screams of the crowd. I turn my attention back to the boxing ring. People are scattered across all levels of the mall, some standing on restaurant counters to get a peek at the action. I can barely make out the figure of a man who's more giant than human.

"His name is Major," Andre explains. "He's one of the first people to ever fight in The Ring. He killed two guys in a fight in New Mexico last year."

The person in front of me shifts to the right, revealing a direct view of the man in question. Major is holding his opponent—a scrawny twenty-something—by the throat. His other hand punches the kid in the stomach. Then in the face. The kid's body cracks like movie popcorn. Blood rushes from the spot in his mouth where his front tooth should be. I grimace, pushing down the taste of vomit on my tongue.

"Oh my god. Won't somebody stop him?"

Nobody does. The crowd left their humanity at the door. Andre's arm moves protectively across my body to stop me from moving, but I would be a fool to step into a fight like this one. This isn't Savannah. Luke at least showed some restraint when I hit him. Here, I'll end up decapitated.

I spot Damon and Luke on the other side of the food court. Damon observes Major like a student admiring his teacher. I dip behind Andre.

The announcer screams, "Major wins!"

A few spectators rush in to help Major's broken competitor off the floor. Blood drips from his jaw down his bare chest. The boy can barely walk. I look away and spot Luke. He nods when he sees me.

I turn back toward the rest of the crowd to find the one person I'm here for. I glance up at the second floor, but there are so many scattered faces that it's impossible to pick one out.

"Next up, Elliott King!"

I push my way through the crowd before Andre can stop me.

The sight of Elliott knocks the wind from my chest. He's a zombie. His eyes are dull, and his hands are shaking, which must be a side effect of whatever drug he's clearly abusing. Like a sheep ready for slaughter, Elliott approaches Major with his head down, his gaze trained on the floor.

Major smirks.

*It's a strategy. Elliott wants him to believe that he's vulnerable.*

I entertain the idea for a moment because it's easier to accept than what I know to be true. Elliott looks like he's given up because he has given up. He doesn't know where I went or why. He has nobody left on his side except for his father, the person he hates most in the world.

Elliott and Major perch about a foot apart from each other. Major growls like a dog, bearing his yellow teeth. Some members of the audience recognize Elliott and chant his name. The sound of it echoes from the towering walls. They don't want him going down without a fight.

A whistle blows.

Major and Elliott circle each other. I find myself praying for the first time in weeks. I'm not sure if it's to a god, or to my mother, or some other greater force of the universe that I can't name. But I swear to whoever the hell it is that I'll do anything, be anything, if it means that Elliott makes it out of this alive.

Major punches Elliott in the right arm. The impact sounds like an earthquake. Elliott stumbles forward, wincing as he grasps his arm, but Major gives him no time to recover. He throws a cross that lands right in the middle of Elliott's bare stomach. He topples over, wheezing. The audience collectively winces as he does.

But Elliott doesn't surrender. He pulls himself back up, sucking in a deep breath of air that fills up his lungs once again. Major grins before hitting him in the exact same spot. This time harder, if that's even possible. Elliott drops.

Then, he gets back up.

The cycle continues until I can't keep watching.

*Why won't he stay down?*

Damon lets out a small sound. I don't know if it's a wince or a sigh of impatience, but Elliott hears it, too. Disappointment radiates from Elliott's father as he watches his son crumple against the floor.

Again, Elliott rises to his knees. Again, Major knocks him into the tile. The dark red blood pooling around him twists my stomach.

"Stay down!" shouts someone from the audience.

A chorus of approving screams accompany it. Elliott responds by spitting a mouthful of blood onto Major's feet.

I realize what he's thinking before anybody else does.

He's not going to surrender. Without me, without the love of his family, without passing grades or a sport that he loves, Elliott has nothing. He'll let himself die on the floor of the ring before going home to his father.

"Elliott," I whisper.

Blood pools from a gash on the back of his head. For all I know, he could be dying already. I stare desperately toward Damon in the hopes that he might intervene, but he doesn't move an inch. Luke swallows like he's going to be sick. I catch his attention, and he nods, confirming what we both know to be true: Elliott's given up.

This can't happen again. I can't lose another person that I love.

"Stop."

The word barely escapes my throat. "Stop," I say it again.

A few onlookers hear this time. One of them gives me a sympathetic stare, as if to say *I'm sorry, little girl, but he's a goner.*
"Stop!"
This time I scream, and it comes from my soul. The crowd silences. All eyes, including Damon's, abruptly land on me.
Elliott's mouth falls open.
Major glances between the two of us.
*Please, Mom.* I silently beg. *Protect me.*
I rush into the center of the ring.

# CHAPTER TWENTY-FIVE

**THE BURST OF ENERGY THAT ERUPTS THROUGH MY BODY IS LIKE NOTHING I'VE** ever felt before.

If I had been able to compete in Andre's competition yesterday, I imagine this is what it would've been like. Pure adrenaline. Impossible strength. A surge of determination. Everything else fades to black as I zero in on Major's carefully crafted smile.

Without hesitating, I slam my right knuckles into his nose. A sharp sting means I've broken my hand, but I push it away for now. Major pauses. He touches his nose as a thin stream of blood spills from it. Although I've watched Elliott punch people in the face before, I never understood why he would want to cause such harm. Now that I'm the one punching, it makes sense. The blood feels like victory, something I've earned, and I want more of it.

Major wraps his hand into the front of my T-shirt. He yanks me forward, but my feet are planted firmly in place. The cloth rips directly down the middle of my body. A rush of cold air sweeps against my newly exposed skin. I drop the remains of the material to the floor and approach him in nothing but a sports bra.

I'm terrified. This man is massive, and he's staring at me like I'm nothing but an insect ready to be squashed. With the adrenaline rushing from my brain to my body, my fear is muted. Anger is all I feel. Because Andre is letting Elliott compete. Because of Damon's willingness to risk his son's life. Because Elliott refuses to see his own worth.

Major snaps. He swings his hips as he barrels toward me.

From the ground, Elliott moves his ankle to block Major's path.

It works. Major falls forward, letting out a stifled groan as he collapses onto the floor. I take the split second to examine Elliott. He's barely moving, and his breathing is unsteady. Crimson covers him, his beautiful tattoos buried in blood, the gash on the back of his head relentless. Slowly, he lifts a finger, pointing toward Major's abdomen.

"One!" the referee screams.

I slam my foot into Major's stomach. I put all my weight onto his body to try and keep him down. He yanks at my hair, and my head whips back. I scream.

I'm not strong enough. I wasn't then, and I'm not now.

I see Harris's face in Major's. He licks his lips. He's starving for blood, and I'm the main course. He sits up from the filthy floor of the ring, a clump of my hair clutched between his knuckles. "Two!"

Elliott's eyelids flutter. He smiles the goofy grin I love before he drifts away again. I wail, the same inhuman sound I let out when I found my mom, but it's not enough to draw Elliott's attention back to me. He's breathing but slowly—too slowly.

This has to end. And not on Elliott's terms. I have to do this myself.

Major's back on his feet.

He releases my hair and grips my throat instead. Immediately, I lose my breath, the pressure of his weight against my windpipe makes spots of color appear.

*Harris grins.*

Major smiles.

*Harris wants my body.*

Major wants me dead.

I gasp for air, but none finds me.

I dig my nails into his hands, but he doesn't flinch. Major shuffles so my neck is in the crook of his elbow. Any chance of escape is lost. His arms are stronger than his fingers. My eyes are stinging, my lungs pleading for oxygen that won't come.

Suddenly, I remember what Elliott taught me that afternoon in Midtown Ring when we practiced alone. He showed me how to escape a chokehold. I move my hands around the outside of Major's arm, and in one fluid motion, I pull with everything I've got.

It doesn't work.

Major's grip is stone. *Shit. Shit. Shit, shit, shi—*

I can't think because I can't breathe. And if I can't breathe . . .

Choking feels like drowning, I realize. Like when I was little and thought I could swim without my floaties and sunk to the bottom of the pool. Like my mom drowned when she took those pills. She let the ocean of her thoughts overtake her, and she couldn't find her way back to the surface.

I hope it was more peaceful than this.

I force my eyes to stay open because if I close them, I'm not sure if they'll ever open again. I study Elliott. Instead of a bloody and beaten mess, I picture him that day in the gym when we practiced. He was strong and loving. He didn't make me feel small as he pressed me against the wall and whispered, "*Never get distracted.*"

I freeze.

Major's so focused on crushing my throat that he's left the bottom half of his body wide open.

So I do what I wish I would've done to Harris Price that night in Elliott's bedroom.

I punch him with all of my strength square in the crotch. Again. And again. And again.

Major wheezes. He crashes against the floor, hugging his knees. I gasp so loud the room shakes as air fills my lungs again. I plant my entire weight on Major's abdomen. Distracted by his pain, he doesn't think to move me.

"One, Two, Three!"

The crowd erupts into a symphony of shouts and applause. One of the men in suits makes his way into the ring and grabs my arm, yanking to pull me away from the ring. But I plant my feet into the floor.

"I won," I mutter, more to myself than to him. He gawks at me like I've grown a second head.

"What the hell do you think this is, little girl? You got lucky!"

"I won," I repeat, my voice louder now, surprised by the steadiness in my voice. I'm transfixed by the envelope of money sticking out of his suit jacket. "If you win, you get the money," I state.

Somebody shouts, "Pay her!"

Screams fill the food court. The suited man stares nervously around the room.

"Do it, asshole!"

"Pay up!"

I tilt my chin. Hesitantly, the man removes the envelope from his suit pocket and opens it. He passes me only half.

"All of it!" another person shouts.

From the floor, Elliott lets out a pained moan.

He needs me.

I grab what cash the suited man will give me and turn to where Damon King is watching. As I approach him, spectators on my left and right hand me bills. Damon leans into my ear. "Major was supposed to win." He glances into the shadows, where I can barely make out the shape of three figures. "We broke their trust," he says. "Elliott will pay for this."

I shiver, but I don't have time to dwell. Elliott can't take the fall for anything if he's dead. I pocket the money and scurry back to Elliott's side. To my relief, he's still breathing.

"Elliott," I say. "Wake up."

From the crowd, Luke steps forward and takes the place at my side. He hoists Elliott up by his arm. Together, we drag him back onto his feet. Elliott mutters nonsense and moans as we move him against his will.

The audience clears a path big enough for the three of us. Women shove bills into my waistband and my sports bra as we leave—twenties, fifties, hundreds, too many to count. I throw open the door, allowing Luke to drag Elliott outside into the freezing November air.

"He needs a hospital," I demand. "Now."

Luke throws me a pair of car keys. Elliott's keys. His black convertible is parked around the corner.

"Take him," Luke instructs. "I'll handle my father."

We guide Elliott to the car and strap his limp body into the passenger's seat. I sit in the driver's seat and press the ignition. Luke slips back inside of the building, where I can hear a fight amongst the crowd break out.

I'm halfway out of the parking spot when I remember I can't drive.

Elliott groans. I don't have time to wait for Gemma to pick us up. I have no choice but to drive.

I count to three and breathe.

I can do this. Elliott is not going to die because of me. I will *not* be too late again.

Thinking back to junior year, I try and recall the week my dad enrolled me in driver's education classes. I slept through most of it.

"Shit," I groan, slamming my forehead into the wheel.

*You've seen Elliott drive. Copy him.*

I put my hand on the gearshift. I press steadily against the gas pedal.

I turn right onto the main road. Like Elliott, I coast above the speed limit instantly, but I don't care. The hospital is a straight shot. The streets are empty. And before I fully realize I'm actually driving, I'm back in the Grady Hospital parking lot. I swing the car into a spot close to the entrance. I slam on the break, narrowly avoiding a concrete pole.

"Rose?"

The sound comes from Elliott. I look at him, but he's already half asleep again. I unbuckle his seatbelt and dive out of the car. There's no way I can pick him up on my own. I leave the car and sprint through the emergency doors.

"Help!" I scream to the first person I see—a nurse dressed in blue scrubs. I point to the car. The nurse nods. She gathers help from staff behind her. One wheels a stretcher outside. I watch as they peel Elliott from the car, lay him down on the stretcher and rush into the building, leaving me in the dust. I stand under the glow of the fluorescent lights of the emergency room frozen like an actor with stage fright.

A staff member from across the emergency room motions for me to take a seat. I collapse onto a plastic chair as Elliott's limp body is wheeled into a room on my right.

I dig my fingernails into my palm until the skin bleeds. The pain is grounding.

One of the nurses guides me into an empty room. She asks a series of questions that I don't have the answers to. She inspects my body for scrapes and bruises. I'm covered in them. Her finger brushes against my right knuckles.

"Does that hurt?" she asks.

I shake my head "no." I can't feel it.

"Your hand is broken."

"Can I please see my boyfriend?" I ask.

"Let me fix this up first, okay?"

I don't have the energy to argue. She brings in a doctor who repeats the same set of questions. He puts my hand in a brace, and as he works, I inspect the door of the room Elliott was wheeled into. It's cracked open slightly. Someone walks out with a mess of soaked bandages.

I shoot up from the bed. Both the nurse and the doctor hold me down. I stop squirming, fearing that they might attempt to sedate me.

"This should help for now," the doctor says, pointing down at the brace on my hand. "But you'll need to follow up to make sure it's healing correctly. Do you have an emergency contact I can call?"

"No," I say blankly. "Can I see him now?"

I'm not sure how much time passes until they finally give in and take me to Elliott's room. A nurse remains at my side, guiding me to the spot in front of his bed.

His blue eyes are closed. He's covered in wires and machines, but his chest is rising and falling. *Alive.*

"It could be a while before he wakes up," the nurse informs me.

Glancing at my phone, I sigh impatiently. It's almost sunrise. I have to get back to the psych wing.

"We found no internal bleeding," the nurse explains. "He has a bad concussion, broken bones, and twenty stitches on the back of his head. Your boyfriend is really, really lucky."

Impossibly lucky. I drift to Elliott's side. He's broken and bruised, but he's here with me. "Wake up," I whisper. "Please."

I squeeze his left hand; the one that isn't wrapped in a cast. His skin is cold and white as a sheet. The nurse slides me a chair, but I don't sit. I'm not sure I could get back up if I do.

"Can you tell us what happened? Is there any family we should call?"

"I'm his family," I mutter, not answering her first question.

She takes the hint. "I'll give you two some space."

I watch as fluid drips into Elliott's veins. He looks like a corpse, and if not for his steady breathing, I'm not sure I would believe he was alive. As I turn to watch the nurse leave the room, a familiar whisper calms every shaking nerve in my body.

"You're bruised," says Elliott.

I stare down at him as he opens his eyes. Despite the bandages and wires, he looks like an angel. A fallen angel. He brushes his thumb against the purple and blue bruise peeking out from the brace around my hand.

"You beat him?" he asks.

A small, proud smile turns the corner of my lips.

"Yes," I reply. "I used my head. Like you taught me."

He grins faintly. His breathing is labored and shrill; each time he inhales, it sounds like grinding metal. Elliott's gasps in terror as he recalls what happened in the mall. I wish I could tell him that everything is going to be fine, that he's free from any pain, that his father isn't going to touch him again. But now is not the time for false promises, so I decide to go with what I know to be true.

"I love you."

He exhales, and this time, it's effortless. He cups my cheek with his broken hand.

"I love you," he says.

Those three words are all I needed to hear. As he speaks, he smiles, and I can tell it takes all his strength. I kiss him gently on the lips, careful not to touch any of his scattered cuts. We melt into each other with ease.

"What happened, Rose?"

"I can't explain it all now," I respond, inching away from him. I don't want to move, but every minute I stay here increases the risk of Gemma and Nishi getting into more trouble. "I have to go. I'm supposed to be in the psych ward."

Elliott's eyes widen, confirming my suspicion that his father never told him the truth about where I was. He furrows his brows. "What do you mean?"

"Call your brother. He'll tell you everything," I mutter, much to Elliott's surprise. "I think he loves you too."

I squeeze his hand one last time, ignoring the shooting pain in my shattered fingers. I would suffer this pain a thousand times if it meant being able to hold him.

# EPILOGUE

**THE MORNING THAT I ARRIVE HOME FROM THE PSYCHIATRIC UNIT, MY DAD COOKS** the biggest stack of pancakes I've ever seen. My mouth waters at the smell of warm batter and maple syrup.

"I still can't believe someone sponsored your hospital bill," says my dad as he flips a pancake over the stove. "Do you have any idea who it might have been?"

"Nope."

A lie. The money I won in The Ring was enough to cover the cost of my stay after insurance and at least ten college application fees.

"You're sure you're not mad at me?" he asks. He plates the last pancake.

"No," I respond, truthfully. I had a lot of time in the hospital to think over my father's decision to keep me in the residential unit. He wanted to help. He didn't want to lose me like he lost my mother. That much I understood.

"I'm glad I went," I confess. "I spoke every day with Dr. Taylor. We came up with a ton of coping strategies. He still thinks I'm ready to apply for college."

He puts down the spatula. "Do *you* think you're ready?"

"Honestly, I'm not sure, but I think I at least have to try. Are you okay with that?"

"Yes," he replies. "If you're ready, I am." He points to the plate of pancakes. "But first I need your help with these."

There's no way that the two of us alone will ever finish the whole stack, which is why I'm relieved when the doorbell rings.

"He's here," I announce. "Please don't say anything about . . . well, you'll see."

My dad nods, confused, as I leave the kitchen.

Dressed in a light blue sweater and knit hat, Elliott smiles when I open the front door. One of his eyes is swollen shut, but he looks so much better than he did when I took him to the hospital. I throw myself against him, wrapping my arms across his body.

I haven't seen him since the night of the fight, two whole weeks ago. After leaving him inside of the hospital room, I slipped back through the window of my room in the psych ward. But going back to inpatient meant no contact with the outside world, so I spent the last fourteen days drawing pictures, talking through my problems with Dr. Taylor, and wondering what the hell happened to Elliott after I left.

I lift my chin. He bends his neck, pulling me in for a tender kiss that makes me forget we were ever apart.

"You look better," I mutter. "Horrendous, but better."

Elliott smirks. I keep my forehead pressed against his until the sound of my father in the doorway interrupts us.

"Hello," Elliott says, holding out his hand.

My father shakes it. He grins at Elliott, ignoring the sight of his beaten-up face and tattooed skin.

"I'm Elliott King. Thank you so much for having me."

"Any friend of Rose is welcome here. I hope you like pancakes."

Elliott's lips curl. "I love them."

Behind him, Gemma and Nishi are laughing. They interlock their fingers as they climb the steps to my porch. Elliott grabs my hand with his.

"Rose!" Gemma squeals.

She rushes forward, squeezing me so tightly that I can barely breathe.

"Hi," I exclaim, pulling Nishi into the hug. "I've missed you guys."

"We missed you too," Gemma says. "School has been so boring without you there. Mr. Ruse made everyone dress up like poets."

I laugh. The school agreed to let me work on my homework from the hospital so I wouldn't fall further behind. It was a nice break from the outside world, but I miss the small things, like eating in the cafeteria with Gemma and Nishi and Mr. Ruse's crazy outfits.

"Food is getting cold," Dad interrupts. "Let's eat."

The five of us manage to get through the entire plate of pancakes.

"That was great," Elliott announces.

A chorus of *thank yous* break out from around the table. My dad stands up and stacks our plates. I drag Elliott, Gemma, and Nishi upstairs to my bedroom. Elliott kicks the princess doll into the air and grabs it. He holds it in his lap on the bed. Nishi and Gemma sit down on the floor beside me.

"So?" I question Elliott. "What the hell happened?"

"Luke came to the hospital the morning after you left and took me home. My dad was with him. He had no idea how you got out. Neither do I, actually."

Nishi, Gemma, and I smirk mischievously. Apparently, Nishi made it twenty minutes running around the hospital before one of the nurses finally grabbed her. They kept her seated in a blood donation room, interrogation style, for two whole hours until I showed back up. Gemma told the staff I paid them to do it. They let them go with only warnings. I guess a poorly executed jailbreak was the least of their problems that night.

"I think Damon's actually quite impressed with you," Elliott adds.

"I thought you might say that," I respond. "So, I bought this."

I pull out the can of pepper spray from my backpack on the ground. Gemma chuckles, and Elliott's face softens.

He says, "My dad told me to thank you, all of you, for stepping in. I don't think he actually wanted me dead."

"Bullshit," I grumble.

Damon King is a wrecking ball. Even if he tries to be civilized, I know he'll find another way to ruin Elliott's life.

"What are you going to do about him?" Gemma asks Elliott.

"I'll be eighteen in a few months. I'll find a way out."

His birthday alone isn't enough to calm my worries, but it's a start. We both have futures that don't involve our parents deciding for us.

"I'm so glad you're both okay," Gemma whispers before turning to Nishi. "We should give them some time alone. Want to get coffee?"

"But we already had—"

Gemma hushes her. I listen as they sneak downstairs and chat with my father.

Elliott leans against my wooden headboard. He raises his uninjured arm, exposing the tattoo of the dagger on his inner bicep. The other arm is hidden inside of a light purple cast. I rest my head on his shoulder and breathe in the smell of him: tobacco and cedarwood.

"Your dad said they'd be angry since Major was supposed to win the fight. Are they? Are you in trouble?"

He shakes his head. "I don't think so. My dad got his ass kicked and swore it wouldn't happen again, so I think we're back to square one. Plus, most of the prize pot stayed intact since that asshole wouldn't give it all to you."

"Okay." I exhale. "Good. That's good."

He picks up the princess doll from next to him and makes her kiss my cheek. "I love you," he whispers.

"I love you, too."

This conversation isn't over. I need details, a better explanation of how he'll quit without getting himself killed, but he's exhausted, and so am I. His fingers twist into my hair. After a few minutes, his breathing steadies. He mumbles a few unintelligible words in his sleep. I watch curiously, smiling every time he says my name.

I'm about to join him in sleep when my phone vibrates. I carry it into the bathroom.

"Hello?" I mutter.

A feminine, unfamiliar voice greets me. "Rosalyn Berman?"

"Um, yes?"

She pauses, then says, "I heard about your fight in Atlanta."

I freeze.

"My name is Kensington Strickland," the voice continues, "I'm in charge of the New York Ring. We plan events nationally and internationally. I'm calling because I think you'd make a great addition to our group here in the city."

*New York?*

I purse my lips, thumb hovering over the end-call button.

"You're mistaken," I stammer. "Atlanta was a one-time thing."

"Doesn't have to be," Kensington responds. "We pay well. People are begging to see you fight again. Crowds love an underdog. And I, for one, would be delighted to watch a girl rise to the top."

Elliott calls my name.

I lower my voice as I respond. "Please don't call me again."

"Consider my offer," she states. "For Elliott's safety. You know how to reach me."

A long beep implies she's hung up.

Elliott's safety. So he isn't in the clear. I swallow, anxiety tightening my chest.

"Who was that?" Elliott asks. Robotically, I leave the bathroom and stop at the foot of the bed.

"Nobody," I lie because he deserves a few more moments of peace. "Go back to sleep."

And he does. I curl up next to him, grateful to rest my head on a pillow that doesn't smell like sterilization. Downstairs, my father sings under his breath as he cleans dishes. Elliott snores, and I melt into him.

This is my new normal. It's not what I imagined, and it's not quite what I want. I want Elliott beside me, but I want him safe. Maybe that's through Kensington Strickland, or maybe it's as easy as getting him away from his father. I don't know the answer yet, but I relax knowing Elliott wants better for himself, too.

Sleep finds me easily.

In my dream, Elliott meets my mother. She holds us both and beams with pride as I tell her stories of everything that she missed while she was gone. Elliott's rugged smile fades from the picture until only Mom and I remain. We sit on the steps of our front porch, enjoying the feeling of the outside air. Sunlight paints her gold.

"You've learned a lot since I left," she says.

I shake my head *no*.

"I still don't know who I am. I thought I was you, but now that I know that isn't true, I'm more lost than before."

She takes my right hand and runs her fingers across the red scar on my knuckles.

"You're exactly who you're meant to be," she whispers. "You're my daughter. You're a strong, unstoppable woman with so much ahead of you."

I raise my head. We look so similar, but the differences between us are now perfectly clear to me. Our eyes are contrasting shades of brown and green. When we laugh, her nose twists up while mine twists down. The lines on our palms vary. Some of them are connected, while others are mismatched, showing that our fates are both intertwined and separated.

"You have something special," my mother states. "Something other people would kill for. I want you to treasure it."

I tilt my chin. "What?"

She holds my hand. The sun threatens to sink below the horizon, enveloping the sky in a beautiful array of orange, yellow, and pink.

"You're a fighter, Rosalyn. Don't ever let that go."

# THE END

# ACKNOWLEDGMENTS

When I set out to write this book, I knew I wanted to tell the story of a girl with anxiety finding her inner strength. Although some plot points changed with each draft, I'm proud the book stayed true to the original concept. To my younger self, who felt disconnected from her body and mind, and who was desperately searching for a character who shared my struggles, this book is for you. You're going to be just fine.

To my team at The Little Press, Monique Jones Brown and Michele McAvoy, who talked me off more ledges than I can count, thank you for taking a chance on In the Ring. You both define what it means to be strong women. Thank you to my literary agent, Tina P. Schwartz, and her assistant, Joel Brigham, who saw potential in this story and never gave up on it. I'm so glad I have you both in my corner. David Habben, thank you for the beautiful cover. It perfectly captures Rose and Elliott.

Thank you to my first readers, Megi and Riley, and everyone in my WY writers group. You have all kept me sane on this long journey towards publication and you're the reason why I never threw in the towel. You're the best cheerleaders I could ask for. I'm so excited to share your books with the world. Thank you to my friends, readers, bloggers, reviewers, TikTokers and everyone else who helped In the Ring take flight. Mom, Dad and Kensi, who have been listening to my stories for the last 23 years without complaint, I love you. To my amazing partner, Jameson, who supports me unconditionally and has read this book more times than either of us can count, I'm so grateful to have you by my side. Thank you to Paras who taught me boxing when I was sixteen. I was terrible but you never judged me. Finally, to Mia, the person who inspired my love for writing, Elliott King would not exist without you.

# DISCUSSION QUESTIONS

• How did Harris' sexual assault impact Rose's life?

• What is Rose's motivation to box? (Strength? Self-Control? Self-Defense?)

• What insight did you gain from Rose's mother's death? How has it informed your thoughts surrounding suicide?

• How does anxiety and depression manifest in Rose?

• Think about the varying family relationships in this story (Rose, Elliot, Gemma). How are they the same or different from your family?

• Think about the romantic relationships in the story (Elliot/Rose and Gemma/Nishi). How are these relationships about more than romance? How do the relationships develop throughout the story?

• Think about the importance of secondary characters like Andre and Sofia. What is their purpose in the story? How do they compare to mentors from other works of art (popular movies and books with significant mentor relationships).

# INTERVIEW WITH SIERRA ISLEY

**Who is your favorite character?**

I love all of the characters, but I feel the strongest connection to Rose. We share a lot of the same struggles with our anxiety and confidence. Rose makes a lot of mistakes throughout the book but she learns and grows along the way. Elliott's voice was a lot harder to capture but I enjoyed the challenge of figuring out what makes him tick.

**What was the hardest thing about writing a novel?**

The book never feels like it's done. I've gone through countless drafts and I never feel satisfied. There's always going to be more of the story to tell, nuances of the characters that I'd like to explore. I wish there was time and space for all of my ideas! But I also think that's the beauty of writing: readers can take what they're given and come up with their own stories about the characters. Rose and Elliott get to live on forever through my readers.

## Why is it set in Atlanta?

I was born and raised in Atlanta, so I wanted to write about an area familiar to me. Living in the city, my high school experience was unique since my friends and I could take MARTA (public transportation) to events and walk to school. I felt very connected to my city as a teenager and I wanted Rose to feel the same way.

## Are you a pantster or plotter?

Regretfully, I'm a pantser. When I started writing IN THE RING, I didn't have a full plot in mind. I knew I wanted to tell Rose and Elliott's story but I didn't know exactly which form that would take. I went through a lot of (failed) drafts until I forced myself to sit down and fill out a detailed plot worksheet. I'll never start a book without a full plot synopsis again!

## How did you get started?

As a kid, I wrote "books" in my journals and read constantly. In high school, I harnessed my passion for storytelling through filmmaking. I made short films with my friends and took classes at a local film non-profit. As a freshman in college, I found myself with a lot of free time and that's when Rose and Elliott's story began. I knew I wanted to write their story in book form. I still love filmmaking and would love to adapt a book one day.

What inspired the book?

IN THE RING was inspired by my own experience coping with anxiety. In high school, I volunteered at a non-profit in a recreation center and one of my instructors brought in a punching bag. He taught me the basics of boxing. It helped relieve some of my anxiety symptoms, and I felt confident in myself for the first time in months. I knew then that I wanted to write about a girl with anxiety who finds her physical and mental strength.

How long did it take you to write IN THE RING?

I started writing IN THE RING in Spring of 2019 and finished in late 2020.

# SIERRA ISLEY

Sierra Isley is an author and filmmaker from Atlanta, Georgia. She currently lives in Philadelphia with her two cats and a mountain of books. In the Ring is her debut novel. You can visit her on Instagram (@sierraisley), Twitter (@sierraisleyy) and online at sierraisley.com.